D1662811

HOOK
LINE
Professor
PART I

Love truly is everything it's cracked up to be. It really is worth fighting for, being brave for, risking everything for.

Erica Jong

- I'll Make You Love Me - Kat Leon
- Bad For Me - Always Never
- Safe and Sound - CLNGR
- Goddamn You're Beautiful - Chester See
- Heatwaves - Glass Animals
- Loney - Laai
- In my Veins - Andrew Belle
- Arcade ft Fletcher -Duncan Lawrence
- On Your Mind - Black Atlass
- Belong - Cary- Brothers
- Half Hearted - We Three
- Feel so close - Calvin Harris
- On The Floor - Jennifer Lopez ft Pitbull
- Tempted To Touch - Rupee
- Renegade - Aaryan Shah
- Untitled - Simple Plan
- Bad Habits - Ed Sheeran
- Hislerim - Serhat Durmus, Zerrin
- Under The Influence - Chris Brown
- My Oxygen - Rupert, Giles Palmer
- Accidentally In love - Counting Crows
- Just Don't Get Enough Of Me - Mindme, Emmi

- Dirty Mind - Boy Epic
- RUOK - Always Never.
- If Our Love Is Wrong - Calum Scott.

To listen to the full playlist Click Here or follow my Spotify.

ACKNOWLEDGEMENTS
&Dedications

Firstly, I would like to thank my family for putting up with my constant cancellations with them to work on this book—especially my hubby and boys for being so understanding and supportive while I worked to finish this book.

Secondly, I want to thank all my readers and supporters for the constant love and encouragement you have given me so far. I am truly so very grateful to you all.

You're all my Angels.

Thirdly, I wanted to say a BIG thank you to Lea for her constant support with proofreading this book in such a tight time frame. You're my rock!

And of course my PA Robyn for always brainstorming and keeping me on track!

I am so blessed to be doing what I love and having you all along side me on this journey.

Happy Reading, Angels!

I can't wait for the buzz in the ShaylAmigas Facebook group!

If you haven't joined... Become a ShaylAmiga

Love always,

Shayla Hart.

ABOUT Shayla

Shayla Hart is an emerging author of steamy contemporary romance novels. Hook, Line, Professor is Shayla's fifth published book with many more works to come.

When Shayla isn't locked away in her writing cave she's busy planning weddings and social events as an Events Co-ordinator. In addition to having a full time job and chasing her dreams of becoming a full time author, Shayla is also a social media influencer.

Follow her socials below for more updates on upcoming works and entertaining videos on her TikTok's where she acts out scenes from her books. Click here

Shayla also has Merchandise for her books which you can find here. Shayla Hart Merchandise

To find out more about Shayla visit her website - Official Shayla Hart

ALSO BY Shayla

CHAPTER *One*

Rein

"Take your seat, Miss Valdez."

"But... there are no chairs, Professor."

"Who said anything about a chair?" I blink and stare at the devastatingly handsome man sprawled out in the absurdly expensive antique leather chair. He's watching me raptly with those glacial blue eyes that make me shudder ever so slightly every time I find myself gazing into them, like staring into the clearest, bluest ocean. His impossibly long, muscular legs spread wide, his large hand rests on his thick and muscular upper thigh.

"I don't..." I begin to say but stop mid-sentence when he stretches out his long index and middle finger and gestures me toward him, his gaze locked with mine. My body moves on its own as if some invisible force was drawing me to him. I count each step I take toward him, my knees shaking a little more each time until I'm standing between his legs, and he looks up at me, silently observing me.

"Did you wear that skirt for me, Miss Valdez?"

My mouth goes dry. "Yes."

"Yes, *what?*"

God. "Yes, *Professor.*"

My eyes flicker down to his full lips when he licks them as he leans forward. I gasp a little when his hands glide my legs until they disappear under my high-rise black and white checkered mini skirt. My black lace thong slowly slides down my legs until they fall around my ankles.

"Bend over the desk."

I smirk, "Ask me nicely."

His dark brow goes up. "Nice? We don't play nice, Miss Valdez."

I lean down until I'm at eye level with him. "That's a shame," I purr. Placing my hands on the arms of his chair, I spin him. He watches me fixedly as I sit up on his desk, the papers crunching under my bare thighs. He leans back against his chair, his hungry eyes raking over me. I lift my legs and place my feet on either side of the arms of his chair, exposing myself to him. "Because you look famished, *Professor.*" I bite my lip and pin him with a sultry look. "And I just so happen to have the perfect snack for you to feast on," I add, raking my fingertips lightly over my smooth thighs.

The Professor watches my fingers inching closer and closer to my most sacred and needy spot.

"Miss Valdez!"

I almost leap right out of my skin when I hear my name echo and bounce off the walls in the lecture theatre. "Huh?" Every head in the room has swivelled and is currently watching me, some with amusement, others with bewilderment, and I redden profusely. I blink and sit upright, shaking my head free of the very lewd, very improper daydream I was just having of Professor Hottie. Speaking of the sexy spawn of Satan, he's looming over me with his six-foot-one, robust frame glaring at me with a face of thunder and eyes shooting beams of red-hot abhorrence. "Yes, Professor H—uh Saxton?" I squeak and clear my throat a little.

"Am I keeping you up, Miss Valdez?"

Oh, yes, you are, you sexy yet broody arsehole.

I shake my head, "Nope. I'm listening. I mean, I've been listening. You were talking about Van Gogh and his most illustrious artwork." I explain, squaring my shoulders and keeping my eyes locked on his with sheer perseverance. This smug bastard has been trying to intimidate and undermine me since the beginning of the semester. I still cannot for the life of me figure out why he dislikes me. Professor Talon Saxton crosses his arms over his chest; the crisp white shirt he's in tightens when his biceps bulge like they were moments away from tearing at the seams. *Good Lord, I bet he can crack a walnut with those guns.*

Those ocean blue eyes don't falter, they crinkle at the corners while he watches me in scrutiny, and he nods once. "Would you care to share your views on the subject and maybe learn a thing or two. Or perhaps you would prefer to resume your nap?" He retorts, his sexy Australian accent compelling me transitorily.

I blink up at him and sink back into my seat.

I sigh, "Starry night is one of the most recognised artworks in the world. It's a timeless piece. The painting is so popular that its fame has almost exceeded its creator. Vincent Van Gogh painted Starry night at a time when he was slowly plunging into depression and having severe suicidal thoughts. As a result, the toning of his paintings got darker. The great thing about Starry night is that it came purely from his imagination. That wasn't the scenery that he was looking out at while he was painting while in that asylum in Saint-Pauls." I answer steadily.

A fleeting look of surprise and a touch of disappointment crosses his handsome face before it vanishes. Come on now, you didn't think I would back down and let you humiliate me, did you, Professor? I didn't work my arse off for years to win a scholarship to Oakhill only to allow a— disgustingly good looking but equally vexatious—college Professor to try and belittle me in front of everyone. Who the hell does this douchebag think he is?

I worked myself to the bone and won a full scholarship to Oakhill School of Fine Arts. I've earned the right to be here. I've just begun my second year or Sophomore year, as they like to call it here in the states. I left my life behind in London and ventured out of my comfort zone, chasing my freedom. I never in my wildest dream thought I'd get into such a prestigious school. It was just a pipe dream, and I figured why not try my luck.

No harm, no foul, right? Much to my astonishment, I got accepted for a full scholarship. So, I packed up my life and moved halfway across the world to Chicago on a mission to find myself. If you haven't guessed already, I'm an Art major. I've always loved painting and photography. I hope to figure out what I want by the time I'm done with college. Maybe I'll teach or open my own gallery someday.

I keep being told that college is a place where you're supposed to 'discover' yourself. But, regrettably, I've yet to do that. I do miss home. Though, I didn't leave much behind other than my beloved aunt Dani and my Grammy. Aunt Dani took care of me after my mother got killed three years ago in a car accident by her psychotic, drug abuser boyfriend. Donny Santos. The monster of a man that wrecked my life. I have nightmares about him. About the very night, he drove that car into oncoming traffic with the intent to kill us all. I've lived and relived that memory for three whole years. I begged her to break it off with him. If she'd listened to me and called the police, she'd still be here.

One day my mum picked up the courage and was determined to leave him after yet another heated argument. I lost count of the number of times I woke up to them screaming at one another. That night my mum shoved everything we had into bags, and we left the house, barely even making it to the car before Donny came barrelling after us. Finally, after begging and pleading with my mother, he convinced her that he would drive us to my Grammy's house.

I had a feeling something wasn't right; he was eerily calm throughout the drive, and that was unlike him—until he deliberately veered the car into the opposite side of the road into oncoming traffic and drove straight into a lorry that killed them both upon impact and me to suffer a myocardial contusion caused by blunt force trauma to my chest where I wasn't wearing a seatbelt and was thrown against the back of the passenger seat from the force of the collision. A valve was torn beyond repair, which meant my heart couldn't function on its own, so I was placed on a ventilator for two weeks while I was put on a waiting list for a heart transplant.

I don't remember much of the moments leading up to the accident, only my mum's screams and Donny's final words to her.

"Even in death, it's you and I, cariño."

My Grammy always says I look just like her with my long mousy brown hair and wide and wondrous eyes. Though my mother, aunt and grandmother all have green eyes, my eyes are... unique. I was born with a rare condition called heterochromia. I have different coloured eyes; the right is light baby blue, and the left is half green and half brown. Often people are fascinated with it, but I hate it. Most of the time, I got teased at school and got called a freak, which caused me to have quite the complex. Now it's not much of an issue, but I wear blue or green coloured contacts most of the time—when I don't forget that is.

My mum was my best friend. It's always been the two of us against the world. I miss her every single day, and there are some days I wish I had died in that crash because living without her is just so hard.

Don't get me wrong, I love my aunt, and I'm so grateful to her for taking on the responsibility and taking me in, but it still hurts not having her around. It was bad enough not having a dad growing up. So how am I supposed to figure out who I'm meant to be if I don't even know where I came from?

My life is, in the literal sense, a big fat question mark. I feel lost. I can't seem to figure out where I belong, like I'm standing in the middle of a crossroad, half terrified and deliberating which route to take to find whatever it is that's missing.

I jump when Professor Saxton tosses the paper I spent all night writing across the desk at me. I gasp when I see the red B- staring back at me. *What the fuck?* I've never gotten a B for anything. *Period.* I'm a straight-A student. I always have been. I sat stunned, staring at the big fat B in absolute horror. My stomach twists with agitation. I look up in time to see him turn and drop assignments to the rest of the students in front of me. *Bastard.* I've honestly had it with him. I have the right mind to go straight to the Dean and put in an official complaint. Who the hell does he think he is?

"Ouch." Paris Miller—my best friend. Actually, I consider her more of a sister than a friend—mutters with a wince when she sees the red pen scrawled across my paper. Note after note on near enough every other paragraph. "That's a lot of red on one paper."

I exhale through my nose slowly to calm the anger burning deep in my gut. I have the urge to get up and storm out of the lecture hall, but I force myself to stay seated, glaring hot deathly daggers at Professor

Saxton. I don't think I have harboured such disdain for one human being in my life... ever.

While he wanders back and forth, talking about our next assignment, I study him closely, starting from his muscular thighs. The dark blue trousers he's wearing fits him snugly around his thighs and taut bum. A firm yet juicy peach I wouldn't mind taking my sweet time indulging in.

My eyes lazily rake up his back when he turns and points to the board behind him. His brilliantly white dress shirt pressed to perfection tightens and stretches across his wide and muscular back. For a brief second, I picture myself digging and raking my fingernails over his back while he drives himself into me.

Judging by the size of hands and feet, I bet he's packing quite the pecker in those trousers. Yes, I know I'm crude, but he's effing gorgeous, and I'm not the only one that practically swoons whenever he walks into a room or through the halls. Yet, despite my cosmic abhorrence for this striking man, I am still human and can appreciate a fine specimen like Professor Saxton. With his deep ocean blue eyes, light brown hair that he cuts short on the sides and back and keeps longer on top and swept back. I bet his hair is soft without any product.

I mean, eighty percent of his class are females. Females that wear very little clothes and way too much make-up with the desperate hope of catching Professor Hottie's attention. Alas, much to their disappointment, he seems impervious to them, or if he is affected in any way, he's darn good at not showing it.

Professor Saxton turns, and my heart leaps up to my throat when our eyes lock across the room. I don't know what it is about him, but he makes me nervous in a way I'm not accustomed to. When he looks at me, I don't know what to do with myself. There's something in his gaze that sends a hot tremor pulsating through me. I'm not shy, I'm a good girl, sure, but I give as good as I get. I'm nobody's damsel, and I sure as hell am no one's doormat either. I can take care of myself, I always have.

I hold Professor Saxton's gaze, every nerve in my body is pleading with me to look away, but I don't, he stares at me, and I stare right back. Even though my stomach is tensing, I don't look away... until he does, and I smirk a little. Success is a series of small victories, after all. For some unbeknown reason to me, the man really doesn't like me. I mean, it could very well be because I spilt coffee on him on his first day on campus, right before his class. It wasn't my fault, I was running late and scampering through the hall to get to my first class, and we crashed into one another as I was rounding a corner.

My triple shot hazelnut latte went all over his crisp powder shirt and my white tank top. And my books and papers fell on the ground, getting soiled in coffee.

"Bloody hell!" I hiss when the hot coffee splatters all over me and my books. "Look where you're going." I fume, looking down at the pile of my textbooks and papers I was carrying to my class.

"Look where I'm going? You're the one that came barrelling into me. The least you could do is apologise." I roll my eyes and kneel to pick up my papers and books, all the while muttering profanities under my breath. When I hear his smooth Australian accent, I lift my gaze from the mess on the ground as he also kneels to help me with my books.

My eyes lock with his, and for the longest moment, I couldn't look away. Every thought in my mind came to a screeching halt. I was mesmerised, spellbound with the deep blue hue of his eyes. "I'm talking to you, are your ears painted on?"

I blink, snapping out my trance and scowl at him while I hastily wrench my sketchbook out of his grasp. "You've got to be joking? Apologise for what? Ruining your precious shirt? You've destroyed my books and paper I spent all night working on. I barely slept two hours, and no thanks to you, not only am I late to my first class with this new obnoxious Professor, but I also now have no assignment to hand in either." I gripe scornfully and gather up my papers before I stand up. *"So, thank you very much, you... yobbo!"* I give him one last look of disdain before I barge past him toward the girls' toilets.

"What did you call me?" I heard him bark after me. His affronted tone hangs in the empty hallway.

"You heard me loud and clear!"

"Psst!" I start out of my thoughts and groan when Paris jabs her bony elbow into my ribs. "You've taken a dive off planet earth again, Rein."

I sigh and sink further into my chair. "I'm contemplating dropping this class, P," I admit sulkily. Paris' hazel eyes grow large, and her perfectly shaped brows fuse.

"What? Rei, you're kidding, right? You can't just up and change your major in the middle of the semester, babe. Besides, you said yourself you've always loved art."

I roll my eyes in exasperation. "I do. What I don't love is the way Professor Knobhead is always trying to demoralise and humiliate me in front of the whole class. Like seriously, what is his problem with me?"

Paris looks over at Professor Saxton and bites down on her thin lower lip thoughtfully. "The man is wound a bit too tight."

I scowl. "A bit?"

Paris smirks sheepishly. "Maybe he's still mad over you spilling your entire cup of hot coffee all over him and insulting him on top of it."

"I didn't. *He's* the one that walked right into *me*." I whisper furiously. "Besides, it's been a whole damn year. Who holds onto a grudge for this bloody long, for crying out loud?" I grouse, sinking into my chair and tapping my finger agitatedly against the desk. Every time I glance down and see that big fat B- staring at me, my annoyance grows tenfold. Finally, ten minutes later, the lecture ends, and everyone starts leaving the hall.

"He's like that with near enough everyone, Rei Rei. I don't think it's an attack on you personally, so don't sweat it." Like *hell* he is. "Any who's, I'm starving and in desperate need of a coffee, or maybe five. Starbies on me. You in?"

I slide my books and notes into my light grey satchel bag and shake my head. "You go ahead. I need to speak to the Professor about this B- he so graciously slapped me with." I utter bitterly and close my bag, sliding the two clips into place until they click and lock.

"Oh Rein, do you really think it's wise to butt heads with the Professor? If you go over there all guns blazing, you're not going to be doing yourself any favours, babe." Paris attempts to talk me down, but it goes in one ear and out the other. I look over at him, gathering his papers, and glance back at Paris.

"P, chill, I just want to talk to him about his notes." I assure her, but she gives me a pointed look that says, *'Yeah right, bitch. Remember who you're talking to'* I give her a lopsided grin, and she shakes her head slowly.

"Don't do something that will get your ass kicked out, all right. Promise me, Rein?"

"Would I ever leave you, sugar tits?"

Paris places her hand on the dip of her waist and flashes me a bright smile, "You better not, bitch tits." I chuckle and shoo her away.

"Don't forget my Caramel Frappuccino," I call out when she turns to leave. "Love you forever."

"I would never." She calls over her shoulder. "Love you always." I exhale and pick up my paper and almost jump when the heavy wooden door slams shut as Paris exits, leaving me alone with Professor Hottie... I mean *Saxton*. I really need to stop calling him that. He's facing away from me as I start to walk down the steps toward him. My palms are clammy, and my heart rate spikes with every step. I've avoided being alone with him for this very reason. I can't tell you what it is, but there's something about him. The moment I step into his aura, I feel... nerve wracked.

"Do you have something you would like to say, Miss Valdez, or are you going to continue standing there like a timorous mute?"

My brows draw together, and I ball my fingers into a fist and swallow the lump that's beginning to form in my throat. "I would like to discuss the grade you gave my paper," I say after finally finding my voice.

Professor Saxton turns to face me after he slides the zipper to his black laptop case. The sound of the zipper reminds me of a dream I had the other night of him slowly unzipping my dress, those sinful lips dragging along my bare skin as he peels the material off my shoulder.

I exhale slowly when he faces me, his muscular arms crossing over his strongly built chest; he leans back against the desk and looks at me impassively. "I'm listening."

"I would like to know the reason you gave me a B-?" I question, my eyes narrowing. Professor Saxton's gaze shifts from mine to the paper I defiantly hold up and then back to me again.

"If you bothered to read through my notes, you would have understood the purpose of your grade, Miss Valdez." He enlightens rather brusquely. I grind my teeth and force down the anger that flares up in my gut.

"I did read your notes, *Professor*. However—and I say this with the utmost respect—I found them to be rather condescending." I almost snarl and notice Professor Saxton's eyes widen a little with surprise. He almost looked insulted... *almost*. Whether it was my choice of words or my tone of voice, I couldn't honestly tell.

"I beg your pardon?"

I push my shoulders back and keep my gaze on his. "I followed and covered every element you highlighted in that assignment meticulously. Did I not?"

"Yes, you did."

"So why did you give me a B?"

He exhales and lets his arms fall from where he had them crossed over his chest. My eyes follow as his large hands grip the edge of the desk his peachy bum is currently perched on. "I gave you a B- because that paper you turned in wasn't your best work, Miss Valdez. It was rushed and felt flat. Compared to the previous assignments you've handed me over the semester, this one had very little to no depth, no passion whatsoever. You may have covered all the elements, but it was all tell and no show. Where was your voice? Your thoughts? To me, it felt as though you didn't even believe what you were writing and did it just because you were obligated." My jaw drops as I absorb his words and stare at him, utterly stunned.

"Art is more than just putting your brush to paper, Miss Valdez. Art is something that stimulates your mind, your emotions, and your beliefs and none of those were reflected in your paper. That is the reason you got the B-."

I exhaled when my stomach aches, like someone had sucker-punched me hard right in the gut. Well, I suppose he did... only instead of his fist; he used his razor-sharp tongue. *Bastard*.

"Well, I don't accept your grade." I utter defiantly, jutting out my jaw. Professor Saxton's eyes narrow, and he licks his lips. "I want to re—"

"No."

I blink, the words dying on my lips before I could even finish my sentence. "No?"

Those blue eyes stare piercingly into my own... unwavering, patent. Sending a chill straight down my spine. I've met my share of arseholes, but this one is the mother clucking Alpha. I couldn't have a sweet older man as my Professor. Oh no, I had to have this infuriating, frosty, yet disgustingly gorgeous Adonis, who just happens to detest me for some bizarre reason.

I look up at him when he straightens and stands at his full height. "No. If getting a B- was going to upset you this much, maybe you should have put a little more time and effort into your work and less time drinking and partying with your friends, Miss Valdez." Professor Saxton tells me evenly and reaches for his bag, and goes to walk off, but I step in his way, stopping him before he could leave.

What a bona-fide prick. I *wish* I were partying instead of working a double shift at Zen's. Slaving away behind the bar and waiting on tables until three in the morning. Maybe my paper was a little flat, but that's only because I was overtired and sleep-deprived. Unlike ninety-eight percent of the students at this school, I don't have wealthy parents that will buy me horses or flash cars or hand me a bank account full of money. No, I came here on my own dime, and I need to work so I can pay for my housing, books, and, you know, other luxuries such as food and clothes. I could tell him I wasn't partying, but I don't really need his pity—not that he was capable of such a sentiment.

"I'm sorry, but aren't you supposed to be *encouraging* your students to do better? Isn't that part of your role as an academic? To inspire and not discourage?" I question.

Professor Saxton's brows knit together, and he bites down on his plump lower lip as he takes a step toward me. My instincts tell me to take a step back, but I ignore them and stand my ground. I won't let him intimidate me.

"This *is* me encouraging, Miss Valdez. I don't nor will I ever spoon feed my students. Any fool can *know*, the point is to *understand*. If you don't care enough to do it right the first time, why should I waste my time nurturing someone when they clearly have no respect for their education nor themselves? In case you've missed the memo, I have very high standards for all my students."

I gape at him in utter astonishment. Ugh, you sanctimonious prick. "No offence, but you seem to be the one that's missed the memo here because I'm a top student in *all* of my classes, including yours, *professor*."

My knees almost buckle when he smirks at me. It was one full of arrogance, but still, I didn't think this tyrant was even capable of cracking a smile. I watch as he goes to walk past me and stops; leaning a little closer, he murmurs, "I don't miss anything."

And with that, he walks off. I spin and watch him walk out of the lecture hall, leaving me gawping after him, completely baffled.

What on earth was *that* supposed to mean?

CHAPTER *Two*

Rein

"What happened, Rei Rei?" Paris questions warily when I all but throw myself into the empty seat beside her in the food hall and drop my head against the table with a clunk.

"I hate him." Comes my muffled reply where I have my head buried in my arm. "God! He has got to be the most aggravating human being —come to think of it, he's not even human; no, he's the devil incarnate."

"That explains the hotness." Paris giggles while she takes a bite of her quinoa salad. I lift my head and give her a flat look, to which she responds with a shrug while she chews gingerly and tosses her honey blonde hair over her shoulder. "Don't look at me like that, Rein. You know damn well he's a real lushy beefcake. God, the things I would let that man do to me." She adds with a breathy sigh, momentarily losing herself in her lewd fantasies yet again.

I roll my eyes and groan. "Well, the gorgeous prick won't let me redo my paper. Apparently, he doesn't want to waste his precious time nurturing someone that has no respect for their education nor themselves." I complain moodily. "I do too have respect for my education, or what the hell am I killing myself for!"

Paris' hazel eyes go round, and her mouth drops in surprise. "What? That's a little harsh. You're like one of the smartest and top students at this school. Are you certain you didn't misunderstand what he meant?"

I sigh audibly and push away the chicken salad sandwich I got for myself to eat at lunch, no longer having the appetite. "Oh, I understood him very loud and crystal clear. I was so close to telling him to shove that B he gave me up his arse to accompany that stick he's got shoved up there, but I caught myself before I did."

Paris sniggers. "I'm glad you did, girl, but I would have loved to have been there should that have occurred so that I could see the look on his handsome face."

"Are you ladies talking about me again?" A familiar voice burrs in my ear. I lift my gaze to look up at Hunter Harris—my boyfriend. His deep brown eyes twinkle when our eyes meet, "Hi, sweet cheeks."

I force a smile on my face, "Hey." I greet him and shift when he lifts me off the chair to sit and pulls me into his lap.

"How's my girl?" Hunter questions adorably, dropping a kiss on my cheek. Hunter and I have been dating for almost three months now. He's the first person I met out of our group of friends. On my very first day at Oakhill, I got lost trying to find my way to the orientation meeting. Hunter found me hopelessly wandering around, looking every bit the lost little damsel trying to figure out where on earth D block was. I've never been great with directions. Aunt Dani has always teased me about it. She refers to me as a pigeon without wings. I'm forever getting lost. Well, I mean, I did fly halfway across the world on my own, didn't I? So evidently, I can't be *that* bad.

After Hunter kindly walked me to the D-block, which was on the other side of the campus, he invited me to join him for lunch and introduced me to the rest of the gang. Paris, who I warmed to immediately, Colton Mills, Hunter's best friend and Sydney Dalton, aka the campus bitch and quite possibly the snidest, phoniest human to ever inhabit this planet. I'm often right with my judgement, and my gut told me not to trust her the moment I laid eyes on her that very first day.

Syd's an absolute snake—an outrageously gorgeous snake with sleek shoulder-length golden hair and piercing baby blue eyes. Perfectly sculpted legs that go on forever and not an ounce of fat on her body. Though I can bet my life the plastic surgery her daddy's fortune has paid for is responsible for the way she looks, but I'm no hater, nor am I one to put someone down or highlight their insecurities to make myself feel better. You can change your appearance as many times as you want, but no amount of money could buy you a new personality.

For the life of me, I can't understand how the rest of the group tolerate her. Poor Paris shares a dorm room with Syd. I do not envy her one bit. I'm thankful I have my own studio apartment. It's not as fancy as the student dorms on campus, but it's cosy. Ah, who am I trying to fool? It's a dump, and I'm paying out of my arse to stay there because there was no space in the dorms. Unfortunately, I left it a little too late to send back my admission forms which resulted in me not getting a dorm as part of my scholarship. I'm on a waiting list though, got my fingers and toes crossed I get to have a dorm next semester so long as I keep my grades up. Until then, much to my dismay, I'm forced into staying in this matchbox, which is a sodding money pit, in case I forgot to mention.

I'm paying eight hundred dollars a month for an apartment that has a front door that barely locks, a leaky tap, a sink that gets blocked every other day and a toilet that flushes when it wants to. Don't even get me started with the non-existent landlord.

I know I could have stayed home and gone to college in London, but this is supposed to be an adventure. An endeavour to find myself. Oakhill is a prestigious school, and I was lucky enough to get a scholarship to my dream school. I just never imagined it being so darn hard. There have been so many days when I packed up my suitcase and almost returned home when I first moved here. I stuck it out, hoping it would get better, it's been a year, and it still sucks lemon balls. I've now surrendered to the fact that this is my life, and I'm determined to try at least and enjoy it as best I can.

"Babe?" Hunter's voice breaks me out of my thoughts, and I lift my gaze to look at him.

"Sorry, I'm a little frustrated," I admit rubbing my forehead. My body still thrums with agitation.

"She got a B- on her paper." Paris leans over and murmurs to Hunter from the side of her mouth.

Hunter's brown eyes grow wide with surprise. "You got a B?" He questions, turning to look at me probingly. I feel the disappointment and annoyance I've been trying to force away flare in my gut again. "Which class?"

"Saxton's." Just saying his name causes every hair on my body to stand.

Hunter grimaces. "Oh yeah, Saxton's a notorious hard-ass. I heard he sets exorbitant standards that students struggle to meet until they burn out and drop out of his class."

You don't say.

"God, I killed myself writing that paper. I was up all night, and sir jackarse said it wasn't up to my usual standard. So, I requested to redo the stupid paper, and he shut me down before I could even get the words out." I complain while Hunter rubs my shoulder soothingly.

"Hey, come on, babe. B- isn't so bad." He offers with a smile, the corners of his eyes crinkling a little. "You'll ace the next one." He adds, brushing his index finger along my jaw and tucking my mousy brown hair behind my ear before he drops a lingering kiss on the corner of my mouth. "Why don't you come back to my dorm later, and I'll help you relieve some of this pent-up tension?"

I groan inwardly. I like Hunter; I really do. He's one of the hottest and most sought-after boys at this school, and he chose to date *me* of all the beautiful, wealthy girls at this school, he picked me! I'm no size two like Paris and Sydney. I've got curves, the hourglass figure most girls claim they would die for, but I feel my hips, arse and tits are just a touch big for my frame—though Hunter and many others have strongly disagreed with my concerns. Despite the compliments, though, I've always had a complex about my body, and it's something I've struggled with for years. I know I should love myself and all that piffle, but it's easier said than done, and I'm working on it, or I'm trying to a little bit at a time.

"Babe?" Hunter's voice breaks me from my train of thought, and I turn to look at him.

"Sorry. Your dorm? What about Colton?" I question warily.

Hunter gives me a lopsided grin and discreetly slides his fingers under my shirt, grazing my flesh lazily. "He has plans and won't be back till late."

I force a smile on my face and nod, returning his kiss when he holds my chin and draws my mouth to his, kissing me tenderly. "Ahem! Some of us are trying to eat here, if you don't mind." Sydney complains, no doubt rolling her eyes in disgust.

"We don't," Hunter mumbles when I start to draw away, but he pulls me back and kisses me deeper. I couldn't help but smile against his lips at his response. I could hear Sydney carping on about PDA and Paris telling her to look away if it bothers her so much.

***

I'VE BEEN LOOKING FORWARD to my double class in the studio after lunch. Even my lousiest mood disappears while I'm painting. That's my go-to when shit gets too real. I park my arse in front of a canvas, and the moment I pick up a brush, I lose myself, and all my pent-up frustration and anger just melts away. Even as a toddler, mum said, I would colour and draw tirelessly for hours on end. I pour all my frustration onto the canvas in front of me without an inkling of what I want to paint, and somehow, it just comes together. It's my escape, my medicine, my way of healing and processing.

I pick up my paint palette and start mixing colours while we wait for Professor Sommers— or *Selena*. She persistently scolds us for calling her Professor Sommers. I just adore her. She's kind, calm, and so passionate about art. When she talks about Monet—her favourite artist, her brown eyes glow with such joy you can't help but feel animated.

The door opens, and my ears pick up on the thudding of heavy footsteps on the dark mahogany solid wood floor. My ears perk, and my eyes snap up at the sound of that silken yet roguishly deep voice that sends my senses into hyperdrive for some bizarre reason. *What the hell is he doing in this class?!*

"Afternoon class. Professor Sommers has taken ill, so I'll be taking over her class for the next couple of weeks. Most of you already know me, and those of you that don't, I'm Professor Saxton."

Oh, hell.

This cannot be happening. I don't think I can tolerate more than ninety minutes with this obnoxious toad of a man. A beautiful toad nonetheless... but let's not get into my foolish crush right now. How am I supposed to focus now? Two whole hours. I lower my gaze to the brush between my thumb and index finger trembling ever so slightly.

Come on, Rein, not the time to freak out. Act like he's not here. Imagine him in his underwear or something... oh no, wait, that won't work! Awe shit, now I'm picturing him in a pair of black, tight fitted boxer shorts and that bulge at the front...

"Miss Valdez." I jump out of my skin when I blink, and he's suddenly towering over me in all his six-foot glory. The brush slips out of my hand and falls on the floor between us. My brain functionality comes to an abrupt halt when I meet his chilly gaze. Those blue eyes chill me right down to my deepest core, but my skin feels like it's sweltering under his intent stare.

We both kneel to retrieve the brush, and our fingers touch. A sudden current of electricity zaps me the moment our fingers brush against one another. I gasp and pull my hand back instantly, and he does the same, fisting his hand, his eyes leave mine to look down at his hand momentarily before they flitter up to mine again. Only this time, I detect bewilderment in his gaze instead of the usual frosty glower I'm accustomed to getting from him.

He recovers quickly, picks up the brush and stands to his full height. I peer up at him until he holds out the brush to me, and I force myself to break the intense eye contact and stand also.

"Thank you." I utter, taking the brush from him. Professor Saxton nods once, and I stupidly watch transfixed as he wets his lips and looks at my blank canvas.

"Better get started." He utters curtly and walks past me, circling the room. I exhale slowly, and it dawns on me that I might not have been breathing for that entire ten-second interaction.

I shake my head and heave a sigh. I'm truly pathetic. What the hell is wrong with me? Why do I keep reacting to him like this? It's like my brain malfunctions, I can't think straight, and I'm temporarily incapacitated.

I swirl my brush through the yellow and white paint while I stare at the blank canvas. I blink, suddenly startled when Professor Hottie's handsome face appears on it. *"Why the dithering, Miss Valdez?"*

What the...

I close my eyes and give my head a swift shake, and his face disappears out of sight. There is something seriously wrong with me.

"*Focus,* Rein, you don't have the luxury to lose focus. Get it together." I mumble to myself as I glide my brush across the canvas.

But for the life of me, I couldn't. I'm very aware of his presence in the room, and it's unnerving me. I keep myself tucked behind my easel to avoid seeing him, but I can smell his aftershave. The deliciously masculine scent lingers in the air as he circles the room. It's a warm, spicy, yet exotically fruity scent I'm finding myself hazardously captivated to.

I finally manage to gather my thoughts enough to focus on my work when I feel someone standing behind me. Not just someone, *he's* standing behind me. Observing me while I work. I turn my head to look back at him, and my eyes interlock with his. There he stood, commandingly tall and enchantingly broad. His burly arms crossed over his strapping chest; chiselled jaw set tight.

I feel tiny in comparison. My mouth goes dry instantaneously like someone shoved a fistful of sand down my throat.

Good grief, he's so darn intense. Why is he not saying anything? I go to speak, but he beats me to it. His eyes move from mine to the canvas behind me.

"Interesting blend of colours."

I gape at him, startled. Was that a... *praise?*

"Um, thank you, Professor," I reply. My heart leaps when he takes a step and moves to stand beside me. I watch his facial expression while he studies my painting.

Professor Saxton nods, "Class ended forty minutes ago."

"Oh," I look around and see the classroom was indeed empty. "I didn't realise class was over," I admit hurriedly while I set my colour palette on the table beside me. "I'm so sorry for keeping you; you don't have to wait around for me. You can go if you like. If you leave the key, I will lock up once I'm done cleaning."

"No need to apologise, Miss Valdez. You seemed to be in your zone, and I lost track of time grading papers while I was waiting for you to finish up." He explains coolly. I keep my eyes fixed firmly on the glass jar of soapy water in my left hand and swirl the brush around to clean off the paint. "Mind if I ask what you're working on?"

I bite my lip and look up at the canvas. I hadn't figured that out yet. I only just painted the background. The left side was a deep midnight blue blending into a warm purple, and the right is orange blending into a bright yellow. "Honestly? I'm not entirely sure yet."

Professor Saxton rubs his jaw with his long fingers while he observes my painting. "I look forward to seeing how it comes together, Miss Valdez."

"Rein." I blurt out before I could stop myself. Those striking blue eyes turn to look at me in bewilderment.

"Pardon me?"

I force myself to look up at him. "Rein, you can call me Rein, Professor."

I don't know, maybe I imagined it, but I could have sworn I detected a ghost of a smile on those luscious, full lips of his. "Be sure to lock up on your way out, *Miss Valdez*." He drawls as he holds out the key to the classroom for me to take. I watch as he walks off toward the front of the class, picks up his leather bag, and walks out of the room.

Oh, that infuriating son of a... crusty old nut sack!

CHAPTER Three

Talon

"Dude, if you don't perk the fuck up, I'll be forced to slap that glum look right off your pretty face!" I wince when my best friend JT slaps me on the back and slides a shot of tequila in front of me. "Drink!" I groan inwardly and take the shot, wincing when the liquid burns my insides. I'm not much of a drinker, or at least I wasn't until recently. "Take a look around, bro. This place is buzzing with talent tonight. Take your pick. Blonde, brunette, look, there's even a fiery redhead over by the jukebox." JT states, flashing his perfect, panty-melting smile at the blonde and her friend sitting at the table opposite us. "Oh, heavenly father, look what you created." I roll my eyes and heave a sigh when he smacks my arm. "Dude, we're getting some serious fuck me eyes over here."

"JT, I'm really not in the mood tonight, mate."

"T, come on, man. Look, I get it. What you suffered was truly devastating, and I get that you're having a hard time letting go of Taylor, but it's been three years since..."

"Stop." I snap, agitated, knocking back the tequila shot and wince. "I can't mate, all right. Tay was my everything, we had plans, we were going to get married, I was getting ready to become a dad, and in the blink of an eye, everything changed."

Jason sighs and stares down into his empty shot glass. "I know, bro, I know, but do you think Taylor would want you to be alone and miserable? She loved you and would want you to be happy. Why are you so adamant on denying yourself any form of happiness?"

"Because it's my fault, Jase. I should have been there; I should have been in that car with her, but I made my job my priority, more so than her and our baby. If I had left a few minutes earlier, I would have made it, and she wouldn't have had to drive in that storm to meet me at the restaurant. I was supposed to pick her up." I grate tersely. "I lost them, and it's my fault."

Jason spins on his barstool to face me properly while I glare irritably down into my empty glass. "Hey, it is not your fault. It was an unfortunate accident. How were you to know that a drunk driver would crash into her car? You can't keep blaming yourself for something that was out of your control, T."

"Who else am I going to fucking blame? When I'm the one that put her in that situation, JT? If it weren't for me, she'd still be alive; they both would. I should have told her to stay home, but I didn't. So now I get to live with that decision for the rest of my life." I explain bitterly with a shake of my head. I can feel the back of my eyelids burn, and my eyes fill my tears that I urgently blink away, averting my gaze from my friend, probably the only person other than my family that knows what I've suffered the past three years.

I still have nightmares of the night I lost my fiancée and unborn baby. It was pouring out; I hadn't even realised there was a storm until I walked out of the building. I lost track of time trying to catch up with grading assignments due to be handed out the following day. My first teaching job was at the Pinebrook University of Arts—the school Taylor and I graduated from. We met halfway through our sophomore year. I'd see her with her friends walking through the hallway to her class; of course, she never noticed me, and I'd always admired her from afar. Taylor was a film production and photography undergraduate, and I was a fine arts undergraduate working my arse off to get my Bachelor of Fine Arts degree so I could one day attain my dream of becoming an Art professor and help others like myself fall in love with the magnificent history of fine art.

My family and I moved out to the states back when I was just fifteen. I was born and raised in a town called Katoomba, a charming town just outside of Sydney. I must admit I had resented my parents for a long time for uprooting my whole life and moving to Ohio. Leaving behind my entire life, my friends, my school, my life. Pops got a new job as a biomedical engineer when LabCorp—the company he had been working for over twenty years went bust.

I wasn't fortunate enough to have siblings. Even though I always wanted a brother or sister, my mother always said they got everything they needed when they had me, so there was no need for another. Yes, I know, that's really cute but try telling that to my seven-year-old self, sitting on my tod and watching the kids in the neighbourhood play with their siblings. I was, however, very fortunate to have great friends. My friends became my siblings. Even though I moved away, we always kept in touch. No matter the distance, whenever we talk or by some miracle, we manage to arrange a get together; it's like no time has passed.

Anyway, I'm shlepping off-topic. I will never forget the day our eyes met as we walked by one another in the hallway. I didn't realise how much I liked her until she smiled ever so warmly at me while she walked on by, and my heart felt like it was going to leap right out of my chest. After that day, we would smile and silently greet one another as we passed each other, neither of us having the nerve to actually talk to each other until one day I saw her at Krayzee Bean, the coffee shop near campus. It was raining out, and she came running in completely soaked. I was sat at my usual table by the window with my tall pumpkin spiced latte working on an assignment when I saw her standing at the counter, ordering her hazelnut cappuccino. While Penny, the Barista, made her coffee, she rummaged around in her bag, searching for something. Finally, realisation dawned upon her face, and she closed her eyes and let out a string of unladylike curses.

I couldn't help but smile when her cheeks went rosy as Penny set the coffee in front of her, and she gave her an apologetic look. "I'm ever so sorry. I think I left my card and purse in my dorm. I can run back and get it." Taylor apologises sheepishly. Penny looked less than impressed and went to take the cup back with a huff.

"Penny, you can add that to my tab." I offer, and both girls turn to look at me. I nodded at her, and Taylor's face turned an even deeper shade of pink.

"Oh no, that's okay. I can run back and get my card." Taylor offers quickly.

"You must desperately need that coffee if you're willing to brave that downpour to go fetch your card." I tease with a smirk, and she smiles back at me beautifully.

"You have no idea."

I gesture to the empty chair opposite me, "Then how about you enlighten me?"

Taylor picks up her cup and slowly walks over to me. She sets her cup on the table and peels off her soaking wet, dark blue denim jacket. "I would hate to bore you."

"I don't bore that easy." I retort with a smirk, and she laughs melodiously while she takes her seat opposite me and wraps her fingers around the steaming cup of coffee.

"Okay fine, but don't say I didn't warn you."

I chuckle and lean further back into my chair, keeping my gaze on her olive-green eyes until she averts hers to look down at her cup. "Something tells me, you're not quite as tedious as you're making yourself out to be."

Taylor smiles and extends her hand to me. "We should probably introduce ourselves. I'm Taylor Reis."

"Talon Saxton." I take her hand in mine and give it a gentle squeeze while I hold her gaze. We sat in that coffee shop for hours, talking and laughing about anything and everything. While she spoke, I inwardly reprimanded myself for deeming her as just a snobby rich girl. But my initial judgement was off by miles. Taylor was the most down to earth, kind-hearted girl I had ever met.

After that day, we spent near enough every day with one another. I fell for her quicker than I had ever imagined possible. Her love took me by storm. To me, she was perfect in every way, and I knew right off the bat that she would be the woman I would spend the rest of my life with.

We dated two and half years and found out she was pregnant toward the end of our senior year. Was I petrified? *Heck yes.* Becoming a dad at twenty-two was never part of my plan. Kids were something I pictured when I was married in my late twenties after I got my Master of Fine Arts and started teaching. And Taylor had plans to open a gallery and sell her photos. Alas, as you could imagine, our plans derailed vastly, so we kept the baby and decided to figure out the rest after we graduated.

I couldn't wait, proposed to her three weeks after graduation, and we rented a two-bedroom apartment ten minutes away from the university I was working at. We were so happy and excited to start our life together. Regrettably, our happiness was short-lived. Until that very night, two months later, I tragically lost the love of my life and my baby. Since then, my life has never been the same—*I've* not been the same. I lost a big part of me the night I lost them.

"There's only one person to blame, T, and he's paying for it. You were not responsible for her death. It was an accident, and you blaming and punishing yourself won't bring her back."

"I know that. I just... I can't forgive myself, and I don't think I ever will. I'm constantly going back to that night and wonder if they'd still be here if I just left when I was supposed to? Or would I have died with them too?" I explain with a sigh. That insufferable ache in my chest intensifies when I relive the moment I drove by and saw the wreckage. I rest my elbows on the bar and cradle my head in my hands. "I miss her every fuckin' day, Jase. I can't seem to shake this heaviness in my chest since that goddamn day. I keep seeing the car wreck and the paramedics pulling her lifeless body out of that car. Like a fucking loop, I'm stuck reliving that moment again and again." Jason squeezes my shoulder comfortingly.

"Of course you are because you're not allowing yourself to move on, dude. You need to accept that it wasn't your fault and stop torturing yourself. Tay would want you to be happy, deep down, you know this too. So, if you won't do it for yourself, do it for her and let her go, bro. Set yourself free of all this pent-up guilt and resentment so you can find peace once and for all." Jase states, squeezing my shoulder a little firmer this time.

I wish it were that simple. I've tried countless times to move on, but I can't. I just fucking can't. I loved Taylor more than anything. She was my whole world, and moving on feels like I'm betraying her somehow. I gesture for the barman to get me another drink, and he pours me another shot of tequila. "You're talking like I've not tried JT, I've tried, I've been trying, but it just doesn't feel right, and I don't think it ever will. So, I'm perfectly fine on my own." I utter sullenly before I knock back the shot.

"If this is your perception of perfectly fine, then we've got a bigger problem than I initially thought, bro. You're a broken shell of a man, and it breaks my heart to see you like this. I miss my best friend, my hombre."

I turn my shot glass over and place it on the bar with a sigh. "I've been a crap mate, I know," I admit and turn to look at him. The moment I do, I detect the pity lurking behind his gaze, and it annoys me. I don't want to be pitied by anyone. That's why I act the way I do. It's not that I'm cold-blooded or unkind I've just found it's easier to shut yourself off than show people your vulnerability and have them use it against you or hurt you. Which they will, eventually. I've loved and lost and don't fancy going through the headache of dating and getting to know someone new or forcing myself into feeling things I'm not ready to feel yet.

"You've not been a crap mate; I'm just worried about you, T," Jason states earnestly.

"There's nothing to worry about, mate. I'm good as I am," I reply and force a smile on my face, but he gives me a po-face look that visibly states, 'nice try, but I'm not buying the bull you're selling' I roll my eyes and chuckle, "Will you get off my back if I fulfil my wingman duties and assist you on closing the deal with that bird you've got your eye on?" I offer, and Jason beams before he scowls at me playfully.

"I wouldn't say no to an assist from my wingman; however, I am more than capable of picking up any chick at this bar on my own, bro. So don't get it twisted. I was hoping to assist you into getting some ass, not the other way around."

I look over at the two blondes flirtatiously twirling their hair around their fingers while they scope us out. They're attractive for sure if you're into the whole cake-faced with make-up, hair extensions, excessively long fake lashes and clothes that leave very little to the imagination. However, I have no doubt Jason would end up going home with both girls; judging by the hungry look in their eyes, they won't need much convincing. "I don't require any assistance mate, thank you for the concern, though. You know me well enough to know I prefer minimalism over whatever *that* is." Jason laughs and glances over at said girls, openly giving them a once over. "I can assure you I use less paint on my canvas than she does on her face."

"What are you talking about? How can you even tell from over here?"

"Because I possess something you don't. Artistic vision."

Jason looks over at the girls, squinting his eyes, trying to tap into his non-existent artistic vision before he gives up with a huff. "Oh-kay Picasso, let's go woo the pretty girls with your *'art can change your life'* drivel they all love so much."

I roll my eyes and allow him to pull me off my stool. It wasn't until I stood that it hit me how much I had to drink when my head whirls and the ground under me suddenly felt unstable. Should have probably eaten something before drinking. I'm already dreading the hangover in the morning.

"How long do you reckon this time till one of them requests I paint them?" I question as we walk over to the table.

"Thirty minutes," Jase answers with a smirk, and I shake my head.

"Fifteen tops." I throw back, and Jason snorts.

"Oh, we're confident. All right, loser buys the next games tickets?" Jason suggests, and I nod without missing a beat.

"You're on, slick."

"ARE YOU AN ARTIST TOO?" Gina, the blonde seated opposite Jason and I, queries.

Jason takes a long swig of his lager and shakes his head. "Nah, I don't possess the imagination nor the patience to be an artist. I work in construction." He answers coolly after he swallows.

"I wish I had the talent to paint." Britany—or was it Bethany—voices while she stirs the swizzle stick in her pina colada and bats her eyes at me. "Or maybe you could paint me? If you ever need a subject, I'm always up for modelling."

I see Jase deflate beside me and smirk triumphally while I glance down at my beloved gold watch—my grandfather's watch he gifted me before he passed away eight years ago.

I go to respond when a crash followed by a smashing of glasses interrupts me. Everyone in the bar stops and turns to look in the direction the clatter came from, including me. And of course, as it is customary, the crowd cheer and applaud whoever broke the glasses. I couldn't see anything but a head of light brown hair piled up into a messy bun fascinatingly enough held together with a pencil. Until she stood up, took a playful bow, and straightened again.

I was about to turn my attention back to Britany or Beth, whatever the hell her name is, when I saw a familiar face in my peripheral vision. I thought I was seeing things until she picks up a tray of glasses and halts when she turned to walk toward the bar and notices me. Those captivating eyes of hers go wide with surprise, resembling an adorable deer caught in headlights the moment she sees me. *She* is my student.

Rein Valdez.

Have I mentioned that I'm a little bit fixated with her eyes? She has the most beautifully unique pair of eyes I have ever seen. The right is a deep blue, a shade lighter than mine with flecks of teal green, and the left iris is a half teal green and a warm amber brown.

Ever since the day she came crashing into me on my first day and spilt her coffee all over me right before I was due to teach, and we locked eyes while I helped her gather up her books that fell on the floor, I was taken aback by the exquisiteness of her eyes.

Goddamn it, why am I still staring at her? What is it about this girl that affixes me into such a trance? Even in class, I need to persistently caution myself to not look in her direction in fear my eyes will linger a little too long.

"What do you say, T?"

Jason's voice and shoulder nudge forces me to break eye contact and look away from her. "Sorry?"

"The girls were just saying we should go back to their place for a nightcap." He iterates, widening his eyes and putting a touch more emphasis on every word as if that's going to convince me to go and hook up with this bird who I'm not even the slightest bit attracted too.

"I can't, I'm sorry. I have an early start tomorrow, so I think I'll pass." I say, paying no attention to the beseeching look Jase is currently pinning me with. "You guys go on ahead. I'm going to head home and hit the sack."

"Oh, come on, dude. How about one for the road?"

I shake my head and drop a couple of bills on the table before I slap Jase on the back. "Nah, you're all right, mate. Girls, it was nice to meet you both. I'm leaving my boy in your capable hands. Send him back to me in one piece, all right?"

"T, you sure you're good to get home, bro? I can drive you." Jason offers, but I wave him off with a chuckle.

"Sweet as. I'm going to jump into a cab; you's have a blast." I declare and squeeze through the crowd of people standing around and conversing. I check the time and see it's gone past one in the morning. How is this place still packed at this bloody time? My eyes scan the faces in the bar in search of *her* as I move toward the exit.

I briefly wonder how long she's been working at Zens. I'm surprised I've never come across her before now.

When I step outside, it's pouring out. The cool evening breeze hits me, and my head spins again.

Fuck.

I groan and pinch the bridge of my nose when I feel exceedingly more intoxicated than I did while I was inside. But, Christ, I shouldn't have had those last two shots.

After waiting for fifteen minutes, I finally see a taxi approaching and jog over to it. The car rolls to a stop, and I pull the door open and get in.

"What the..." I still for a moment and slowly turn my head to look to my left when I hear a voice beside me.

You've got to be kidding me. "Miss Valdez?" I utter surprised.

"Professor..."

Rein

WHAT A NIGHTMARE OF A SHIFT.

I am absolutely wiped. Friday nights at Zen's is always chaotic, especially between four and five when we have happy hour. Because it wasn't busy enough, Raymond—the owner—decided to add a happy hour where patrons can purchase one drink and have the second free.

Ten minutes in, I lost count of how many cosmos and mojitos Clay and I had to make. Clay is the head bartender at Zen's. When I finally got my licence to serve alcohol, he took me under his wing and taught me everything he knew. I am so grateful because the tips are why I can afford to keep a roof over my head. Imagine Tom Cruise in the movie Cocktail, and you get the idea. He's got the cocky bartender charm down pat in conjunction with a smile that leaves girls almost swooning across the bar on a nightly basis. Clay plays the game well, racks up the tips, and goes home to his long-term girlfriend Leila and eleven-month-old baby boy, Jackson, at the end of the night. It must be nice to have someone to go home to.

"Rein, you look whacked." Clay says when I lean against the side of the bar and rub my sore neck. "Don't worry about closing tonight, sweet cheeks. I can manage, you go and get some rest. You look like you're about to pass out." He adds thoughtfully while he tosses a white cloth over his shoulder after he wipes down the bar.

"Are you sure? I can stay if you need me?"

Clay shakes his head with a chuckle, "I don't need you. Go home before you go and die on me."

I sigh tiredly, "Thank you. My feet are aching, and my body feels like I've been hit by a freight train." I groan, stretching my arms over my head with a yawn.

"Do me a favour; before you head out, can you grab the empty glasses for me?" Clay requests pointing to the table by the jukebox, and tosses the cloth at me. I catch it and nod before I walk over to the table, tray in hand. There are so many empty glasses and bottles that it takes two trips to clean up the damn mess they left behind. As I carry the last of the empties to the bar, I step on something wet on the wooden floor and almost slip but only manage to catch myself before I hit the floor. My heart leaps in sheer panic, but I couldn't catch the bottle and two-pint glasses that topple off the tray and smash on the floor.

I close my eyes and groan when everyone around me cheers and applauds. I look over at Clay, who throws his head back and laughs while he cheers along with the crowd. I do a little bow and throw the towel at him and set the tray on the table beside me. "It's not funny, arsehole. Handover the dustpan and broom."

Clay catches the cloth I dashed at his head and reaches over to grab the broom. "Here's your dustpan and broom." He drawls teasingly, imitating my British accent and doing a terrible job of it, might I add.

"Such a twat." I throw over my shoulder and laugh when he scowls playfully and throws a peanut at my head. Clay comes over and takes the broken glass to dispose of it out back while I pick up the tray of glasses and turn to walk to the bar. The moment I turn to walk over to the bar, I freeze when I see a familiar pair of eyes watching me across the room.

Those eyes.

What on God's green earth is he doing here? I stare at him, surprised, and he stares back, seemingly equally surprised to see me. I grip the tray tightly in my hand when the glasses and bottles clink a little when my fingers tremble ever so slightly.

Wait, why am I so nervous? Cheese and rice Rein, pull yourself together. I'm tired, that's all it is. Thankfully the other guy at the table veers his attention from me, and Professor Saxton glances away, breaking eye contact. But, shit, it's like the man possesses the power of medusa for fuck's sake. Sure, I've not turned to stone, but I feel almost paralysed whenever he looks at me. My legs lock, and I forget to breathe.

What is that?

I watch him for a couple of seconds, conversing with his friend and the two blonde girls at his table. He's on a double date. He seems to be more laid-back and relaxed than he is in class or around campus. Due to his position at the school, it's easy to overlook the fact that he's quite young. The three-piece suits he wears to work makes him look much older than he really is. The outfit he's in currently is more fitting to him, in my opinion. You wouldn't think he's a professor at a college looking at him now dressed in a pair of black designer jeans ripped at the knees and a plain black, tight short-sleeved, fitted button-down muscle shirt. He looks like a normal guy on a night out with his friends.

"Rein?" I gasp when I hear Clay call my name from behind me.

"Huh?" I spin and look at him.

"What are you staring at?" Clay questions leaning against the bar, his brown eyes darting around the bar.

I shake my head quickly, my mouth opening and closing like a fish out of water while I think of an excuse. "Uh, I'm not staring. I wasn't staring. I just zoned out for a second."

Clay chuckles, "Okay, girl, chill. I won't tell your boyfriend you're checking out other guys." He teases, reaching over and tweaking my nose. I swat his hand away with a pout. "Go on, head home before you keel over." I would argue with him, but I was too darn tired. So I just opt to giving him the finger instead. "Good night to you too, sweet cheeks." He hands me my bag and light blue denim jacket where I had stashed it under the bar.

I smile gratefully and make a beeline toward the back exit. But, unfortunately, the moment I open the door, I'm greeted with a downpour. I thought the weather in England was bad, though it rains just as much here in Chicago and the winter is freezing; the summers are roasting hot and suffocatingly muggy.

The late-night chill runs straight through me, seeping deep into my bones. The rain soaks me the moment I step outside and wrap my arms around myself to hold onto what little body heat I have to keep myself warm. It's a fifteen-minute walk to my place from Zen's but fuck walking in this downpour. I literally can't afford to get sick at the moment. I see a green and yellow taxi approaching and jog over to it, waving my hand to catch the driver's attention. I silently thank the heavens when he rolls to a stop, and I pull the door open, and I all but haul myself into the car. I close the door and turn to place my bag on the seat and freeze when I see someone beside me. "What the..." I'm ready to go in all guns blazing, preparing to battle it out for this cab, when I see Professor Saxton sitting beside me, dripping wet, looking like every girl's wet dream—especially mine.

"Miss Valdez." He utters, surprised.

"Professor Saxton?" I reply, finally finding my voice after gawping at him like a piteous mute. Good grief, I can only imagine how shit I must look right now. I probably resemble a drowned rat. My hair is wet and stuck to my face. My mascara is likely smeared down my face. God, why do you hate me? I just want to go home, take a shower and sleep. "Fancy seeing you here in *my* taxi." I blurt out before I could stop myself.

Professor Saxton's brows draw together for a moment before he starts looking around the car as if in search of something. I watch him in bemusement. What the bloody hell is he looking for? Is he high? "Lose something?"

"Hm?" He turns to look at me before he lifts his eyes to the roof of the car. "Oh no, I was just looking for some imprints or a carving of your name in the car that signified that it is *yours*." He drawls sardonically, his left brow rising a little in contest.

Oh, that sarcasm, it makes my blood heat up.

My eye narrow, "Ever hear the expression first-come, first-served, Professor? I was here first, so..."

"I think you may be a little disordered there, Miss Valdez. I think you'll find *I* was here first—ergo... my cab." He throws back at me, shifting, so he is facing me properly. We glare heatedly at one another until the cab driver clears his throat.

"I don't have all night, make a decision and make it quick before I kick you both out." He informs us both, watching us through the rear-view mirror.

"Excuse me, Mr..." I lean over, squinting my eyes to look at his badge displaying his name. "Chui..mon? Chimoni?" I utter and turn to glare at Professor Saxton when he starts to chuckle at my attempt to pronounce the drivers absurdly complex last name. "What are you

51

cackling at? If you can pronounce it better, please, by all means, be my guest." I snarl, jutting my jaw toward the badge and crossing my arms defiantly over my chest.

I bite my lip and watch as he leans over to look at the badge. "Chimonier."

"Actually, you're both wrong." The driver states, turning his head to glare at us both. I snort, and Professor Saxton veers his gaze to me, his ruggedly handsome face aglow with annoyance. "If you don't mind, I've got a long night ahead of me, either decide or get the hell out of my cab. You can embrace the rain and continue your quarrelling out there."

I sink back against the faux leather seat and fold my arms over my chest, looking out of the window to assess the rain. It's picked up since a couple of minutes ago. If I walk briskly, I could make it home in fifteen minutes. I'd be soaked, no doubt about that. However, as much as I get a kick out of giving shit back to the hot, soaking wet Adonis sitting beside me, he's still my professor, and he could make my life a living hell if I step on his toes any more than I already have. So, it would be wise to perhaps learn to shut my mouth occasionally.

I exhale slowly, mentally bracing myself to jump out and get soaked. My teeth clatter just at the thought of walking against the nippy wind. "You take the cab, Professor; I can walk," I say, reaching out to pull the handle and push the door open, but I feel his warm fingers curl around my wrist, stopping me before I could make my exit.

I swallow the gasp that almost escapes me when surges of the warmth of his touch fires through me like some hasty wildfire. Something shifts between us; the air suddenly feels thick, and the car way too hot. My eyes flitter down to his hand on my arm before they slowly lift to meet his. "No. Miss Valdez, you can't walk in that. We can share. If that's all right with you?"

It takes a moment for my brain to catch up, and I shake my head. "Oh no, Professor, really it's fine. I only live fifteen minutes away. I don't want to put you out of your way." I reply and turn to leave, but his fingers tighten around my arm.

"Please, I insist." I bite the inside of my cheek, considering his offer. I nod once, and he withdraws his hand from my arm, and I find myself longing for his touch almost immediately.

What the actual hell? When did I stoop to this level of gimcrackery, like seriously? The last time I had this sort of crush was back in secondary school on a boy named Neal, and I couldn't stop myself from acting a fool in front of him just to get his attention. Although in my defence, I was fourteen, and he was totally gorgeous and eons out of my league—come to think of it, I see similarities between him and Professor hottie. Light blonde hair, blue eyes, tall and athletic. Yes, okay, it's becoming apparent that I have a type. Although, ironically, my boyfriend has brown eyes, dark brown hair, and is just shy of five-foot-eleven.

Want to know the real kicker? I've been desperately trying to convince myself that I'm attracted to him when deep down, I know I'm not. I was quite happy keeping him firmly in the friend zone, but Paris kept going on and on about how great we would be together and how I've been single for too darn long, and I should give him a chance. So, I gave into peer pressure and said yes to a date—begrudgingly and don't get me wrong, he's great. This is going to sound really cliché, but it's not him. It's me. I'm the problem; I'm always the problem.

I should break it off. I know it's unfair to him, but I still care about Hunter, and I truly cherish our friendship. I just can't seem to shift him from my friend to my boyfriend for some odd reason.

I don't nor have I ever experienced any of that—what do they call it 'the honeymoon phase'. You know, the excitement or crazy lust when you can't keep your hands off each other. Those are the feelings that should come naturally with a new relationship. Only, I've never really had that with any of my past relationships. Although do they class as relationships if they were all less than three months?

I know what you're thinking; I have commitment issues. Maybe I do, but trust me, I'm not without my reasons.

"Miss Valdez?" I swiftly shake out of my thoughts. Shit, I've been staring at him without a word for longer than I would have liked.

"Okay. I mean, thank you."

Professor Saxton nods and looks over at the driver briefly. "If you can head to Oakhill University, please. We'll drop her off first."

I lean forward a little, "Uh, actually, if you could please drop me on Eden Avenue."

"Sure, no problem." The driver utters back and indicates to pull away from the curb muttering incoherently under his breath to himself. I'd bet my life he's regretting ever stopping to pick us up.

I glance over at Professor Saxton, who watches me with his brows fused as I lean back. "Why Eden Avenue? That's quite the walk from the student residence."

I avert my gaze to my fingers when I begin to nervously twirl my silver infinity ring Paris got me for my twentieth birthday. "I don't live on campus. I rent a studio apartment."

His brows rise to his hairline. "I was under the impression you were on a full scholarship?"

I nibble on my lower lip and nod as I force myself to lift my eyes to look at him when I answer. "I am."

He stares back at me beautifully and utterly bewildered. "So why the apartment?"

I exhale slowly and twirl my ring around my finger restlessly. "I'm on a waiting list. Unfortunately, all the dorms were already taken by the time I got here, so I didn't really have much choice in the matter. It was either rent an apartment or be homeless."

Professor Saxton just looks at me wordlessly for what feels like an eternity, but in fact, it was only a second or two before he nods again, rubbing his index finger along his jaw thoughtfully. I notice from the corner of my eye that he was about to say something but the cab rolls to a stop outside my apartment building, and he closes his mouth, his curious gaze darts around the dark street.

I curse inwardly when I see the two drug heads sitting on the steps of my apartment building. I often lower my gaze and slip past them, ignoring the lewd remarks and catcalls they slur as I fumble to open the main entrance. I fish out my keys and still when Professor Saxton leans a little closer to get a better look at the five-floor building or what's left of it. "This..." he points to the building and shifts his gaze to me. "...is where you live?"

I hold his gaze for a beat and nod, turning to look up at said building. It resembles something out of a horror movie. It's an eerie looking building that's falling apart due to inattention. It's evident the landlord spends as little as necessary to keep the place upright and not a dime on the upkeep of the building. As a result, the exterior has deteriorated considerably. The brown bricks stained white from moisture damage and discolouring. Don't even get me started on the state of the inside, for heaven's sake. It's not even a fixer-upper. It's in desperate need of bulldozing.

"Temporarily... I hope." I answer, reaching for the door and hesitate when I see the two guys leering at me like I'm a juicy shish kebab they can't wait to sink their rotting teeth into. "Oh, I almost forgot." I lean forward toward the driver. "Excuse me, what's my share of the fare, please?"

I catch a glimpse of Professor Saxton shaking his head at the driver when he looks back at us through the rear-view mirror. "Don't worry about the fare; I got it."

My brows draw together, and I turn to look at the Professor. "I can pay for my cab fare, Professor."

"Miss Valdez—"

I take out a twenty-dollar bill from my jacket pocket and hold it out to the driver while I keep my gaze locked with his. "Good night, Professor." I pull the handle and go to push the door open when I feel his fingers grip my forearm.

"At least allow me to walk you to your door?" I turn my head to look back at him.

"Why?"

I notice his eyes dart over my shoulder fleetingly before they find mine again.

What in the waffle.

Is he... *concerned* about *me*? I almost chuckle out loud at the absurdity of that very thought. No, no bloody way, the man detests me. He's likely fretting that he'll be the prime suspect should my lifeless body be discovered in the morning, considering he was the last one to see me alive.

"Because Miss Valdez, I would feel a great deal better knowing you got to your apartment safely." He replies evenly.

"As opposed to..."

"Not."

How very suave.

I lean a touch closer, "Do you provide this assistance to all your other students too, Professor? I didn't realise walking your students to their doors in the middle of the night was part of your job description."

He smirks and licks his lips while leaning in also. *Don't swoon, Rein, do not fucking swoon.* "Are you insinuating that you're special, Miss Valdez?"

Oh, how I wish I were. I feel my cheeks grow hotter by the second. But, hold on a bloody minute; what is happening here? Why is he so... courteous and pleasant all of a sudden?

Me? Special? That's laughable. I wouldn't even know what that felt like even if I were. I cock my head to the side and narrow my eyes a little while I study his handsome face. "Are you eluding the question, Professor?"

The corner of his lip curls into an amused smirk, and he shakes his head, his eyes find mine, and he holds my gaze. "When you ask a question worth answering, I will. But, until then, I bid you good night, Miss Valdez."

And just like that, he goes back to his usual stand offish demeanour. With an inward sigh, I push the door open, and the chill of the wind feels kind of nice against the heat radiating off my face. Thank the Lord it's dark out, or he would have seen my cheeks contorting through every shade of red known to humankind. "Good night, Professor Saxton." And with that, I climb out of the car and push the door shut behind me. I can feel him watching me as I near the two guys sitting on the stairs to my building. They both look up at me, eyes wide and rimmed red as I approach. I inwardly pray that they move aside to allow me through and not say anything. I'm way too exhausted to deal with a couple of crackheads slurring lewd remarks at me.

Thankfully, they shuffle aside, and I walk up the steps to the main entrance. I slide in my key and turn it until I hear the click. I tell myself not to, but it seems my body just doesn't want to pay any attention to the signals firing from my brain. I turn my head and look back at my devastatingly gorgeous Professor still in the cab, his window rolled down, patiently waiting for me to go inside to the 'safe' confines of my apartment. When he smiles and gestures with his brows for me to go in, my stomach went all funny.

I've got a feeling there's more to Professor Hottie than he allows people to see, and I'd be lying if I said it didn't pique my interest.

CHAPTER *Five*

Talon

I really need to stop going out drinking with JT. Nothing good ever comes from it, and tonight was yet again another reminder of that little statement. Of all the bars in town, the idiot drags me to the one my student happens to work at. The last thing I need is my students witnessing me necking shots and getting pissed as a fart. I'm not even getting into the whole walking her to her apartment nonsense that sprouted out of the darn blue. The words just fell out of my mouth before I could catch them. Would it have been deemed inappropriate that I was simply looking out for the safety of one of my students? I think not.

Clearly, she thought otherwise. Oh, who am I kidding? I was bald-facedly flirting with her, and she was giving it right back. Why is it troubling me that she may be unsafe in that abomination she considers an apartment? I keep wondering what might have happened if I weren't with her. I saw the vile look in the eyes of those two meth heads, and I didn't like it. Did she even make it up to her apartment? What if they followed her in after I left?

I pace back and forth in my living room, my mind conjuring up the worst. I sit on the sofa and curl my fingers in my hair. Images of Taylor being pulled from that car wreck replays in my mind.

Fuck!

I shake off that image. Stop it, Talon. Get a damn grip. She's going to be in class Monday morning, and you're going to feel like a fool for overthinking this whole thing. She's a big girl; she's not your problem, you idiot.

It's the alcohol. It's causing my thoughts to go haywire. I'll take a shower, go to sleep and wake up back to my usual self. With a bit of luck, I'll be unable to remember the way she smells sweet like vanilla and cinnamon, like the mouth-watering aroma of freshly baked cupcakes, or the way her wet shirt clung to her full breasts under her jacket.

Hell, Talon, she's your student!

I wince and almost slap myself out of the lewd thoughts my brain was starting to conjure. Thoughts a professor should most definitely not be having of his student eight years his junior.

Jesus, when did I become such a degenerate?

MONDAY MORNING, I got up at the arse crack of dawn and went for a run. Another restless night has left me feeling exhausted, but I'm determined to power through and not allow my disarray of emotions to drag me down a path I've got no business moseying down. So I exhale deeply while I pull the jacket onto my navy-blue three-piece suit and tug the sleeves of the white shirt, so it's aligned with the sleeve of the jacket—not that it matters, I'll take the jacket off ten minutes into class anyway.

Fuck, I loathe Mondays.

"Good morning, Professor Saxton." I halt the moment I step out of my office when I hear her voice. Please tell me she wasn't loitering outside my office this whole time waiting for me.

Oh, bloody hell. I could do without this shit today. I curse my damned luck and turn to face Polly Montgomery—the Professor of Media Arts who has been incessantly hounding me for a date. I'm running out of excuses and polite ways of rejecting her.

"Good morning, Miss Montgomery," I answer with a tight smile and go to sidestep her, but she jumps in my way.

"How was your weekend, Professor? Do anything fun?" I grit my teeth and shove down the wave of annoyance rising from my gut.

"Not particularly, no. Just caught up with some reading. I'm sorry, but if you don't mind, I'm running late and don't like to keep my students waiting." I answer tightly and move to walk around her.

"Professor, before you go." I look down at her fingers curled around my bicep. I lift my gaze to hers and wait for her to continue while silently counting to ten to calm my irritation that's simmering beneath the surface. "There's an art gallery opening tonight, and I was wondering if you would like to join me?" I open my mouth to refuse, but she cuts me off before I can get a word out. "My apartment is in dire need of some sprucing, and I don't quite have an eye for art as you do, so I thought maybe our prised professor would help out a girl in need?" Polly requests with a sugary smile, batting her brown eyes at me flirtatiously, her fingers slowly trailing down my forearm. "Maybe after I can buy you dinner as a thank you."

Good grief, she's laying it on thick this morning.

"Miss Mont—"

"Polly," She interrupts me, dragging her tongue along her bottom lip.

"Uh, *Polly*, I'm afraid I already have plans for this evening. And while I appreciate the offer, I don't know what your apartment looks like or what piece would fit where. The piece you choose should resonate with the viewer; it should speak to you personally. Then, when you see the perfect one, you'll know. If you still have trouble, my advice would be to ask the art curator at the gallery. I'm sure they would be happy to advise you on which piece would suit you and your home best." I explain, tug my arm out of her hold, and smooth out the creases she left on my jacket when she squeezed my arm. "Now, if you'll excuse me."

"Boy, you sure are a hard man to pin down, Professor Saxton." Polly purrs, stepping closer, deliberately pressing her breast against my arm. I try my best not to cringe.

"Excuse me, Professor Saxton?" I still when I hear that familiar silky voice that sends an electric pulse through my body. I look over at Rein standing a couple of feet in front of me in a knitted beige sweater dress that hugs her curves to absolute perfection and a pair of thigh-high black boots. Her shoulder-length light brown hair down and windswept, likely from her walk to campus.

For the love of God Talon, do not give her the once over man. Don't fucking do it.

"Miss Valdez?"

"I'm sorry to interrupt," Rein apologises and smiles warmly at Polly, who crosses her arms over her chest, not even bothering to hide the fact she's annoyed at the interruption. Rein's gaze flitters to me, and she bites her bottom lip. "I seem to have misplaced my copy of the assignment for next week you handed out Friday, and I was wondering if you had another copy?"

I nod. "Yes, I do. It's saved on my computer in my office. If you follow me, I'll print one off for you. Excuse me, Miss Montgomery." I gesture Rein toward my office, and she follows me. I cannot express how thankful I am that she showed up when she did. I have got to find a better way to shake that bloody leech of a woman.

I place my briefcase down on the chair and walk around my mahogany desk while Rein walks in and closes the door behind her, and leans against it. I keep my eyes on the task at hand and search through my documents to find the paper she's requesting. If I'm honest, her presence in my office is making me perspire a little under my three-piece suit.

I finally found the document and hit print. While she casts an eye over my office space, I observe her. Bloody hell, she's beautiful. Rein walks over to a painting I have on the wall above the fireplace to the room's left. I lean against the desk and watch her as she stares up at the painting in awe.

I walk over to her after I collect the papers from the printer beside my desk. "The Storm of the Sea of Galilee by—"

"Rembrandt Van Rijn." She finishes for me and turns to look back at me, "I know. The painting that got stolen from the museum in Boston in 1990 and till this very day still remains missing."

I smile and nod, holding her gaze until she turns to look at the painting once again. "That's right. The paintings disappearance remains quite the mystery. It's referred to quite often in popular culture." I say, and Rein turns to face me when I hold out the papers to her. "Try not to misplace this one. I would hate to give you another B."

Rein rubs her forehead and looks down at the paper in my hand. She winces a little. "Actually, Professor, I didn't misplace my copy. It's in my bag." She admits sheepishly.

I stare at her, my brows fusing tightly. Did she seriously come in here to waste my damn time? "Excuse me?"

"Uhm, I was on my way to class and noticed you were cornered and looking mighty uncomfortable with Miss Montgomery, so I may have fibbed a little that I misplaced my paper to help you out of a sticky situation." She offers with a shrug. Every instinct in my body was telling me to grin like the cat that caught the canary. I can feel my lips curling against my best effort to stop it, so I rub my index and middle finger over my lip to veil the smirk while I compose myself.

"Let me see if I got this right. You saw me talking to a member of the faculty and took it upon yourself to come over and what... save me?"

Rein's eyes grow wider when I take a step toward her, her pouty mouth drops open, and she stares up at me, no doubt trying her best to think up a viable justification for her actions. "Tell me, Miss Valdez, do you often make a habit of going around rescuing your professors or..." My eyes lock with hers when I lean in a little closer. "Am I just special?"

Rein shakes her head quickly, her eyes never leaving mine. I notice she's wearing green contacts, and I hate it. Why would she cover up those mesmerising eyes of hers? Is she ashamed of them? Self-conscious perhaps?

"No," she fires back quickly. "Consider it a thank you for looking out for me on Friday night."

I lick my lips and nod when she averts her gaze from mine, "I see. So, I suppose you now assume that this makes us even then?"

Rein juts out her jaw in a defiant manner and nods once. "I don't like to be indebted to anyone, so yes, this makes us even."

I smirk.

"Well then, that makes two of us because if my memory serves me right, Miss Valdez, you stole my cab and then paid for it. So if anyone is indebted to anyone, it's me to you, wouldn't you agree?" I question, leaning back until my backside is resting upon the desk.

Rein smiles and walks over to the door. "Well, Professor, in that case, take back the B you gave me on my last paper, and we'll call it even." She offers with a cheeky smile before she opens the door.

Laughing, I shake my head. "Nice try, Miss Valdez." I commend her.

"See you in class, Professor. Try not to be late." Rein glances back at me once more and shrugs before she walks out of my office and closes the door behind her.

I tilt my head back and turn my gaze heavenward. "Christ."

I DON'T KNOW what is wrong with me. While I'm talking throughout my class, my eyes keep drifting over to her, and I'm fighting with myself to look away. It's almost like she's the only person in the room. My brain is completely disregarding the rest of the fifty students sitting in my class.

This is bad—no, it's worse than bad. I'm in real deep shit here. I think I might have an attraction to my student.

Fark me dead. This cannot be happening.

The silk tie around my neck suddenly feels like a noose suffocating me. I loosen it and exhale slowly. It wasn't so bad seeing her for ninety minutes, once a week, but now I'm covering Selena's classes until she's back—God only knows when that will be—which means I'll now see Rein three times a week at least.

Jesus, where did this attraction creep up from? I was fine. I was fine before Friday night when I saw her at the bar. But, something between us changed in that taxi. Whatever that change was its screwed everything up.

Nah. I'm overthinking this. I have to be. I can't be attracted to my student. It's forbidden, against the rules. It's unethical.

I tap apprehensively at my keyboard, pretending to work while the class reads the pages that I have assigned for them. I'm neither blind nor stupid, I'm fully aware of the attention I get from the girls around the school and gossip that often circulates about me, but I've learned to block it out over time. Being a young professor teaching at this school doesn't help matters, nor does the nickname Professor Hottie that the students have rigged me with.

I've had to report many students for the inappropriate comments, making eyes at me or the secret love notes they kept sliding under my door with their underwear. It was out of control for a while until I became impervious, made them believe I was cold and unyielding to throw them off and it worked... sort off. Of course, I still get the flirty remarks, but I brush them off and put a stop to it before it escalates and gives them the wrong impression. I'm here to teach. I took a loyalty oath, and I didn't work myself to the bone for years to throw everything all away.

But why *her*? What is it about Rein Valdez? How and more importantly, *when* did I allow her to get under my skin?

Maybe it's because whenever I'm around her, it eases the immensity of guilt that I've been carrying in my chest for the past two years? That guilt that's been eating away at me every day since I lost Tay and my baby. Or maybe it's because she reminds me of Tay? Whatever the case, I need to be responsible, and more importantly, I must steer clear of her.

The question is, how?

CHAPTER Six

Rein

"COME ON, REI REI, PLEEEEEASE!"

I wince at the shrill tone of my best friend's voice and drop my pen with a huff before I look at her.

"No. P, I already told you I don't like to make a fuss about my birthday. You know this." I remind her and go to pick up my pen, but she grabs hold of my hand and pokes her bottom lip out at me.

I raise a brow while I stare at her straight-faced. "For me? Puhleeeease? It's your twenty-first birthday. This is a big deal."

"No, it really isn't."

Paris stares at me, her eyes growing wider by the second.

"Ugh, fine. No party, just a dinner with friends. You swear?" Paris beams and squeals excitedly while bouncing in her seat. Ugh, I'm dreading this already. "Yes, totally."

I scowl and point my pen at her. "Swear it, or the deal is off."

"I swear!"

I stare at her warily for a moment and nod, turning my attention back to my assignment. "Great, do you think you can bugger off now so I can finish this paper before Professor Saxton slaps me with an F to go nicely with the B- he already gave me?"

Paris giggles and twirls her hair around her index finger while she sighs lustfully. "Have I mentioned how jealous I am that you get an extra two hours with him a week?"

I roll my eyes and sigh in exasperation. I'm not getting this paper done for shit today. "Mentioned? You've not shut up about it, P." I grouse irritably and scowl at her when she reaches over and plucks my pen from my hold, and points it at me. "What you consider lucky, I deem a damn inconvenience. In case you've forgotten, the man harbours an immense abhorrence toward me." I utter with distaste and go to take my pen, but she moves it out of my grasp.

"Hm, this is true. Although, I did read in Cosmo last week that men tend to act like jerks to women they feel intimidated by. It could very well be a defence mechanism to hide his true feelings."

I reach over and hastily snatch my pen back from her, "P, what on earth are you yapping on about? Why the hell would he be intimidated by *me*? The man is a renowned professor in a prestigious school, and I'm just a student on a scholarship. I'm hardly a damn threat to him, am I?"

Paris leans back in her seat and crosses her right leg over the left, and grins mischievously. "Uh-huh. What if you are a threat, though? But in a manner that surpasses the boundaries of the student-professor relationship?"

I stop writing and turn my head to look at her. "Care to justify?"

"Just saying, I felt a vibe between the two of you the other day in his class." Paris voices with a shrug.

I snort, "You need to go get your head examined, P." I answer dismissively, slamming my notebook shut and gather my papers. It's evident I'm not getting anywhere with the assignment with her around. "If you're about done with your daft delusions, I have a shit ton of work I need to catch up on before my shift later."

"Hey, you ever hear the expression there's a microscopic line between lo—"

"P, zip it!" I throw over my shoulder as I walk toward the exit of the library.

The thought alone that Professor Talon Saxton is intimidated by me or is acting like a colossal jerk toward me because he has the hots for me is preposterous.

Pfft. He's just another pretentious, entitled asshat, and that's all there is to it.

———

"REIN VALDEZ, you get that sexy butt out here right this second!" Paris calls out to me from behind the wooden door. The following day, Paris drags me out to pick a dress for my birthday. I stare at myself in the full-length mirror in the changing room and tug the figure-hugging, sparkly pink mini dress down, but it doesn't budge. When I pull the hem of the dress down my legs to cover my arse, it reveals the ugly fading scar between my breasts from the surgery. I brush my fingers over the scar and close my eyes when images of that night flood my mind. "Rein!"

I sigh. "Paris, I can't wear this."

"Nah-uh. Don't you start with that I'm too fat bull, all right? Open the door and let me see you." Paris replies, her voice closer, and I can picture her pressed up against the door, her thick yet perfectly shaped brows drawn together.

"P, this dress isn't me. It's too short; my butt cheeks are practically hanging out, for goodness' sake. I don't have the body shape to pull off a dress like this." I complain, turning to look back at myself.

"Lord, here she goes again." Paris groans and I know she's pinching the bridge of her nose. "Rein, you're being ridiculous. You're an absolute Goddess. Do you have any idea how many girls would kill to have your figure? Some even pay for it! Look at Kim K! Now get out here or so, help me God, I will crawl under the opening at the bottom of the door."

I exhale and unlock the door. Paris pulls the door open and looks me over and smiles broadly. "Holy hot mamasita, look at you! You look fire, Rei Rei!" I wrap my arms around myself and shake my head. "Kim Kardashian, eat your heart out."

"I feel naked, P."

Paris sighs and takes a step toward me, and pulls my arms away from my chest. "Rein, I wish you would stop allowing these insecurities of yours to control you. It's all in your head, babe. You're perfect just the way you are." Paris affirms, taking hold of my hands and squeezing encouragingly. "Don't hide away in the dark when you're clearly made to shine. Look at you!"

I smile appreciatively and bite my bottom lip. It's not the dress. I'm uncomfortable in my own skin, I always have been, but a girl like Paris, with her slim waist and long, slender legs, could never understand what that feels like. I lower my gaze and smooth out the dress with a sigh. I wish I did possess the self-confidence to pull off wearing such a sexy dress.

But I don't, and that's no one's fault but my own.

Despite what everyone says, all I see is an ogre smothered in shimmery pink staring back at me in the mirror.

The good friend she is, Paris notices the uncertainty written all over my face and whips out a satin red midi dress with a high slit on the front. "Okay fine, no mini dresses. This baby right here will look bomb as fuck on you, though, bae." I eye the dress warily, and she thrusts it at me and ushers me back into the changing room. "Go on, shoo."

I only just manage to get the dress on before Paris knocks impatiently at the door. I don't bother with the buttons on the back. "Come on, Rei; I'm dying out here!"

How she lasted a whole nine months in her mother's womb, I'll never know. I smooth out the dress and unlock the door before I push it open. Paris' eyes rake over me, and she grins. "Oh my gosh, yes, I love it. Please, tell me you love it because we have to get you this dress, please Rein, please don't say no." Paris pleads, pressing her hands together and pouting.

"P, I love you, I do, but there is no way in hell I am allowing you to spend three thousand dollars on a dress for me. Absolutely not."

"We'll take it!" Paris chirps excitedly.

"No! No, we won't." I shake my head at the shop assistant, who smiles and nods, completely ignoring me. "I don't need a three-thousand dollar dress! Paris, get back here. I'm talking to you!" I call out to her, and she waves me off, turning and pulling the shop assistant toward the shoe section.

"I'm thinking a pair of six-inch, open toe, glitter, champagne coloured Jimmy Choo sandals will go perfectly with the dress." I watch her in astonishment as she burbles on and on about finding the perfect pair of shoes to go with the dress.

Did she just say Jimmy Choo's? The closest I have ever gotten to designer shoes was when I borrowed my Aunt Dani's knock off Jimmy Choo's for prom. Now that I think about it, I think they were called Timmy Who's.

I look at the price tag on the dress and heave a sigh. I know Paris means well, and she's an incredibly generous friend, but whenever she buys me these expensive gifts, it makes me feel beggarly.

Growing up, we didn't have much money, we weren't exactly broke. We got by, but my mum and aunt Dani always taught me that if you want something, you work hard and earn it. So being sheathed in expensive gowns and designer shoes and jewellery is something that's vastly foreign to me. I know it shouldn't because it's not meant maliciously to make me feel bad about myself, I cannot tell a lie, it sure did wound my pride a little... okay, *a lot*.

"Damn, babe, you feel so fucking good." I squeeze my eyes shut and arch my back while Hunter thrusts himself into me.

Come on, Rein, focus. You can do this, just relax, and it will come.

You will come.

Hunter pulls his head back from where he had it buried in the crook of my neck and peers down at me. "You okay?" He pants, his thrusts slowing. I nod, curling my fingers at the nape of his neck; I draw his mouth to mine and kiss him.

"Yes, feels good. Don't stop. Keep going." I murmur into his mouth, wrapping my legs around his hips. I rock up, meeting his thrusts. "Fuck me harder, Hunter."

"Fuck, you're going to make me come." Hunter groans, grabbing a fistful of my bum and slamming his hips against mine. "Come with me, baby."

Oh crap. I would if I could, for fuck's sake.

"No, no, don't come yet." I whimper, curling my fingers in his hair. "Not yet."

Hunter presses his forehead to mine and bites his lip. "Fuck, I can't hold back. You feel too good. I'm coming."

Goddamn it.

I sigh and stare up at the ceiling while Hunter grunts, his body trembling while spilling his seed into the condom. I loosen my legs around his hips, and he rolls off of me after dropping a quick kiss on my lips. "You're awesome."

The hell I am.

What the hell is wrong with me? Why can't I seem to reach orgasm? It's so frustrating. I can get myself off, and it feels great, but I've never had an orgasm with any of my boyfriends. I get close, but I can never seem to go over the edge, or they finish before I can even get there.

Statistics show that twenty-five percent of women don't climax during intercourse. It sucks lemon balls that I'm part of that percentage. I'm doomed to have boring, run-of-the-mill sex for the rest of my life. Maybe I'll join a nunnery and stop wasting my damn time chasing a fantasy that is likely never going to happen. All three guys I've slept with and nada. I should make an appointment to see a doctor. What if there's something seriously wrong with me? Perhaps there's a pill they can give me to help things along?

With a defeated sigh, I sit up and pick up my black lace bra from the floor where Hunter threw it after almost tearing it off me when he struggled with unclasping it.

"You're leaving?" I nod and don't bother looking back while I do up my bra and reach for my jeans. I can hear Hunter cleaning himself up after he disposes the condom in the bin under his desk.

"Yeah, I need to head back home. I've got a ton of research I need to get through before my class tomorrow." I tell him while I pull my jeans on and button them up.

It's not a complete lie, I do have research to do, but it wasn't due until next week. I lied simply because I didn't want to spend the night listening to Hunter's dorm-mate Mr-no-boundaries-Colton, and his flavour of the month screwing on the bed next to ours. The last time I made the mistake of spending the night, Colton brought back some emo girl early hours in the morning, and they shagged for a solid hour... right there in front of us as if we weren't trying to sleep less than ten feet away.

I don't remember ever feeling so uncomfortable in my life, and I've witnessed some crazy shit back home.

Hunter grabs my wrist and pulls me back down on the bed, his muscular body covering my own as he crawls up and over me. I peer up at him questioningly. "It's past midnight. Happy birthday, baby." I smile and part my lips, accepting his kiss when he presses his mouth to mine.

"Thank you." I brush my fingers through his dark and messy bed hair. Hunter presses a kiss to my wrist, his brown eyes glittering as he stares adorably into mine.

"I guess I'll see you tomorrow night for your birthday dinner?" I brush my index finger along his jaw and nod.

"You mean secret party?" Hunter's eyes grow a little wider, and he fights off the urge to smile.

"So, you know about the party?" I nod again.

"Yes, I know. I love Paris, but she's not exactly the best at keeping things on the DL. In true Paris fashion, she's going all out despite me insistently telling her I don't want a party or a fuss. I'd prefer a night in with my friends chilling and eating pizza."

Hunter's face contorts to one of dissatisfaction.

"Seriously? You'd rather spend your twenty-first birthday sitting indoors eating a pizza? We do that most nights, babe. You only turn twenty-one once."

I sigh and resist the strong urge I get to roll my eyes. I wasn't meant to live to see my eighteenth birthday, let alone turn twenty-one. I almost voice my thoughts, but I shove it down and force a smile on my face.

"You're right."

Hunter smiles and winks. "I'll be seeing you tomorrow then."

"You sure will. Paris wants us to get ready together, so I'll be in her dorm."

Hunter smiles handsomely and brushes a kiss over my lips. "Even better. I'll just pick you up from her dorm then."

I roll him over and straddle his hips. Hunter grabs hold of my hips and smiles as he leans up to kiss me, but I pull back, grinning teasingly. "I have to go."

I jump off the bed, and Hunter falls back on the bed with a sigh. "Can't you just do your research here?" He questions, hugging the pillow and gazing up at me with his eyes all big and pleading. "You can use my laptop?"

I grin and shake my head. "The problem isn't the hardware; it's you, Mr Harris."

"I'll be good."

I pull my jacket on and shake my head, pin him with a knowing look, and he smiles, watching me as I tuck my phone in the back pocket of my light blue jeans. "I'll see you tomorrow, boyfriend."

"You sure will, girlfriend."

An hour and a scalding hot shower later, I'm sprawled out on my bed staring up at the chipped white paint on my ceiling, not a wink of sleep in me. I pick up my phone off the nightstand and look at the time.

1:05am

I'm feeling frustrated, so very beyond frustrated, but I can't seem to pinpoint the reason why. The thoughts going round and round in my mind are chaotic, incoherent, and I think that's what vexes me.

And the constant dripping sound coming from my tap is only adding to my state of annoyance. Oh, sod it. There's only one sure-fire way I'll fall asleep, and it's not by laying here listening to my drippy tap. Instead, I reach over to my nightstand and pull out the purple butterfly vibrator I bought myself a year ago. While my fingers get the job done just fine, sometimes a girl just needs that extra boost to heighten the pleasure, and that's what this gives me. Toe-curling, head spinning, clutching at the sheets, losing your breath kind of pleasure I only wish a man could give me.

God bless the British doctor that invented the vibrator back in the nineteenth century. But, of course, it was initially designed for male physicians because they simply grew tired of 'examining' aka masturbating their female patients using only their fingers to diagnose a condition referred to as Hysteria which was manually treated by a 'pelvic massage' until the patient reached a hysterical paroxysm, after which the patient appeared miraculously restored.

Imagine that... all she needed was an orgasm, and she was right and rain. I've got to get myself one of those special examinations. Perhaps a sinfully handsome doctor in scrubs can help make me hysterical with blissful gratification.

Mm, now there's an image I can work with.

I slide my thong down my legs and kick them off, dropping them on the floor beside the bed and glide the silk straps up and tighten them around my hips and thighs, positioning the butterfly over my clit. I push the power button on the remote, and the butterfly comes to life, vibrating at the lowest setting. A breathy gasp escapes me. I bite down on my bottom lip when that familiar yet desperately craved rush of tingles works its way up from the base of my spine.

I slowly push the dial-up, and the vibrations get more intense. My back arches, and I whimper, rocking my hips up, unable to stay still because of the intensity of the pleasure thrumming through me.

"Uhhh." I drop the remote and reach up, fisting my pillow. My hips shook as I slowly near my release. I close my eyes, and the moment I do, as always, I see *him*, watching me with those penetrating blue eyes of his. He lifts my legs up and over his broad shoulders while his large hands splay out over my hips, and he grips tight, keeping me still while his tongue circles teasingly and sucks my clit like a man that's starved. The pressure in my groin builds, the blood flowing in my veins goes hot and my heart rate soars, thrashing wildly against my ribcage.

"Ahh, fuck, yes, yes." I whimper breathlessly while I linger on the edge of sweet release. That transient moment when your entire body tenses, every muscle goes stiff, and liquid heat rushes straight between your legs. My toes curl, my back arching up off the bed reflexively as I let myself free-fall off the edge into an abyss of earth-shattering rapture.

"*Professor.*" I cry out for him, again and again with every wave of pleasure that fires through me, with every tremor of my release, until I collapse onto the bed, a sweaty, breathless mess.

While I lay there, savouring my post orgasmic bliss, it hit me how wicked it is that I fantasise about my professor instead of my boyfriend while I pleasure myself. It also occurred to me it's not the first time either; it's been happening more and more frequently—especially the last few weeks.

Of course, we're all allowed to have fantasies, but does it make it right? Is what I'm doing considered emotional cheating? Especially if I know deep down my heart is not in the relationship?

When you get more pleasure out of a fantasy than you do your boyfriend, it's time to acknowledge the reality that's staring you in the face and act.

And that's exactly what I'm going to do.

I'm going to break up with Hunter.

CHAPTER *Seven*

Talon

"Yes, mother, for the tenth time, I'm coming home for thanksgiving." I huff as I hurry through the bustling corridor to my next class, which I'm running late for.

"Excuse me for not taking your word for it, love. You've only flaked out on us countless times already over the last three years. I'm starting to forget what my own son looks like!"

I roll my eyes and shake my head in exasperation. "Mum, we Face-Time twice a week. I assure you I've not changed much since Tuesday, all right?"

"Don't get smart with me, young man. You promised you would come home for Thanksgiving and Christmas this year."

I sigh, closing my eyes briefly. "And I'm keeping my promise. I'll see you in two weeks. I'm looking forward to eating your homemade iced Vo-Vo's and Milo balls."

I hear my mother chuckle, clearly amused and smile. I miss her and my dad so much. I'm looking forward to indulging in her cooking. "I'll make you all the Milo balls and Vo-Vo's your heart desires love, so long as you come home, so I can see your handsome face. We miss you terribly."

My heart constricts at her words. I can hear her voice thickening while she tries her best to hold back her emotions. "I miss you guys too. I'll be with you soon." I say as I reach the door to class. "Ma, I'm running late for my next class. I'll call you later. I love you."

"I love you too, be safe, love."

"Always." With a sigh, I hang up the phone and stare at the dark wooden door in front of me with the words 'Art Studio' decaled in big letters in the centre of the wooden panel. All right, I'm going to walk on into that class like every other and not even acknowledge her. She's nothing you need to fret over, just another student out of the hundreds you teach.

You've got this, Tal. Find your fucking bollocks and get it together, you dick.

I loosen my tie a little before I reach for the door handle and pull it open. The smell of fresh paint surrounds me the moment I step into the room, and oddly it eases the tension throbbing in my temples. The students stop talking when I enter the room, and all eyes turn to look at me.

My eyes inadvertently scan the room, taking in each face and zeros in on the one I just spent a good twenty seconds convincing myself I wasn't even going to glance at. Rein lifts her gaze from her painting, her hand holding the brush halts mid-air when our eyes lock across the room.

"Afternoon everyone, apologies for my tardiness. I got a little held up in my last class. Please begin working on your projects, and if you need any help, give me a shout, and I'll be happy to assist you." I say and edict myself to direct all my attention on taking out and firing up my laptop and not allow my gaze to loiter on the five-foot-six brunette standing less than a hundred feet away from me.

Fuck, why does she have to be so beautiful? With a subtle shake of my head, I click a file on my desktop and open the coursework I assigned to my last class last week that I've got to grade and return Monday. I could do it over the weekend, but hell, I'm in desperate need of a distraction right now.

Half hour, that's how long I managed to keep my mind and eyes occupied before they—of their own accord—flitter up and watch Rein paint. The canvas in front of her is obstructing my view of her. All I can see is the left side of her face, her bottom lip between her teeth, and her eye narrowed as she concentrates on her work. Her long light brown hair is braided neatly to the side and draped across her shoulder. While I discreetly admire her from behind my screen, I envision my fingers gripping that braid and tugging her head back till her delightfully feminine neck is exposed for me to bite and suck till I leave my mark on her olive skin.

Damn it. I bet she tastes incredible too. My mouth waters at the mere thought of spreading her out in front of me on my five-thousand-dollar desk and overindulge till my appetite is satisfied.

"Professor?" My thoughts come to a screeching halt when I hear someone calling for me. I see Melanie watching me, her arm in the air, fingers wagging to get my attention.

Ah fuck, I've only gone and got a damn stiffy. I suck in a couple of deep breaths to control the bulge in my trousers. "Give me a moment, Miss Andrews. I'll be right there." I stare at my screen, re-reading the same sentence over and over till my cock slowly slackens.

Okay, we're good.

I rub the back of my neck, avoiding looking in Rein's direction as I walk over to Melanie. "Yes, Miss Andrews?"

"Professor, I'm having some trouble with the shading. I can't seem to get it to reflect off the water as I want." I nod and rub my chin while I tilt my head to the right and observe her work. She's painting a landscape of a meadow lake surrounded by trees and a campfire.

"May I?" I ask, and she nods and hands me the brush and palette. I pick up the red paint and mix it with a little yellow to create a deep orange, and using a soft brush, I softly guide my brush over the water with slow horizontal strokes until the fire from the campfire reflects off the surface of the lake. "Don't worry too much if your reflections don't resemble exactly what's on the bank. Nobody will notice." I hand her the brush and point to the section I just painted. "While your paint is still wet, use the clean side of your brush and gently pull horizontal across the reflection. This will give you a very flat-water effect, and you'll achieve the shading you desire. Next, use your palette knife add some white lines to the edges of the bank to add some ripples."

Melanie smiles appreciatively. "Wow, thank you so much, Professor. It looks so much better already. You truly are as gifted as people say you are."

I shove my hands in my pockets and stare at her painting. "Thank you, Miss Andrews. You're not so bad yourself." I nod courteously. "Carry on."

I circle the room, stopping to observe each painting for a couple of minutes. As much as I took my time, I eventually made my way to Rein. She's got a pair of earphones in, and she's completely lost in her work. I stand behind her and watch while she dexterously guides her brush over the canvas with precision.

Her painting is a mixture of a deep purple on the left and a combination of orange and yellow to the right. She's currently working on the outline, a silhouette of what looks like a woman with a slim frame and long hair. It takes her a long moment to sense someone is behind her. Her head slowly turns, and she looks back at me, clearly surprised to see me standing behind her. I avert my gaze from her painting, and my eyes skim over her pretty face till they meet hers. I'm greeted with her wide and inquisitive gaze watching me. She pulls out the left earphone.

Rein's lovely dark arched brows rise a little. "Miss Valdez?"

"You look as though you've got something you want to say, Professor?" I bite back the urge to smile at the slight tartness to her tone. I'm noticing she goes straight into the offence whenever she's around me, and I wonder if this is something specific for me or is she like this in general?

I shake my head and take a step closer, averting my gaze to her painting while I move to stand beside her to her left. "Not at all. I'm just curious about your work. Most of the class have chosen to paint landscapes or abstract pieces. It's nice to see something a little different. I feel like there's a story here." I voice, and Rein turns her attention to her canvas, her brows knitting together looking adorable while she loses herself in her thoughts for a moment.

She sighs, "There is."

I look at her. "Care to share?"

The sudden spout of gloom that descends upon her delicate features doesn't go unnoticed. Rein drops her paintbrush into the jar of warm water and picks up a white cloth to wipe the paint off her hands. "Can I ask you something?"

I nod, watching her closely when she swivels on her stool to face me. "Have you ever had to break someone's heart you genuinely care a great deal for?"

Okay, not what I was expecting. I thought her question would be more about art than personal. I scratch the top of my eyebrow thoughtfully. "I think we're all guilty of breaking a heart or two. Whether it be intentional or for some unselfish reason that we believe would be in the best interest of the other person." I answer truthfully, leaning back against the window and crossing my arms over my chest. I regard her curiously. I shouldn't, but fuck it, I'm asking. "May I ask, who is this unfortunate fella whose heart you're gearing yourself up to break?"

Rein chews on her bottom lip, wincing a little. "My boyfriend Hunter's. I care about him and don't want to lose his friendship, but I..."

Oh damn.

Hunter Harris is her boyfriend? He's the golden boy of the school. I see that little twerp flirting with other girls all the time, and here she is feeling guilty about breaking his heart when I can bet my life, he's screwed half the girls at this school. I clench and unclench my hands by my sides. That piece of information has truly gone and fucked me right off. "I see."

Rein shakes her head and laughs softly, her cheeks turning rosy. "Ah, I'm sorry, Professor. I don't even know why I'm telling you any of this. Ignore me."

I frown and straighten, "Don't apologise, Miss Valdez. I may not know the specifics or the state of your relationship, but I know one thing for certain. If something doesn't feel right, ninety-nine percent of the time, it's your gut trying to tell you something." Rein's eyes slowly lift to mine when I take a step closer to her, momentarily distracting her from the task of neatly folding the wires to her earphones in an attempt to avoid looking at me.

"Trust your instincts. A woman's intuition is her greatest weapon, and it doesn't lie." I add solemnly and allow my gaze to linger on hers for a second before I walk back toward the desk at the front of the class. I glance at my watch and see there's fifteen minutes to the end of class. "That's all for today, guys. I'm seeing some great pieces. Please clean down your stations, and I will see you all next Friday." I close my laptop and gather my papers, stuffing them into my brief-case. "Miss Valdez?" Rein's head whips around, and she looks over at me questioningly. "Would you please lock up?" She nods.

"Sure."

"Have a great weekend, everyone." The students utter a goodbye as I open the door and exit the classroom.

I stand by the door for a minute processing the conversation I just had with Rein. Did I just inadvertently encourage my student to dump her boyfriend?

Christ, I'm a right fucking dill.

LATER THAT NIGHT, I pop open a bottle of Bud and throw myself onto the comforts of my soft brown leather sofa skimming through Netflix, trying to find something interesting to watch.

Damn, has it been a week.

I scroll through the tv shows until I find one that piques my interest. I push play and get comfortable when my phone pings alerting me of a notification on Insta. JT tagged me in a photo of himself out at our bar 'Aura' with two birds. The boy doesn't give his knob a bloody rest; JT and I both invested three hundred thousand dollars into this bar last year as silent partners. Craig—one of our buddies who has a solid background in managing clubs, pitched the idea to JT and myself, and we decided it was a great investment. Being a silent partner suits me just fine. I have no time or desire to manage a swanky bar. Craig seems to have everything under control.

I like the photo and mindlessly scroll through my feed. A girl that resembles Rein catches my attention, and I stop scrolling, staring at the picture. I find myself comparing her to Rein—only there is no comparison. Rein is naturally more beautiful. She has this unique beauty that shines even without her trying.

I wonder if she's got an account. Before I can talk myself out of it, I'm typing her name into the search bar. The first account that comes up is hers, and I'm clicking on it at nerve-wracking speed. Jesus mate, eager much?

Fuck.

She posted a photo twenty minutes ago with her friend that always sneaks into my class... Paris, I believe, is her name. They're both dolled up, clearly ready for a night out. Posing side by side with their hands on their hips and smiling broadly. Rein is clad in a mid-length red dress with a high slit on the front, showing off her shapely tan leg. Her long hair is falling around her shoulders in loose curls. I recognise the neon blue sign behind them. They're at Aura. The caption under the photo read, *'Another year older, but definitely none the wiser. I'm only here for the cake she promised me. #cheersto21'*

I smile.

It's her birthday. I jump out of my skin and drop my phone in my lap when it starts ringing. "Shit." I pick it up and see it's JT calling. Fucker scared me half to death. I push the green answer button. "Yes, mate."

"Dude, it's Friday night. Tell me you're not sitting at home like some boring old fart." JT shouts over the loud music and noise in the background.

I chuckle and take a long swig of my beer. "It's not boring when you happen to enjoy your own company."

"Fuck that! You, my friend, need to fix up and start acting your age and snap out of this middle-aged persona you've stumbled into. Come out. Aura is lit tonight, bro."

I have my excuse lined up and ready, but I hesitate. A change of scene might be nice. The kid does have a point. I'm twenty-eight, not fifty, after all. I'll have a drink or two and come back home. "You may be right, mate. I'll swing by for a drink. I have been meaning to drop by to see how things are going."

"Wait, what? You're coming? Wow, I had a whole argument ready to go. You've stumped me."

I laugh and get up off the sofa, sipping my beer as I stroll to my walk-in wardrobe, "Sorry to disappoint you, kid. I'll be there in thirty minutes. Have my double Chivas waiting."

JT laughs, "You got it, bro. Aye Craig, Sexy Saxy says to have his Chivas ready for him." I shake my head as I look through my shirts. "Craig said there's a bottle with your name all over it."

"Fuck, I'm not looking to get trolleyed, mate. Let me get dressed, and I'll see you soon."

"Sweet as, we're in the VIP lounge."

"I'll find ya." I hang up and toss my phone on the bed. I choose a pair of grey plaid trousers, a white polo neck sweater and a grey tweed jacket. I'm going for a preppy smart, yet casual look. After I style my hair and spray my aftershave, I grab my keys off the kitchen counter and head out.

I got to the club in thirty minutes. Traffic was unusually light for a Friday night in Belmont Central, where the club is located. There's a line around the block with people waiting to get in as I drive up to the gate beside the building. Killian, one of the bouncers, recognises me and opens the gate so I can pull into the reserved car park for VIPs.

The moment I step out of the car, I can hear the music filtering through the doors.

"Talon, it's good to see you, my man." I smile and fist bump Dennis, the head of security at the club. "You've not been around these ends in a while."

"I know. Works been kicking my arse lately. It's good to see you, brother. You keeping well?" Dennis smiles, nodding, and opens the door for me to enter.

"Ahh, never a dull moment here."

I chuckle, "Jase in his usual spot?"

He nods again, taking a pull from his cigarette, "Sure is, bro."

I walk in and make my way through the crowd. The music was thundering at deafening levels, the ground under my feet vibrated as I squeezed through the crowd toward the VIP floor on the third floor. The two stories above are reserved for the rich and famous. So often, you'll find celebrities, politicians and wealthy kids throwing around daddy's cash.

"There he is!" Jase shouts, waving me over. He's got two girls on either side of him, one of them practically draped across his lap. I greet him with a nod and shake Craig's hand. "Girls, meet my boy Talon Saxton."

I nod politely and take the glass of whiskey from Craig before I take the seat beside him. "Ladies."

"I almost dropped dead when you agreed to come out tonight, bro. Not that I'm complaining, but what gives?"

I savour the first sip of my whiskey; that rich, smooth taste and the burn as it goes down was almost orgasmic. "I told you, I needed a change. It's been a long week, and I need to burn off some fuel."

"I hear you, fella. I'll drink to that." Craig holds out his glass to me, and I toast him with an inward sigh.

The fact Rein Valdez is somewhere in this club had absolutely nothing to do with my decision. Not one little bit.

And yet, my eyes are against my better judgment, scanning the club in search of her.

CHAPTER Eight

Rein

"BOTTOMS UP, SUGAR TITS."

I wince as I watch Paris slide another blue kamikaze shot in my direction. "P, you're killing me," I complain, swaying on my feet while I stare down at the drink. I've currently got a nice buzz going, but if I keep downing these shots, I'm going to get zonked beyond belief.

"Don't be such a lightweight. It's your birthday. You're supposed to get pissed. So come on, drink, drink, drink!"

I clink my glass with hers, and we down the shots. I grimace and shudder at the bitter aftertaste. I knew Paris would pull a stunt like this, so I made sure I had something to eat beforehand so I didn't drink on an empty stomach. I mean, I know some of these people, but most I don't even know. They're all her friends from her dance performance class. And why she invited Sydney is beyond me, and the fact she even showed up baffled me even more.

I look around and frown when I notice Hunter is missing. "Hey, have you seen Hunter?" I ask Paris, and she shakes her head and takes my hand, pulling me through the crowd toward the dance floor.

"He's probably gone to the bathroom. Come on, sugar tits. We're going to dance till our feet fall off." Paris shouts over the music.

My feet were already aching in these stupid shoes. You'd think a pair of shoes that cost more than a kidney would at least be comfortable, but nope. 'Tempted To Touch# by Rupee starts thundering through the speakers. While I dance rather provocatively with my best friend, Hunter finally emerges with Colton and joins us. I feel his arms snake around my waist, and he draws me back against him.

"There's my girl." He drawls in my ear while we sway together. Something inside me recoils when he calls me that. Shouldn't I be giddy when my boyfriend refers to me as his? Instead, I feel almost repelled.

Professor Saxton's words replay in my mind. *"Trust your instincts."*

I promised myself I would break up with him after tonight. Because every moment I'm with him, I feel worse for leading him on. I'm not being true to my feelings nor his. I'm starting to feel like such a fraud, and that is something I'm not. It's becoming exceedingly difficult trying to play the doting girlfriend when I feel nothing of the sort.

We all continue dancing, me with Hunter while Colton is grinding rather heatedly with Paris beside us. Nothing new there. Paris has slept with that man-whore more times than I can count. They've got that I hate you, but I love to fuck you thing going on.

I gasp when Hunter spins me, pulling me against his chest, his hands gripping my hips while he grinds himself against my bum, his lips nipping at my pulse point. I sigh, and I'm not even sure what made me, but I open my eyes and look up to the level above us and almost swallow my tongue when I see none other than Professor Saxton watching me, a glass of whiskey in hand while he's leant against the glass balustrade.

I'm hallucinating. I must be drunker than I thought. There is no way he's standing there. I squeeze my eyes shut and shake my head a little, half-convinced I'm losing my mind, and he will disappear when I open my eyes again.

I slowly open my eyes and gasp. My mouth goes dry the moment our eyes lock. Oh my God, he's actually here. He takes a slow sip of his drink, his eyes never leaving mine until Hunter spins me again, so I'm facing him.

Oh hell.

What the ever-living fuck is he doing here?

The song changes to Calvin Harris' 'Feel So Close'. The lights flicker to the beat of the music, and smoke fills the air. Aura is one of the best clubs in Chicago, so it could very well be a coincidence that he's here. Hunter stops one of the shot girls and hands me a shot of gold tequila. I don't even hesitate. I knock the shot back, my eyes discreetly lifting to the balcony to see if he's still there. I shudder at the acidic taste of the tequila after I swallow it. The lights dim even darker, but I could still see him every time the blue neon light rotates or flickers. He's talking to a beautiful brunette girl, leaning in close to speak into her ear. Whatever it is he says to her she throws her head back and laughs with gusto, squeezing his bicep flirtatiously.

"Have I mentioned how sexy you look tonight?" Hunter slurs in my ear as we continue to dance together.

I force a smile on my face and nod. "Once or twice." I answer and instantly regret that last tequila shot when my head whirls. I lean against Hunter's chest and he wraps his arms around me, his lips trailing down the side of my neck. I close my eyes and swallow thickly when my stomach turns. I pull away from him and look around for Paris but she's disappeared with Colton. *Fuck sake.* "I need to go to the bathroom." I shout over the music, and Hunter nods, he opens his mouth to say something but stops when he notices a group of his friends waving him over on the dance floor.

"Go ahead babe, I'll be here." I resist the urge to roll my eyes and squeeze through the crowded dance floor in search of the bathroom. Not that I need a goddamn escort, but an offer would have been nice.

My head spins, and the floor under my feet suddenly felt alarmingly unstable. I grabbed hold of the first person I could reach before I fell. "Hi gorgeous, are you lost?" I hear a deep voice in my ear, and I exhale, shaking my head. I let go of his arm and push him off me.

Jesus, when did I get this drunk? I was fine a moment ago. I'm one drink away from being utterly wasted, and that is exactly what I've been trying to avoid. After much effort, I finally spot the bathroom and push the door open and stumble in almost losing my footing. "Wow, that is one heavy door." I utter to no one in particular while I stare up at the big wooden door and giggle drunkenly. There's a group of girls touching up their make-up and chatting.

I slowly walk over to the free sink beside them and run the cold water. I bow my head and groan, fighting the urge to throw up every time my stomach lurches in protest.

I lift my gaze and stare at myself in the mirror. My face is flushed, lips tinted red where my lipstick has worn off. I press some cold water to my neck and cheeks to try and sober up a little and cool down my flustered skin. It's like an inferno in that club.

I hear laughter and when I open my eyes, I see the brunette Professor Saxton was talking to earlier was among the group of women standing a couple of feet from me. "Ari, you're so bad. Tell me you're going home with that fine specimen of a man you've been eye-fucking all night."

The brunette named Ari smirks and glances back to her friend while she applies her nude lipstick. "Possibly." She rubs her lips together and cleans up the edges of her lips with her finger. "You know he's a professor? There seems to be a mysterious streak to him, and I dig it. He doesn't give much away; I can't really tell what he's thinking." She voices and turns to face her friends after she drops her lipstick in her clutch. "But you know me girls, I love a good challenge, and something tells me this one is definitely going to be worth the trouble... if you know what I mean." She adds with a suggestive wink as they walk out of the bathroom.

I snort in a very unladylike manner and shake my head. Of course he's going to leave with her. If I were a guy, I'd leave with her too. She's outrageously beautiful, a perfect ten out of ten and I...

Wait a bloody minute? Why do I care who he takes home and fucks? And more importantly why am I even standing here comparing myself to her like I would ever stand a chance with a man like Talon Saxton. Firstly, he's like eight years older than me. He's smart and successful and the man is my *professor* for crying out loud! Satan will be ice-skating to work before he and I ever came close to becoming anything at all.

No, Talon Saxton will remain securely where he belongs—as my deepest, lewdest fantasy.

When my head finally stops spinning, I walk out of the bathroom and push through the crowd toward the VIP floor. The music changes to Jennifer Lopez's 'On the Floor' and I can feel the bass thumping painfully in my head as if someone's beating my head against the wall.

I couldn't see anyone through the sea of people jumping and dancing on the dance floor. Where the hell are Paris and Hunter? I need to get out of here. I push through toward the stairs at the side and stop when my knees wobble in protest at the mere thought of trying to climb up one step.

The elevator, there's an elevator somewhere that we took up earlier. I turn, my eyes scanning the club and see it tucked away behind the spiral staircase. I make my way over to it and push the button twice.

I can't wait to take these goddamn shoes off and dive into my bed before I projectile vomit all over the place. Finally, the doors swing open, and I go to walk in and stop dead in my track. I stare unblinking at the couple sucking each other's faces off like they wanted to swallow each other whole.

Everything around me slows, the music fading away, my heart beating hard in my ears as I stood there like a fool watching Hunter sucking faces with Sydney, his hand up her dress, fingering her.

"Oh God," I whisper, pressing my fingers to my mouth. I should have said something, *did something*, but all I could do is pathetically watch my boyfriend pleasuring another girl. Not just a random girl. Fucking Sydney!

My stomach rolls at the sight, and the alcohol I consumed slowly makes its way up. I had the urge to take off my shoe and hurl it at the bastard's head, but I couldn't even muster up the energy, my limbs felt like lead. I couldn't bear to watch anymore, so I spin on my heels and almost topple over when the room spins with me. I walk straight into a solid figure; my knees shake in warning.

I gasp when a firm grip on my upper arms steadies me before I hit the floor. My eyes sluggishly rise and I blink when I see Professor Saxton standing tall and imperious in front of me, those icy blue eyes of his fixed firmly on Hunter and Sydney still going at it, completely oblivious to their surroundings.

The lump in my throat grows bigger with every passing second as I helplessly look up at him. His jaw clenches and unclenches when he lowers his gaze to mine. I don't know what he sees in my eyes and in that moment, I couldn't care less because whatever it was made him wrap a brawny arm around my waist and guide me through the throng of people.

"Where's your friend?" I hear him ask and only muster a shrug in response. Professor Saxton looks down at me thoughtfully and guides me to the back where a giant of a bouncer is guarding a door, "Did you bring anything with you?"

I nod and hold up my wrist where I had a wristband to the cloakroom where I left my bag and jacket. I hazily scan the club in hopes I'll see Paris but no avail, she's probably in a dark corner with Colton. Jesus, that boy brings out the worst in her.

Professor Saxton speaks to the bouncer, and when he touches my arm to get my attention, I look up at him. The bouncer walks ahead of us, and I feel Professor Saxton's hand at the small of my back, guiding me through the door toward the corridor to the exit. I thought we would stop to collect my things, but before my mind could register, the wristband was already off and handed to the bouncer.

"Wait, what about my stuff?" I question drunkenly, looking back at the bouncer heading toward the little hut cloakroom while we near the exit.

"Dennis will bring your stuff to the car."

I look up at Professor Saxton, "Dennis?"

"Yes, Dennis, the big bald bloke you saw inside. He's the head of security here."

I blink, and as we step outside and the fresh air hits me, my legs momentarily turn to jelly. I sway on my feet a little; everything around me spins; it felt like the world was spinning on its axis at hundred miles per second. Professor Saxton stops and steadies me by holding onto my shoulders.

"Are you all right?" I hear him ask through the thumping of my head while I fight the urge to throw up.

Am I all right?

I couldn't say yes. I couldn't say no. It suddenly felt like the most complicated question in the world to me at that moment. I couldn't really place my feelings. Was I heartbroken? Definitely not. Do I feel betrayed? Absolutely. Even if I had plans to break up with Hunter, I never imagined he would ever cheat on me. If he could do that in a club where I was present on my birthday, imagine what the rotten bastard got up to behind my back.

I feel so stupid.

I should have known something was up, I should have trusted my gut, but I didn't. Why would the most popular and sought-after guy at the school choose to date a nobody like me? Now that I think about it, it wouldn't surprise me one bit if Sydney put him up to it to fuck with me.

And to think I felt bad that I was going to hurt him! When all the while he's been screwing fuck only knows the entire time we've been dating. Arsehole.

You've truly crossed over to a whole new level of pathetic Rein; well fucking done.

"I want to go home," I whisper, peeling my eyes open when every-thing stops spinning and look up at him.

Professor Saxton nods once and guides me toward an all-black Mustang GT. "Come on." He sighs and guides me around the car to the passenger side. He unlocks it and pulls the door open for me. I stop before I get into the car; with a frown, I stare up at him.

"Wait, wait, there's a very high possibility that might throw up in your car," I mutter, pointing my index finger at his flash car. Professor

Saxton's blue eyes narrow at the corners while he watches me and licks his lips while he stares into my eyes as if he's trying to see straight into my soul and unveil my deepest darkest secrets.

"If you chunder in my car, you'll be cleaning it up, Miss Valdez." I look over his face, searching for any signs that he might be jesting but the surly look on his face tells me he's dead serious.

I gulp.

"Get in." My step falters, and I stumble a little as I get into the car, clumsily falling into the plush red and black leather seat. I watch as he pushes the door shut and walks around the car to the driver side just as Dennis—the head of security, walks over with my black leather jacket and silver clutch bag in his hands and passes it to Professor Saxton.

While they stand outside conversing, I kick off my shoes and groan at the throbbing of my toes and the unpleasant ache at the balls of my feet. I'm convinced that the person who invented heels hates women with a vengeance. I honestly don't know how some women prance around in these godforsaken torture devices all damn day. It would hurt less walking barefoot over broken glass.

While I rub my aching feet, I glance around the car. Even in my drunken state, I couldn't suppress my nosey side from prying a little. It's dark, and I can't really make out much, but it looks pristine, and there doesn't seem to be any sign of a woman's presence.

Holy crap on a sesame cracker, I'm sitting in Professor Saxton's car!

Am I dreaming? When I woke up this morning, I certainly didn't expect my night to wind up with me being cheated on, and my hot as sin professor, who I was sure loathed me stepping in and rescuing me —not that I needed saving. Of course, I can take care of myself, but I can't deny that it feels *nice* to be protected.

While I was adrift someplace in my thoughts, I didn't notice Professor Saxton opened the door and was in the car until the door shut, and the dull thud caused my heart to leap up into my throat. I take my jacket and clutch from him when he holds it out to me and gently set them on my lap.

The car roars to life, and we drive out of the car park of the club. I stay quiet and stare out of the passenger side window. My mind stuck replaying the moment the elevator doors opened, and I saw Hunter with Sydney.

"Are you okay? Do you need me to pull over?" I turn my head to look at Professor Saxton while he drives. His cerulean eyes on the road, his fingers gripping the steering wheel.

I shake my head, "No, I think I'll be all right." I answer, and he nods. When I don't look away, he notices me staring and gives me an inquisitive side-long glance.

"You look like you've got something you want to say, Valdez."

"I may be a little more intoxicated than I initially assessed, but... I didn't just have some weird trip and hallucinate back there, right? That was my boyfriend Hunter kissing and finger fucking Sydney Dalton in that elevator on a night we were supposed to be celebrating my birthday?"

Those dark brows of his draw together, and he averts his gaze back to the road. I keep my eyes on him, waiting for a reaction and deflate a little when I get nothing but a stoic expression. "I'm afraid so."

I sigh, chewing agitatedly on my bottom lip while I rake my fingers through my hair and sink back into the leather seat. "What a sack of shit." I gripe hotly. I feel my phone vibrate in my bag and pull it out. I see Hunter's name flash across my screen and stare at it for a beat before I push the green button and answer it.

Professor Saxton watches me. "Oh, look who finally decided to come up for air long enough to remember he has a girlfriend."

I hear music playing faintly in the background, "Rein, baby, what are you talkin' about? Where are you? I've been lookin' for you." Hunter slurs drunkenly.

"Oh, piss off, you stupid prick. Looking where exactly, in Sydney's mouth?"

"Baby, come on—"

"I am not your fucking baby, and I sure as shit am not your girlfriend —in fact, why don't you go and suck on Sydney's bony arse a little more and forget my number like you did our relationship, you fucking arsehole!" I spat stormily and hung up the phone.

I pinch the bridge of my nose and exhale slowly to calm the rage twisting in my gut. When I finally look up, I find Professor Saxton observing me, his blue eyes swimming in sympathy. "Stop looking at me like that."

He frowns as the car rolls to a stop at a traffic light. "Like what? How am I looking at you?"

"Like I'm some heartbroken damsel. I'm fine. In fact, I feel great. I've been stewing the past couple of days, trying to figure out how I will break up with him. I should thank the prick for saving me the trouble." I utter irritably, crossing my arms over my chest and staring at the red traffic light waiting for it to turn green. I lean forward a little when I notice huge columns of thick black smoke surging into the sky. "Is that..."

Professor Saxton follows my gaze, and he looks up to see the smoke. "It looks like there might be a fire."

My heart dives into my stomach. The light finally turns green, and we drive up onto my street, and I see the flashing blue lights of the three fire trucks and ambulances parked up outside my apartment building which was engulfed in flames. I don't think I've ever sobered up so fast in my life. I stare up, utterly stupefied, at the building engulfed in flames before me.

And just like that, the rat hole I once called my own is now... gone.

CHAPTER Nine

Talon

A WHOLE FIVE-SECONDS, REIN AND I BOTH SILENTLY STARE UP at the burning building. Flames burned red and amber, engulfing it from every side.

"No..." I hear her whisper beside me, and I tear my gaze away from the horrendous sight before us and look over at her. I see the curiosity from a moment ago quickly turn to horror when every bit of colour drains away from her pretty face. She unbuckles her seatbelt and reaches for the handle to open the door. I follow suit and swiftly unbuckle my seatbelt and jump out of the car. The acrid stench of the smoke burns my nostrils as soon as I step out.

Rein runs barefoot toward the crowd of people, helplessly watching and sobbing while their homes burn right before their very eyes. I jog after her, pushing through the group of people trying to get to the front. "What happened?" she frantically questions one bystander. "How did this happen?" She asks another couple, and they shake their heads forlornly. Rein curls her fingers in her hair and looks up at the building. "Oh my God."

"Rein, wait!" I call out after her when she runs toward the burning building. I manage to catch up with her, pushing people out of my way so I can get to her. I catch her arm and pull her back to me.

A firefighter steps in her way and shakes his head. "Miss, you need to stay back."

Rein shakes her head, fighting in my hold "No, please, you don't understand I live there. Apartment 5b. I have something valuable up there. I need to go get it!"

"I'm so sorry, Miss, but whatever your valuable item is, I assure you it's unlikely it will make it out of that fire. However, your insurance will replace whatever losses you have incurred."

Rein shakes her head slowly and stares up at him pleadingly with eyes full of tears, "Insurance? Insurance can't replace what's up there! Please, just let me by, and I'll go and get it myself."

"Rein, stop, stop. Come here." I tighten my grip on her arm, and she falls against me. "You won't make it up there alive long enough to retrieve whatever it is you want to get," I tell her, and she sobs, pressing her hand over her mouth. "You heard the firefighter; he said it's unlikely anything will be salvageable in a fire of this scale."

Rein shakes her head. "You don't understand. It's all I had left of her." Rein utters, tears spilling over and rolling down her cheeks.

"Left of who?"

"My mum." She whispers woefully and pulls away from me, looking up at what was once her home. The flames reflecting in her sorrow-filled eyes. "The necklace she gave me when I turned eighteen, just before she died. I left it on the nightstand by the bed." She explains, lifting her fingers to her bare neck as she speaks. "I told her I would never take it off, and now it's... it's just gone." She sobs quietly; her head hangs low.

My chest constricts at her confession. I'm all too familiar with that feeling of wanting to hold onto something of someone you've lost. I've got the strongest urge to gather her into my arms and hold her while she cries, but fuck, I couldn't. So instead, I fist my hands by my side and watch her sob like an insensitive prick acting like I didn't care. But deep down, I do care, for some reason unbeknown to me.

I cared when I saw the betrayed look on her face when she saw her boyfriend necking off with some bird on a night they're supposed to be celebrating her. I was ready and willing to get my punch in, detach his fucking jaw from his head, but lucky for him, I'm no hothead. I'm a man that exercises control in all things, and she's not mine to protect. Above that, Rein is my student. I already took a colossal risk of being seen leaving the club with her.

Rein wanders off toward the curb on the side of the road and sinks down on it, burying her head in her hands. I walk over to the fire-fighter that was talking to Rein a moment ago. "Hey mate, can I ask you a quick question?"

He turns to look at me and nods, taking off his helmet and tucking it under his arm. "My friend left a necklace in her apartment that's very valuable and holds a great deal of sentimental value. What's the like-lihood of it being recovered after the fire has been put out?"

"Honestly, it depends on the karatage. If it's gold or platinum, then it's likely to be recovered with minimal damage." He kindly explains and I nod, taking out one of my business cards and handing it to him.

"Thanks mate, I appreciate you taking the time to answer my ques-tion. Take my card, her apartment is 5b, if you happen to find a neck-lace on the nightstand by the bed, please give me a call."

104

"Sure thing, pal." I shake his hand, and he nods, tucking the card into his jacket pocket and walks toward his co-workers. "Any casualties?" I ask the police officer standing guard at the barricade.

"None as of yet. A couple minor injuries, some smoke inhalation. They all got lucky. It seems everyone made it out just before it reached the second floor." He explains turning to look over at the paramedics treating a couple of people.

"Luckily. Any idea what happened?"

He shakes his head, rubbing his hands together to warm them up. "Not yet, once the fire is extinguished the fire marshal will investigate and report back what caused the fire."

"And all these people? Where will they go?"

"Their insurance will cover a hotel for a couple nights until they can make arrangements," I nod and glance over at Rein sitting on the curb, I can see she's trembling all the way from here. She must be absolutely freezing in that dress.

"That's good to know. You got any spare emergency foil blankets going?" The officer nods and walks over to the back of his police car and comes back a moment later with a folded-up foil blanket. "Thank you." I unfold the blanket as I walk over to Rein and when I reach her I wrap the blanket around her shoulders. She jumps, startled and looks up, her eyes rimmed red, her button nose pink from being out in the cold. Her gaze softens when she sees it's me and visibly relaxes, sinking into the warmth of the blanket with a heavy sigh.

"Thank you, Professor." She whispers gratefully.

I nod, perching down in front of her. My fingers itch to reach out and brush away the hair that has fallen over her face, covering up her left eye. "I spoke to the police officer, he said hotels are being arranged for those who have lost their homes due to the fire. Your insurance will cover your stay for a couple of nights while you make arrangements. You'll need your policy number."

Rein's eyes fill with a fresh batch of tears, and she shakes her head slowly, a bitter laugh escaping her while she angrily swipes away the tears that stream down her face, "Insurance? I don't have insurance." She sniffles, "I don't even have a rental agreement or contract."

I stare at her unblinking. "What do you mean you don't have a rental agreement? You must have signed a leasing document before you got the keys when you paid your security deposit, right?" Rein shakes her head and I frown.

"I didn't pay a security deposit. The landlord said he would waiver off the security deposit if I didn't sign an agreement because it was only a short-term lease because I was a student and didn't have three months of pay checks."

"Jesus, Rein." I sigh tiredly, pinching the bridge of my nose. "I can understand the renter's agreement, luckily you obtain some rights, but without renters' insurance, you won't be able to claim any of your losses."

"I didn't know the building was going to burn down, did I?" She snaps hotly while gesturing to the building. "I was only supposed to be in there a couple of months while I waited for a dorm to open up, but it never did, so I was stuck there. I just about manage to scrape together the rent for this shithole. It was either pay twenty-two dollars a month for insurance or spend that money on food; I chose the latter."

I shove a hand through my hair and glance down at my watch. The time was almost three-thirty in the morning. Rein hastily stands and wraps the blanket tighter around herself. "You should go, Professor. Thank you for bringing me back home and sticking around, but I'll manage from here on."

I slowly stand, and she looks up at me. "You'll manage? And how exactly do you propose to do that, Rein? Where will you go?"

She shrugs, averting her gaze from mine. "I can take care of myself. I'll figure something out. I always do. You've already done more than I can ever ask for, so please, just go home. I've ruined your night enough as it is."

Like hell I'm leaving her out on the streets on her own. "I'm not comfortable leaving you out on the streets on your own. Is there someone you can call or someplace I can at least drive you?" Rein's eyes lift heavenward and she exhales, a cloud of condensation emitting from her mouth. "How about your friend? The girl you were with tonight?"

"I called her, she didn't answer. She's probably passed out drunk in Colton's bed right about now."

Wow.

"Anywhere else?"

"I appreciate your concern, Professor, but I'll just stay at Zen's or something." I stop rubbing the back of my neck and stare at her perplexedly.

"Zen's? You're going to sleep in a *bar*?" I question incredulously, and she shrugs, looking down and shuffling from foot to foot. I follow her gaze and scowl when I see she's standing barefoot on the gravel in this freezing weather. Fucking hell, she's going to wind up catching pneumonia. Rein walks past me, and I watch her retreating back as she walks toward my car.

I follow her and unlock the door when she tugs on the handle. "You can't spend the night in a bar."

"Yes, I can." She utters tiredly, "There's a room in the back; it will suffice for tonight and tomorrow. I'll just... I'll find the first flight out and go back home."

I'm knocked for six by her response. Home? Home as in back to London? "You're going back to London? What about school, Rein?" I question as I move to stand by the passenger side door. Rein picks up her clutch bag and sits on the seat so she can put her shoes on.

"What about it, Professor? I think it's evidently clear that this whole thing was a big, big mistake. I should never have come out here. I don't know who the hell I thought I was, fooling myself by thinking I could make it on my own. I'm done, and I want to go back home." There's an ireful undertone to her words.

I can wholly understand where she's coming from and why she feels like giving up, but she's got such a bright future ahead of her; it would be a dire shame for her to throw all of that away with only a year to go to graduation. Rein curses when she drops her shoes while she struggles to put them on.

I can sense the frustration leaching off her in waves, so I perch down and pick up one shoe and look up at her. Rein watches me back warily and bites her plump bottom lip when I gently wrap my fingers around her ankle and slide the shoe on her dainty foot. I repeat the process with her right foot, all the while battling with the voice in my head, telling me to keep my distance and respect her wishes. I've already crossed the line by miles tonight.

I don't know what the hell I'm doing, if I'm honest. I don't know what it is about this girl that makes me want to burn the old rule book and break every single one of those promises I made to myself about fraternising with a student.

It's the feisty in her. It's stirring up a side to me I've kept dormant for many years. The starved beast inside wants to claim her in every filthy way possible.

"If you're willing and have the heart to throw away all the hard work you've put in over the two years you've been here, then maybe you should go back home," I tell her evenly as I stand again. Rein looks up at me and blinks, her brows drawing together.

"You think I want to, Professor? You have no idea what I've been through. Look at me; it's clear that I don't belong here." She states, gesturing to herself. "I've tried okay. I've beaten myself down for the past two years. I worked myself to the bone. I've starved for days on end so I could buy the books I needed for classes or trips. I've damn near killed myself trying to fit in, but it's not working." She cries dejectedly. "Just when I convinced myself that I had everything under control, it unravels all over again, and I've lost everything." Tears stream down her cheeks, her bottom lip quivering. She holds her arms out to her sides, "This, what you see, is all I have left. I don't have the strength to start over again; I just don't."

"Rein—"

"Please don't, just go, Professor." She side-steps me and goes to walk off, but I grab her arm and stop her before she can.

"You're wrong, Rein." She stares ahead. "You do belong here. Unlike most of the students at that school, you've earned the right to be here through all your hard work and all the sacrifices you've made. It takes guts to up and move across the world to follow your dreams, but you did it. You're going to be faced with challenges in every aspect of your life. How far do you expect to get if you up and quit each time you trip and fall? You shouldn't let the challenges you've experienced deter you. Don't throw away everything you've worked so hard for because you've come across another hurdle. Take it from me; living day in and day out with regret is far worse, especially when you've come so close to the end." I explain and loosen my grip on her upper arm a little when she turns her head to look at me.

"Why are you helping me, Professor?"

We stare at one another wordlessly for a long moment while I gather my thoughts, "Because I see tremendous potential in you. You've got a real gift, Rein, and it would be a real shame to see it go to waste." I answer and watch her closely. She sighs and looks ahead again.

"I appreciate you saying that, Professor Saxton. Coming from you, that's truly a huge compliment. As hard as it is to believe, given the shit I've had to endure, it means a lot to hear it." Rein states earnestly and pulls her arm free of my hold before she wraps her arms over her chest to shield herself from the chill of the wind. She exhales heavily, "You should go; I feel terrible for dragging you through all this mess. I'll be fine, honestly."

I shake my head and rub the back of my neck, resisting the urge to groan when a dull ache shoots down my spine. "I'm not leaving you until I know you've got someplace safe to go."

"I already told you I have. I'll spend the night at the bar and figure something out tomorrow."

I sigh inwardly, fucking balls; she's stubborn as fuck. I held the passenger side door open for her and gestured for her to get in. "Fine, at least let me drive you. I've got a feeling those shoes are not suitable for long walks with evening dew in the freezing cold."

I almost break into a full-on grin when she doesn't argue and slides into the passenger seat. The drive to Zen's from her place was no more than five minutes. I pulled up outside and observed the pitch-black eerie-looking bar and almost drove off again.

Something doesn't sit right with me. I can feel my stomach twisting like a pretzel, and I really don't like the idea of leaving her all alone in an empty bar.

"Thank you for the ride, Professor."

"I'll walk you in." Rein stops as she reaches for the door handle and gapes at me, stunned. I kill the engine and take out the key. "After you." I gesture toward the door once we both get out of the car.

"Professor, you really don't have to—"

"Are you going to open the door, or are we going to keep lurking around out here like two of the world's daftest criminals?" Rein sighs and takes out a set of keys from her purse, and unlocks the door. A beeping of an alarm system greets us the moment we walk in. Rein uses the flash on her phone and punches in a code on the panel by the door disarming the alarm.

A moment of silence falls between us as we stand in the dark side by side with only the flashlight on Rein's phone illuminating the area in front of us. The irritatingly loud humming of the fridges behind the bar was already starting to bother me. "Are you absolutely certain you want to spend the night here? It's rather uncanny, and it's freezing."

"It is a little on the creepy side after hours, but I'll be fi—" Rein gasps aloud and almost leaps into my arms when we hear a loud bang from somewhere in the bar. It wasn't until a couple of seconds after that I realised, she was pressed up against my chest, my arm wrapped protectively around her waist holding her against me.

Oh hell.

Rein sluggishly lifts her gaze to mine, her fingers curled in my polo-neck sweater. I can feel her heart beating wildly against my ribs while we stare into each other's eyes.

CHAPTER Ten

Rein

I HATE MY LIFE.

I truly feel like my guardian angel has buggered off on annual leave or some shit and is currently lounging in a deck chair on a beautiful beach in Hawaii, sipping on Mai Tai's while someone up there is sitting around with a big bag of popcorn just enjoying watching my life fall apart one stinking bit at a time.

I'm on a downward spiral here, and I don't know how to stop it. Let's just shove aside the fact that I'm now homeless, and I just lost everything I worked so hard to get in that unfortunate fire. I currently have a total of a hundred and two dollars to my name. Bearing in mind, I still have two and a half weeks before getting paid from Zen's.

How am I supposed to survive with a hundred and two dollars for two weeks? Even the tips have been coming in dribs and drabs as of late, so I can't even rely on that as it's so close to Thanksgiving and Christmas, people are saving up.

I could ask Raymond for an advance on this month's pay, though I highly doubt he will agree. The man is so tight he would skin a fart.

I will have to speak to Clay and see if I can convince him to talk to Ray about allowing me to stay in the back room for a couple of nights till I can save up enough to plan my next move.

That was my plan until I hear a loud crash somewhere in the bar and unconsciously throw myself into Professor Saxton's arms—who, might I add— gallantly wraps his arm around me, shielding me from an imminent threat.

My heart jack-hammers against my chest, and I'm inwardly praying he can't feel it where I'm pressed so closely against him. He's so warm and firm. I want to lay my head against his strapping chest and fall asleep with the smell of his expensive, intoxicatingly masculine after-shave surrounding me.

I must admit, in my absolute shoddiest moment, he's the last person I ever expected to be by my side. I wish I could scream how lonely and scared and helpless I felt at that very moment, but I couldn't. All I wanted was for someone to hold me and assure me everything was going to be all right. That *I* was going to be all right.

This whole 'you've been blessed with a second chance make the most of it' malarkey is honestly horse shit. Life has been nothing but unkind to me. It's been testing me since I was eighteen years old.

I can feel the life being siphoned right out of my veins.

I'm falling apart.

Feeling daring, instead of pulling away, I lift my gaze and look up at him. The flashlight from my phone—which I dropped in my panic dimly lit up the bar enough to give us just enough light to see one another. When I look up at him, he's already watching me. My mouth suddenly goes bone dry when our eyes finally meet. I couldn't look away, and it seems neither could he. I find myself momentarily captivated by the startlingly deep blue hue of his eyes. That second or two we stood staring mutely at one another felt like hours to me.

"You're not staying here." Professor Saxton states stiffly. It wasn't a request or a suggestion. It was an outright directive, one that clearly wasn't up for discussion.

"Professor, I don't really have a whole lot of options," I reply, taking a step back and leaning over to pick up my phone. My head spins, and I almost topple over, but a firm grip steadies me before I face plant on the floor. Huh, turns out I didn't sober up that much after all. "I'll be fine, really. I'm a big girl. I can take care of myself. I'll figure something out in the morning." A chill rushes straight through me without his body heat, and I visibly shiver.

Professor Saxton pins me with a disbelieving look, and I sigh, wrapping my arms around myself. "Even if by some miracle you make it to morning before you die of hypothermia, you've consumed quite a bit of alcohol, and I'm worried you'll fall over and wind up breaking your neck if I leave you here all alone."

"What do you suggest then, Professor?" I voice with an apathetic shrug. "Because it's either I sleep here or under a bridge or a park bench somewhere. Those are the only three options I have right now."

Professor Saxton shoves a hand through his already dishevelled hair and heaves a frustrated sigh. "I have a spare room at my place, you can spend the night there, and when you've had a good night's sleep and sobered up in the morning, we can devise a plan."

I gape at him, stunned. I think my eyes just bulged out of my head.

Did he just invite me back to his place? Has this outrageously gorgeous man gone and lost his marbles? If anyone ever gets a whiff of this, he could lose his job. I can't do that. I won't be the reason he loses his job. I shake my head and take a step back, my feet wobbling in these stupid heels. I'm sure my toes have all fallen off, considering they've gone numb, and I can no longer feel them.

I keep my eyes on his, "Professor, that's truly kind of you to offer, but I'm going to have to respectfully decline."

"And I'm going to have to respectfully *insist*. I refuse to leave you here. If something were to happen to you, I'd never be able to forgive myself for abandoning you in this place, in the cold, wearing..." His eyes skim down the length of my body, and despite the freezing weather, I flush under his gaze. "That."

Huh, do I detect a touch of desire in those gorgeous blue eyes, or is my boozed-up mind imagining things.

I turn and walk toward the bar. I use the term 'walk' loosely because I'm sure I must've resembled Bambi on ice as I stagger toward the bar. Didn't help that I could feel his gaze penetrating the back of my head as I did. "While I appreciate your offer. I'm more than capable of taking care of myself. I've made it this far... all things considered." I state, pushing the door open to the back room and flashing the light so I could see better. The tatty brown two-seater sofa bed I had planned on sleeping in is now the resting place for a massive, filthy LED sign that we use for happy hour.

"Shit." I lift my gaze to the ceiling and sigh. '*Why do you hate me?*' When I feel movement behind me, I glance over my shoulder and see Professor Saxton leaning against the bar, arms crossed over his chest, eyes narrowed a little while he patiently and coolly watches me.

I slowly turn to face him and lean back against the wall feeling utterly defeated. "Okay," I cave and hold my hands up in surrender. "I'll go with you; I just need this night to be over with already."

Professor Saxton nods, gesturing for me to walk ahead of him. "After you then."

I push myself off the wall and walk toward him, keeping my eyes on his as I brush past him. After I lock up the bar and enable the alarm, we're back in the comfort and warmth of his mustang, cruising through the empty streets of Chicago at four in the morning. I stare out of the passenger side window, watching buildings and lights zooming past me. I literally blink, and the next thing I see is Professor Saxton leaning over the panel between the two seats and saying my name in that sexy Australian accent that makes my vajayjay tingle in the best possible way. "Rein."

My eyes feel heavy, almost like they're glued shut, but I peel them open and gaze up at him drowsily, "Professor." I murmur; reaching up, I brush my fingers along his carved jawline. The coarseness of his stubble makes my stomach flip nervously. "I like it when you call me by my name."

He stares down into my face, and I can feel his jaw clenching and twitching under my fingers until he wraps his fingers around my wrist and slowly pulls my hand away from his face but not entirely. "Let's get you upstairs so you can get some sleep—"

"I can sleep here." I sigh, snuggling into the plush leather seat. "Just leave me here."

Professor Saxton sighs, "Rein, I can't leave you here. There's a big bed upstairs where you'll sleep more comfortably."

"Your bed?" I smirk impishly, and he glowers at me, his brows drawn together tightly.

"No Rein, not *my* bed, *a* bed." Before I could respond, he was out of the car and walking around toward the passenger side. The door opens, and he sticks his head in, leaning over me to unbuckle the seatbelt. "Come on, up you get, easy does it."

Despite my protesting, I'm hauled out of the car; losing my footing, I fall against Professor Saxton's strapping chest.

Mm, his sweater is really soft and smells too damn good.

"I was wrong about you." I sigh, tilting my head to look up at him. Professor Saxton glances down at me after he pushes the car door shut and activates the locks.

"You were? How so?" He questions, those cobalt eyes peering inquisitively into mine.

"Well, you're not as obnoxious as I had pegged you to be." His brows rise with intrigue; he licks his lips, glancing around the quiet car park of what I'm assuming is his apartment building before they settle on me again.

"Not *as* obnoxious, huh?" He states sceptically, "I suppose I'm still fairly obnoxious then?"

I couldn't contain my smirk at the tetchy tone of his voice, "I've not seen you genuinely smile, not even once. You're always so reserved and stony with pretty much everyone. Why is that?"

We start walking through the underground car park toward the elevators. Well, he was walking. I was just staggering along, trying my best not to fall flat on my face. If it weren't for his hand on my back, I probably would have, but the warmth of his fingers pressed against the small of my back not only distracted me but practically singed my skin in the most delightful way.

"Maybe I just don't have a whole lot to smile about." He retorts as he reaches over to push the button to the elevator. I shift and lean against the elevator door, observing him closely. "Rein, don't lean on that."

I smile and bite down on my bottom lip, "Come on, Professor, that can't be true. I bet I can make you smile."

Professor Saxton watches me intently, jaw set, handsome face devoid of any form of amusement. "You'll lose that bet. Many have."

"I'm not like many," I reply evenly. The elevator dings, and the doors swing open quicker than I could catch myself. I gasp when Professor Saxton's arm swiftly darts out and grabs my wrist, and yanks me toward him before I fall into the elevator. I peek up at him, my chest rising and falling quickly against his, all the while my heart racing at an unnatural pace. Half from fear of falling, the other from once again being pressed up against him.

"No, you're not." He says, his eyes lowering to my lips briefly before they flitter up to mine again. "You're very disobedient, Miss Valdez."

"And that bothers you?"

"Yes." He counters precipitously, "I just told you not to lean on the doors, and you blatantly ignored me and yet again put yourself at risk of getting seriously hurt."

My brow goes up, "Oh? I hadn't realised that you cared such a great deal for my well-being, Professor. Very few do."

"Miss Val—"

"Rein," I interject, licking my lips while I gaze at his sensuously full lips. "Just call me Rein. There's really no need to be so prim, Professor. We're not on school grounds right now; the rules don't apply here."

Professor Saxton's Adam's apple jumps when he swallows. I notice a shift in gaze, those delightfully blue eyes darken, and he takes a step forward, slowly forcing me back into the elevator, my right arm still firmly locked in his grip.

Oh Lord, have mercy, there's something so very primal in the way he's looking at me, and it makes my stomach coil tightly and burn with exhilaration.

The elevator doors slide shut when he presses a blue card to the panel and the button to the sixteenth-floor lights up, his eyes never leaving mine. "Rein, you've had quite a bit to drink, so I'm going to chalk this behaviour down to that, but let me make something abundantly clear to you. Those rules you're referring to are in place to protect us both. I'm your Professor; whether we're on school grounds or not doesn't change that fact. Do not mistake my kindness for anything more because you'll be left disappointed. Understand?"

Ouch.

Even though his words stung me, I kept my composure and smiled broadly. I almost laugh but think better of it and take a step back when he lets go of my arm. "While I'm all too familiar with the conception, I can assure you I'm wholly used to being left... *disappointed* in every sense of the word, so don't sweat it," I state impishly. Professor Saxton's eyes narrow, and he shoves his hands in the pockets of his trousers while he studies me intriguingly. "Although I think you misunderstood me, which I get it, you must have students throwing themselves at you left and right, so you're well within your right to get your back up and protect yourself. I only said that because you are now saving me twice, we shouldn't feel the need to be so formal. I wasn't trying to seduce you." I add with an amused and boozy chuckle.

The elevator slows and comes to a stop interrupting whatever professor Saxton is going to stay. The doors swing open, and he holds the door open, gesturing for me to go first.

I stroll out into the dimly lit hallway and wait for him to come out and lead the way. Instead, he walks around me, and I follow him to the left of the corridor. It's a short walk to the apartment, I'd say less than two hundred feet. While he unlocks the door, I glance around my surroundings and kick off the blasted shoes that have murdered my feet one toe at a time. Light plush cream carpet swallows my feet the moment I step into it; it's so soft I had the urge to lay down and curl on the floor and drop off into la-la land. The walls are painted a pale eggshell colour that goes nicely with the carpet. There's one other apartment at the opposite end of the corridor mirroring his. Only two apartments on one floor? I noticed a couple of abstract paintings hung on the wall, adding some colour to the otherwise boring design.

I stare at Professor Saxton's back; I can't believe I'm spending the night at his place. Paris would die if she knew. I would never tell a soul that he brought me here; a part of me wishes I could divulge and see the envy on Sydney's fugly face. It's no secret that she's exhausted every trick in the book trying to catch his attention.

The door swings open, and I linger outside the door for a second until Professor Saxton turns and looks at me. "Come on in."

I don't know why, but I hesitate, my nerves kick in, and I'm suddenly very aware that we're all alone in his apartment—which is stunning, by the way. Nothing like I imagined and unlike any bachelor pad, I've ever seen. Much like his car, his apartment is gleaming. The house is dimly lit, especially at night, but the walls are painted brilliant white from what I could make out; the light grey flooring added a nice touch to the décor.

I stand awkwardly by in the entryway taking in the elegance of his apartment, completely awe-struck. No wonder he was so shocked when he saw the state of my building. This place makes my apart-ment look like a shit-shack... which, let's face it, it truly was. But, on the other hand, I can bet my life prisoners probably have better living conditions than I ever did. A wave of nausea hits me, and I can feel it working its way up my stomach despite my best effort to keep it down.

"You look confused."

I blink and turn to look at him, "No. I um, I feel a little..." I gesture to my stomach and wince when my mouth fills with saliva. "Bathroom, I need the bathroom."

Professor Saxton looks alarmed and gestures to the grey door to his left, and I race over to it, making it just in time to empty out all the alcohol I consumed. My stomach lurches, and I hurl until there's nothing left.

I am never drinking again.

While I sat in a heap on the cold tile floor, my head buried in my hands, in my Professor's enormous bathroom, reality came thundering down on me once again.

I literally have nothing. No place to call home, no clothes, no art supplies or books, barely any money. What am I supposed to do now?

I don't even know where to begin picking up the pieces this time.

I pull my knees to my chest and let the tears I've been fighting flow free. How ill must my fate be to keep losing everything dear to me?

My Grammy always says life will never deal you more than you can handle. Well, I sure hope that's true because I'm honestly not sure I can cope with any more tribulations.

"Rein?" I lift my head and look over at the grey door when I hear Professor Saxton calling my name from the other side of the door. "Are you okay?"

"I think I am the furthest I have ever been from being *okay*." I sigh, resting my head back against the tiled wall. "But life goes on whether you're ready to face it or not, right?"

"Can I come in? Are you decent?"

"It's your house." I drawl mordantly. "And I've not stripped naked if that's what you're worried about." The door's silver handle spins, and the door swings open, revealing his sexy highness, eyes full to brim with apprehension while he looks down at me sat pathetically beside the toilet.

"You done chundering?"

I blink up at him. "Chundering?"

Professor Saxton walks further into the bathroom and hands me a bottle of cold water. "Throwing up."

"Chundering. I like that." I say with a chuckle before I greedily guzzle half the bottle of water. Each drop feels like absolute heaven as it washes down my scratchy throat. "I don't feel so good."

"I'm not surprised after all the drinks you've consumed. You're definitely a snowflake."

I pout like a putout child, "I am *no* snowflake." I argue, poking at his chest. "I assure you I'm more than capable of handling myself." I stop and hiccup a little. "Tough as old boots, I am."

When he chuckles, I gape up at him, astounded. My God, did he just crack a smile? "See, I told you I'd make you laugh!" I giggle drunkenly and reach up so I can give his cheek an affectionate squeeze, to which he, of course, responds with a scowl. "I won the bet. Hand over my prize Professor Hottie."

"You sure did, snowflake, and I don't recall us betting on a prize."

I blink up at him, "Well, that's boring. Let us renegotiate."

I sway on my feet a little as I walk toward the door, leaning against the frame for support. "That won't be necessary. How about we focus on getting you into bed in one piece so you can sleep off the booze you've consumed?"

I nod, resting my head against the doorframe. "Yes, sleep sounds... really, really good. I'll just sleep here for one minute." I murmur, dozing off when my eyes grow heavy.

"Rein, no, no, you can't sleep here." I vaguely hear him say until I feel him tapping at my cheek to wake me up, "Rein, wake up."

"Shhh, P, one more minute. Professor Hottie is waiting to ravish me in my dreams." I huff blearily and snuggle against the door with a lustful sigh.

"Oh Christ," I gasp and stiffen when I'm suddenly lifted off the ground and cling to him for dear life. No one has *ever* swept me up and carried me before, so it's not something I'm used to. While it felt nice, it sent my anxiety through the roof in fear he would drop me flat on my arse. "Rein, relax. I've got you." Upon hearing his voice in my ear, my body slackens, and I melt into his strong arms; my face nestles into the crook of his neck, the familiar scent of his aftershave comforts me enough that I fall asleep.

The next time I opened my eyes, it was because of the throbbing ache in my temples and the dryness of my throat. It felt like I swallowed a mouthful of cotton balls. Oh, and the incessant buzzing in my head didn't feel delightful either. When I finally managed to peel my eyes open, I stared up at the plain white ceiling for a solid minute before my eyes focussed. My brain acknowledged that I was in a foreign bed in a bedroom that wasn't mine. My roof isn't pristine white; it had stains of God only knows what and damp. In a panic, I sit up, check myself and sigh when I see I was still in the dress I wore to my birthday party.

Oh, I feel like death. My head feels like it's about ready to fall out of my arse.

Where the hell am I? My eyes scan the room, and I wince against the sheer brightness of the room. The sun is beaming through the window, melting away my corneas.

The room is painted a brilliant white; a soft, light grey carpet covers the floor. The furniture in the room is minimal, with two white bedside tables, one built-in floor to ceiling mirrored wardrobe opposite the bed, broadly displaying how unsightly I look in all my hungover glory.

My usual soft brown hair was a tangled mess of waves, my mascara and eyeliner smeared around my eyes like a drowned panda, and my lips tinted red from the lipstick Paris generously slapped on me despite my complaints that it's a tad too 'hooker' red for me. Did she listen? Of course not.

I slide to the side of the bed and swing my legs over, sitting up as I do my best to recall how I got wherever the hell I am? Where the hell are Hunter and Paris?

Oh God, what if I got smashed and came home with some rando? I bury my head in my hands and groan. No, I wouldn't do that. Maybe we all wound up in this place for an after-party? Yes, that makes more sense.

There is absolutely no sign of fornication of any kind. No empty condom wrappers, no clothes strewn about on the floor. I'm fully dressed. I think I'm safe on that front.

I cautiously push myself up onto my feet and hiss when the balls of my feet ache. Consequences one must pay after strutting around in seven-thousand-dollar shoes, I suppose.

The apartment is quiet as I warily tiptoe my way out of the bedroom. I scan my surroundings and frown when I see no sight of anyone. The apartment is stunning—not overly lavish like Paris or Hunter's residence, but whoever lives here must have paid a pretty penny or two.

I hear a dull 'thump' 'thump' 'thump' coming from down the corridor, and before my brain could react, my feet already make their way following the sound. I halt in front of the door and stare unblinking at the man running topless on a treadmill.

Oh, good, God.

Not just any man, Professor *fucking* Saxton.

Oh, be still be my beating vagina.

CHAPTER Eleven

Talon

"Professor Hottie is waiting to ravish me in my dreams..."

Run Talon, fucking run.

Forget whatever you heard; she was raging drunk and waffling. It was just drunken jargon, that is all.

I am such a moron. Why would you bring her to your apartment? Take her to a hotel and let her sleep it off, you absolutely dipshit.

Fuck, like that was a bloody option. I couldn't just abandon her in some hotel room in her state. Anything could have happened to her.

I've been running the past forty minutes trying to calm the chaos in my head, but I can't seem to get her words from last night out of my mind. It just keeps going around and around in my head, picturing her beautiful face flush when she stated lustfully that she has sex dreams about me ravishing her.

God help me, did I want to ravish her in every fucking way possible. I've lost count of the number of times I woke up in a hot sweat from a sordid dream I've had about her the last few weeks. I've had more stiffys and wanks than I can count—like an unnatural amount no thanks to her.

Maybe I ought to take JT's advice and just bite the bullet and get my dick wet. Three years is a long time to be abstinent, and while it's not really been a problem, it sure is becoming one now. A mighty big one, might I add.

Don't get me wrong, I've obviously been jacking off every now and then, like once a week, just to take the edge off, but it wasn't anything astounding. Just your run of the mill Monday morning wank. But lately, fuck, it's been different. That all-consuming urge I've not felt in a very long time has surfaced, and I'm finding myself rock hard at all hours of the day. Dragging out each session, every slow stroke, each jolt of pleasure causing my body to jerk uncontrollably while building up to an orgasm so intense it fires scorching shockwaves through me.

And it's all because of her.

From the corner of my eye, I catch a glimpse of red and glance over to find her standing in the doorway, eyes almost bulging out of her skull, her luscious lips parted slightly while she observes me running on the treadmill. I hit the red stop button, and the belt instantly slows and eventually stops.

I shouldn't, I know, but I like the look of wonder and desire tinged on her pretty face whilst she openly gapes at me. I can bet my life I'm the last person she expected to wake up and see.

Panting, I grab the towel I had hanging over the side of the treadmill and step off the machine while patting the sweat off the back of my neck, all the while I keep my eyes on her. I cock my head to the side and narrow my eyes a little, "Morning. How are you feeling?"

Rein opens her mouth to speak, her face contorts to one of absolute confusion. "Uhm," She utters, timidly wrapping her arms around herself; she licks her lips. "Like I'm standing on death's door waiting in line to take a number."

I smirk and nod, "Hanging hard, huh."

Rein winces, rubbing her temples. "Out of my arse, literally. There isn't a fibre in my body that doesn't hurt right now." She complains with a groan.

"Yeah, getting shit-canned will do that to you."

Rein stares at me pensively for a beat as though she's trying to recall something. "I um, I can't seem to recall much of last night, everything is a blur, but I do remember seeing you at the club. You were there, right?"

I throw the towel over my left shoulder and nod, leaning back against the treadmill. "I was."

"So," Rein looks around the home gym before her gaze reverts back to me again. "How did I end up *here* in your apartment?"

I sigh inwardly; it was hard enough watching her break down over losing everything in one night. I don't know if I can stomach witnessing her relive it all over again. I straighten and walk over to her, "Let's get something in your stomach to soak up the alcohol you indulged in, and then I can fill you in."

Rein watches me warily as I near her, "Okay."

Eight minutes, three small bites of toast and two cups of coffee later, Rein is sat helplessly on a stool at the white marble kitchen island, looking every bit as devastated as she did last night. "Oh my God, it's slowly starting to come back to me. My apartment building... it was up in flames." She states, horrified, her fingers tremble as she presses them against her mouth while she recalls the events from the night before. I can see her eyes glistening with tears as she fights to hold them back. Her hand slides from her mouth down to her neck, and her eyes grow wide in alarm. "My necklace." She gasps. "I left it, I left it in the apartment."

"Rein—."

I watch as she slides off the stool and frantically paces back and forth. "I need to go. I need to find my necklace." I catch her arm as she makes a beeline to walk out of the kitchen.

"Rein, stop." She looked up at me, and the devastation in her eyes made my gut twist painfully. "Even if you go down there, you won't be allowed to enter the building. It's not safe."

Rein shakes her head and tugs her arm out of my hold. "I don't care! You don't understand what that necklace means to me. Even if the entire building collapses on top of me, I'm going to get it." I sigh and straighten from my leaning position and peer down into her upturned face.

"Rein, I get it. I know how much it means to you. It's a gift from your late mother. I'd have to be utterly dense to not comprehend the significance of that necklace but let the fire marshal do the investigation. Then, when he gives us the all-clear, we can go and get your necklace. Okay?"

"I can't lose that necklace." She whispers sullenly, her eyes brimming with tears. "It's all I have left of her. I promised her I would never take it off."

I almost reach out to pull her into my arms and hug her but catch myself just in time. The misery in her tone combined with the forlorn look on her face cut me someplace deep. If I've learnt anything about Rein Valdez in the last semester, it's that she's a fighter, and I'll be damned, I find her perseverance admirable.

Jesus, what the hell am I supposed to say? How am I supposed to comfort her? "Rein, I know it feels like you've hit rock bottom right now, but everything will be all right. You're going to pull through this."

"How?" She laments, hastily wiping away the tear that rolls down her cheek. "How is it going to be all right? Look at me, Professor." She turns to face me fully and gestures to herself. "I've lost *everything*. I'm homeless. The apartment I lived in may not have been much, but at least I had a roof over my head. I had a place to call my own, even if it was a shoebox. What do I have now? I just about have enough money to get by for a day or two if I'm lucky. I can't afford to start all over again, nor do I have the energy anymore. I'm tired of constantly fighting a losing battle. It shouldn't be this goddamn hard." She vents with a frustrated shake of her head. "Moving out here was a mistake. It's clear now more than ever that I just don't belong here."

I take hold of her shoulders, keeping her still, and those eyes that I've spent one too many countless nights fixating over slowly lift and lock with my own. "Rein, listen to me. You coming here wasn't a mistake. Giving up and walking away from your aspirations—especially when you've worked so hard to get to where you are—will be a mistake you will regret for the rest of your life." I affirm earnestly. "I can't force you to stay if you really want to go, but I assure you, I've been where you are, and I understand. I've felt alone and lost and almost came close to packing up and leaving, but my professor at the time stood before me and told me the same thing I'm telling you now. You possess more talent in your little finger than ninety-nine percent of the students I teach could ever reap in a lifetime. It would be a real shame to see such remarkable talent go to waste."

Rein's shoulders fall a little, and she shakes her head slowly, her eyes lowering to stare at my chest. A distant look in her eyes tells me she's lost someplace deep in her thoughts. "I don't have much of a choice in the matter. After all, not everyone gets the opportunity to achieve their dreams, right? I've been foolishly deluding myself, trying to reach for the stars in hopes I'll catch one, but all I ever got in return for my efforts is a grander sense of failure each time I get wrenched back down to reality." Rein admits dejectedly.

I realise I'm still holding onto her upper arms, and a part of me revels in the silkiness of her skin against my fingers. I let her go and push my hands into the pockets of my grey tracksuit bottoms to keep them under control. "There is nothing wrong with setting your expectations high, Rein. As long as you pace yourself, take it one step at a time and be patient, you will get to where you're meant to be."

Rein heaves a sigh and turns her back to me; she looks around the kitchen, her hands placed at her hips. "When you're so accustomed to losing every good thing in your life, it's rather difficult to set your expectations high, let alone try and live up to them. I think I've reached as far as I can, Professor. This was me attempting to accomplish my goals and exceed my expectations, but alas, life has yet again shown me that it's just not meant to be."

I nod in understanding, "I get that, but life isn't always what we expect it to be. Unfortunately, if you want the rainbow, you've got to put up with the rain." I express taking a step toward her. "You were given this life because whether you want to believe it or not, you are strong enough to live it."

Rein turns and gazes up at me, looking like she wants to say something but thinks better of it and sighs instead. "I, uh, I should go." She blurts out suddenly, glancing around seemingly in search of something. "I'm truly sorry for ruining your evening. I'm sure the last thing you expected was to babysit a student all night." She voices with an adorable wince, her nose crinkling while she scratches her temple awkwardly. "Also, thank you for taking care of me, letting me crash here *and* listening to me vent about my shitty life."

"Rein, wait." She turns and looks at me inquiringly. "If you don't mind me asking. Where are you going to go?" I question.

Rein shrugs, gracefully tucking her hair behind her ear; she averts her gaze from mine. "I don't know, but don't worry, Professor, I'll figure something out."

I don't like the sound of that, and I can't ignore the ambiguity in her tone either. I hate the idea of her walking out of here with nowhere to go, especially in that fucking outfit. "Look, Rein, I don't have any plans for the rest of the day, so you don't have to rush off with nowhere to go," I assure her. "I've arranged some clothes for you. You look as though you're about to pass out. Which isn't a surprise after the night you've had. So, just take a shower and freshen up first. Then, you can figure out what you're going to do when you've recovered a little from your hangover."

I see the relief and gratitude sweep over her pretty face, and she nods, her shoulders sagging a little when her body relaxes. "A steaming hot shower sounds... tempting, but I really don't want to impose on you any more than I already have." She admits combing her fingers through her wavy hair and scratching her scalp.

I take a large step closer to her, keeping my eyes on hers. "You're not imposing, I'm offering. I assure you, Rein, if I didn't want you here, you wouldn't have spent the night in my guest room, and you certainly wouldn't be standing in my kitchen right now."

Ah shit. Why did I say that? I just openly admitted that I *want* her here.

Well done, Talon, way to put your foot in it. We wordlessly stare at one another, neither of us breaking eye contact for a good couple of seconds until she nods and lowers her gaze, licking her ruby lips.

"Not that I'm ungrateful by any means for your benevolence, but why am I, Professor?"

Careful Talon.

I shrug unflappably and smirk at her, "Perhaps I'm going soft in my old age, don't go getting used to it. Now stop asking questions and go shower before I change my mind." Rein's lips curl in a faint smile, and she nods.

"I'm going, I'm going." She says, holding her hands up as she backs away toward the door, "Uhm if you could point me in the direction of the bathroom..."

I gesture with my head for her to follow me as I walk out of the kitchen, leading the way toward the bathroom. "There are fresh towels in the white closet to the left of the shower; the clothes are on the basket," I say, and my eyes sweep over her body. "I'm hoping they'll fit. You look about a size eight."

Rein looks up at me, eyes all wide with surprise. "I am a size eight."

I smile and rub the back of my neck rather awkwardly while she gapes at me. "I'm pleased my guess was right then. If you need anything, just shout." I say and turn to walk toward my bedroom.

"Uh, professor?"

I halt and turn to look back at her, "Yes?"

Rein hesitates, her cheeks flush crimson, she wrings her fingers almost anxiously. "My dress—it's a button-down, and Paris buttoned it up for me because I couldn't reach..."

Oh fuck. She's not asking what I think she is.

It's my turn to stare at her, completely stumped. The thought alone of undressing her is rousing feral ideas in my head that should definitely not be there. The sudden look of apprehension on Rein's face when she peeks up at me through her dark lashes conveys that she's feeling rather foolish of her request when she notices my reaction—or lack of. "Actually," She winces, instantly regretting ever asking and turns to walk into the bathroom. "Ignore me. I can manage."

"No," I blurt out before I could stop myself. Rein looks back at me over her shoulder. "I can give you a hand, of course."

"Professor, you honestly don't have too. I can manage," she asserts and I shake my head.

No, if I cower away, she will think I'm affected by her, and I can't have that. So I must remain impervious, aloof. I'll just unbutton the damn dress swiftly and hightail it out of there. I study the small buttons down the back of the dress and sigh. It's all the way down to the bottom of her spine, for fuck's sake. There is no way she will unfasten all of those buttons by herself. The dress is so tight she can't even lift it over her head. "Something tells me you'll be in there a while attempting to unfasten all of those tiny buttons by yourself." I gesture for her to enter the bathroom and follow her in.

Shit, my heart is racing like a preadolescent teen that's never touched a girl before. Fucking hell, Rein, what are you doing to me. "Believe me, this dress wasn't my choice of attire. I've made a mental note to not let my best friend pick out my clothes moving forward." She admits turning her back to me.

Not your choice? For some strange reason, I am not the least bit surprised to hear that. Maybe it's the way she carries herself. Still, for a twenty-one-year-old, she's very mature, nothing like the girls at school, running around in skimpy outfits and high heels soaking up every little bit of the attention they get from every bloke desperate enough to notice and be affected by all that nonsense. But Rein, she's the opposite. Either she's too modest for her own good or lacks confidence and isn't comfortable in her own skin. My bet is on the latter.

I fist my hands at my sides while I stare at her hair cascading down her back. I swallow hard. "May I?" I probe, motioning to move her hair out of the way so I could get to the buttons on the dress. Rein looks at me through the mirror and nods.

"Oh, sure."

While a part of me is hoping she would move her hair over her shoulder, the silly boy deep down inside is thrilled that I get to brush my fingers through the silky strands as I've been longing too for far too long. I've had one too many fantasies where I'd notice her in class working. A strand of her hair falls over her lovely face, and I get the urge to walk over and brush it away while she looks up at me with those magnetic eyes.

Fuck me, I can feel my cock grow hard already, and I've not even touched her yet. I'm fretful I'll combust and come right in my boxers the moment my fingers graze her olive skin.

I've not been affected by anyone like this since—well, since Tay, if I'm honest, and even with her, it was never this intense. I don't know. Maybe I'm just overthinking this. It could very well be because, with Tay, it was easy, uncomplicated. Sure we had the passion, and we were very much in love, but I've not had this primal urge with anyone for a really long time. And that's what's alarming me.

Just as I imagined it would be, Rein's hair is silky soft. The stands glide through my fingers as I carefully sweep her hair over her left shoulder, exposing her dainty neck. My stomach goes tight. My eyes sweep over her neckline, and I press my molars together, suppressing the fervent need to dip my tongue in the hollow of her collarbone and suck hard till I leave a nice red mark behind.

I drag my eyes up and see Rein watching me through the mirror when I start unbuttoning the dress, popping one button out of its loop at a time. I wonder what she'll think of me if she knew the lewd thoughts that are crossing my mind at this moment. Would she be as repulsed as I am with myself right now?

Momentarily losing concentration on account of my train of thought, I fumble with one of the buttons halfway down her back. Unfortunately, every sodding button I undo exposes more of her back, and I can't seem to focus on the task at hand, especially when the straps to her dress loosen and provocatively falls over her shoulders. I curse the idiot that designed this dress. While it's sexy as fuck, who would even think to put so many buttons on a dress?

If she were any other girl and not my student, I would have ripped this dress off her in five seconds flat and had her on her knees while I fuck that smart mouth of hers. But, instead, my fingers halt when I reach the last four buttons, and the lace waistband of the red underwear that she's wearing becomes visible.

Oh, fuck me, just when I thought I couldn't fancy her more, I noticed she has Venus dimples. Christ, this is fucking torture.

I know I'm not alone when I say this, but I've always found Venus dimples sexy. If you're wondering what Venus dimples are, they're the little back dimples some girls have at the base of their spine. It sits high on the list of things that get me all hot bothered.

There isn't a snowball's chance in hell that I'm getting rid of the raging hard-on I'm exhibiting right now. So, before she notices, I need to get the hell out of this bathroom and as far away from her as possible.

I clear my throat and take a step back, avoiding looking at her. "All done."

"Thank you, Professor."

I get called Professor all day long by many, but the way it sounds coming from her lips and the way it rolls off her tongue is driving me crazy.

"No worries." I throw over my shoulder as I turn to walk out of the bathroom. I hurriedly pull the door shut behind me and walk to my bedroom at the end of the corridor. I kick the door shut and press my palms against the door, eyes closed, head hung low, my shoulders rising and falling with every frustrated breath that escapes me.

Why, why, why am I allowing this girl to affect me? At what point did I allow her close enough to get under my skin.

"Come on, Tal. You're better than this; get your fucking shit together, man." I whisper under my breath and press the side of my fist against the door crushing the urgent need to pummel my fist straight through it.

There is nothing special about this girl. She's just another student, just another body among the many at that school, that is it.

That *has to* be it.

THE LAST TIME I spent longer than ten minutes in the shower was when I was living with my folks back in Ohio. I was sixteen years old, and the only place I could peacefully whack off was in the shower. Today, I feel as though I've reverted back to that boy. I've honestly not jerked off this much since I've become infatuated with Rein Valdez. She's the ultimate taboo. My student that I can never have, I shouldn't want but desperately do.

The images my mind conjures up while I relieve some of the built-up tension she's caused was downright worrying, especially since she's here, in the same house as a guest. Fuck, the thought alone of her being naked and wet in my bathroom is enough to drive me senseless. What I wouldn't give to be in there with her right now. It wouldn't be so bad if I were alone, but now, I need to go out there and look her in the face after beating off while fantasising about her... *again.*

I'm a damn disgrace to my profession.

When I finally bolster the nerve, I leave the safe confines of my bedroom and walk to the living room, where I find Rein staring at the picture sitting on the mantel above the fireplace of me and my parents at my graduation.

There's a faraway look in her eyes while she studies the photograph, her arms wrapped around herself. While she's preoccupied, my eyes take in her appearance. The make-up she wore the night before was all gone, leaving her face bare and vibrant. The clothes I had Julie from the front desk pick out for Rein fit her perfectly. She did great. I must remember to tip her generously. The tight black jeans hug her hips and shapely arse flawlessly, and damn, that plain baby blue crop top is frying my brain; her breasts look sensational. I've always been a sucker for a nice pair of tits, but Rein Valdez has the best of both. A pair of full, natural—I'm guessing D cup breasts and a sexy peachy arse a starved man like me would fucking die for.

So much for not perving on her.

I sigh and once again shake off the inappropriate thoughts before I walk over to her. "Feeling better?"

Rein jumps, startled and spins to look up at me, surprised. Oh, the contact lenses she's been wearing are now gone, and those eyes that captivate me stare up at me all wide and wondrous. Great, how am I supposed to keep my focus in check now? "Yes, much better. Thank you." She replies, placing her hand over her chest. No doubt to calm her beating heart after I startled her.

"Good," I hold out a bottle of water and two pain killers for the headache she's likely suffering. Rein looks down at my hand and then up at me again. "For the headache. You need to stay hydrated, at least two litres of water to flush out the alcohol you consumed." I advise, and she nods, removing the hand she has pressed over her chest to take the two pills sitting in the centre of my palm.

"Thank you, Professor."

"Come have a seat." Rein's eyes follow me toward the living room as she washes down the pills and joins me. I gesture to the glass dining table, and she warily slides into a chair, resting her hands in her lap, playing with her fingers tautly.

Do I make you *nervous*, Rein Valdez?

I slide a key across the table toward her. Rein stares at the key for a long moment and then slowly raises her eyes to meet mine. Dark brows drew together, disclosing her obvious state of confusion.

"What's this?"

"A key," I answer, resting my arms on the table. Rein looks at the key and shakes her head; her eyes grow wide in panic. I suppress the urge to laugh at the startled look on her face. Judging by the horror on her face, she assumes I'm asking her to move in with me.

"A key to... where?"

"Not here, so you can relax," I state and smile when her shoulders visibly relax, and she exhales. I lean back in the chair, cross my arms over my chest, and fix her with a probing look. "The idea of living with me scare you that much, does it, Miss Valdez?"

Rein shakes her head, her cheeks flushing crimson while she scrambles to find something to say in response to my question. "No. I mean, it is a little out of the—"

I chuckle and hold my hand up, "Relax, Rein, I'm only winding you up. The key is to my mate's place across the courtyard." Rein's mouth drops open, and she looks at me blankly, so I continue, "The apartment is in the complex opposite mine. Michael got a job in London and moved out there two months ago. He's a telecoms specialist and works on a contract basis, so he'll be gone for at least a year. He asked me to take care of his place until his contract runs out and he returns home. When I agreed to keep an eye on the place, I didn't realise he meant I had to water his plants three times a week."

Rein's lips twitch, and she presses her lips together to stop smiling. I roll my eyes. "Do I look like the type of guy that knows a damn thing about botanical plants?"

Rein shrugs and crosses her arms over her chest while she lets her eyes openly roam over me. "Hm, I don't know. There may be some potential there."

"I can assure you there is zero potential and even less interest." Rein smiles a little, picks the key up and looks at it pensively for a long moment.

"What exactly is it you're offering here, Professor?" She questions, narrowing her beautiful eyes at me in scrutiny.

I shrug. "I'm offering you a safe place to stay temporarily till you can make other arrangements. You need a place to stay; the apartment is empty."

"And what does your friend have to say about this little idea of yours? I highly doubt he would want a stranger living in his home." Rein states tersely as she twirls the key between her fingers.

"Michael is fine with it." I assert, standing up and leisurely walking around the table. "I'm not so cunning that I would go behind my friend's back and offer out his home to random people without his knowledge or consent, Rein." I declare, resting my shoulder against the window.

Rein pushes her chair back a little and stands also. "I know. I didn't think you were, Professor." I watch her intently as she carefully tucks the chair under the table and walks over to me. "Thank you for your kind offer, Professor, I truly appreciate it, but I can't accept it. I'm not, nor will I ever be, the type of girl that easily accepts handouts from anyone. You've already done more than I could ever repay you for. I wouldn't be comfortable living in someone else's home. But, of course, if I were paying rent, that's a different situation... not that I could ever afford a place like this, but at least I wouldn't feel like a freeloader."

I frown.

"Rein, this is not a handout, and you're not freeloading. It's a temporary arrangement till a dorm room becomes available." I explain evenly, and she shakes her head. I can see the misery radiating in her eyes despite her best effort to mask it; she doesn't want to show any weakness.

"I'll figure something out." She holds the key out to me, and I stare at it motionless while she looks at me expectantly. Straightening, I take a step toward her, my eyes fixed firmly on hers as I inch closer. I push the key into her palm and close her fingers around it.

"Don't be stubborn, Rein. If you continue with this mentality, your pride will cost you everything but leave you with nothing, and the only person that will suffer is you." Rein looks down at our hands and sighs. "I understand and admire your intention to want to stand on your own two feet and not rely on anyone, believe me, I've been there. But why drown when you can walk over a bridge that someone is offering to build for you?"

Rein remains quiet, which is unusual for her. I'm so used to her firing a catty response back right away that it throws me off a little. I wonder what happened in her past to make her so... cynical. "I don't need anyone to build a bridge for me, Professor. I'm not some pathetic damsel in need of rescuing. I am and have always been more than competent in finding my way. I'll struggle, maybe, but I will get there eventually. At least that way, I can't blame anyone but myself when it all falls apart." She asserts sombrely, freeing her hand from my hold; she places the key in my palm and forces a smile on her face. "I'll pay you back for the clothes as soon as I get paid."

Christ, she's exasperatingly stubborn.

"Rein, that won't be necessary." I blink and shut my mouth when she only smiles up at me with her brow raised, pinning me with a look that clearly states she's not going to accept no for an answer. "Can I at least drive you wherever you're planning on going?" I offer, picking up her purse off the table and holding it out to her. Rein takes the bag and shakes her head.

"No, I'll call an Uber. I'm sure you have much better things to do on your day off than drive me around. I'll be fine, honestly. Thank you again, Professor." She declares, holding out her hand to me. I drop my gaze to her hand and begrudgingly slide my hand into hers and squeeze gently. The softness and warmth of her dainty hand in mine made me feel all fuzzy deep inside. Shit, I want to tug her to me and ask her to stay. I don't like the thought of her leaving here with no inkling of where she will end up. She'll likely go to her friend Paris. Or will she go back to her boyfriend? Maybe she'll forgive him for his indiscretions, and they will wind up getting back together and having wild make-up sex.

What the actual fuck, Talon? How is it any of your business who she screws? Christ, get a grip man, she's not your responsibility. Let. It. Go.

I let go and drop her hand rather abruptly, and Rein gives me a quizzical look when I abruptly stuff my hand in the pocket of my dark blue jeans. I reach over and open the door for her, leaning against it as she goes to walk through it. "Goodbye, Professor."

"All the best, Miss Valdez." She doesn't leave right away; she lingers while we hold each other's gaze. I couldn't make myself look away, and it seems she couldn't either. I can feel the sadness and uncertainty she's trying so hard and failing to conceal in her eyes deep in my gut.

One second, I'm staring into her eyes and the next, she's pushing up on her toes and pressing a gentle kiss to my cheek. I did nothing to stop her. I should have pulled away, but I couldn't even react. It happened so fast, yet it seemed the world itself stopped spinning on its axis, trapping me in a stupor.

Shit, shit, shit.

Rein stills before she slowly draws back, taking her scent and warmth with her. A look of immediate regret is clear as day when she realises what she has just done.

I swallow hard and push the door closed when she goes to take a step to leave. Rein stares at the door, her chest rising and falling, then slowly turns her gaze up to look at me. I take a step toward her, and she retreats until her back hits the door.

I placed my hands against the door on either side of her head and lowered mine till I was at eye level with her.

"Care to explain what that was back there, Miss Valdez?"

CHAPTER Twelve

Rein

OH GOD, OH MY GOD!

Holy shit balls, what the fuck did you just do?!

My brain decides it's time to power down and leave me to deal with the predicament I just went and plonked myself into.

I just kissed my Professor! What in the ever-living shit were you thinking, Rein?!

How am I going to explain myself? How could I possibly justify kissing him? It was impulse; I didn't even think, and before I could get control of myself, I was already kissing his cheek.

Oh, how I wish the ground would open and gobble me up right now. I'm so embarrassed I don't know what to do with myself. I'm almost certain I'm still a little bit drunk. I must resemble an overcooked lobster right now if the heat radiating off my face is any indication.

I can't fucking breathe. I'm sweating. Why is he looking at me like that? Why am I pressed up against the door like we're about to devour one another?

"I'm so sorry, I didn't mean to... *do that*." I squeak pathetically. "I don't even know why I did. It just... happened," I explain in a flurry, my voice barely an octave over a wavering whisper.

Professor Saxton's blue eyes narrow a little while he continues to stare at me intently, little by little robbing every drop of air right out of my lungs. "It just happened." He intones gruffly. "A kiss doesn't *just happen*, Miss Valdez. Do you go around kissing all your professors on the cheek impulsively?"

"No!" I exclaim, forcing myself to peek up at him. "I just... I..."

"You just what, Rein?"

I close my eyes and sigh, "I'm sorry, I wasn't thinking. For a fleeting moment, I forgot that..."

Professor Saxton observes me fixedly, patiently waiting for a reasonable explanation for my behaviour. "You forgot what? That I'm your professor, and you're my student?"

I gape at him, unsure of what to say while he glares at me with those glacial eyes of his much like he used to before lines got blurred between us, only this time, they weren't as frosty. There's a trace of something there, but I can't for the life of me decipher it. "Maybe, I guess." I stammer. Jeez, I can't think straight with him standing this close to me. "As you're aware, I've had a really shitty twenty-four hours, and you've not exactly been your usual standoffish self. I just thought..." I shake my head and take a second to choose my words carefully. "I wanted you to know that I was grateful. That's all." I admit, lowering my gaze to the floor. I can feel him staring into my head.

"Rein, look at me." No, please don't make me. "Look at me." My eyes flitter up to his, and I'm surprised to find them softer, sympathetic even.

He shakes his head and licks those sinful lips before he speaks. "The last thing I want to do is give you the wrong impression here. I told you this yesterday, my concern for your safety and wellbeing is only and strictly on a professional basis. My benevolence isn't specific to you only. I would do the same for any one of my students."

I find that hard to believe. Does he honestly think I'm that naive? He assumes I don't notice how he looks at me when he thinks I'm not paying attention? The way he was watching me in the club while I danced with Hunter. That is not the way a professor looks at his student. Or is this all in my head? Could I be projecting my own feelings?

"Do you press all your students intimately up against the door also, Professor?" I question austerely before I lose my nerve. A look of surprise falls upon his handsome face, and he stares at me wordlessly, then drops his arms and straightens.

"I can't say that I have. But, then again, none of them possess the bravado to kiss me." He states coolly, placing his large hands at his narrow waist.

"Or you haven't let them close enough to try," I reply.

His eyes narrow. "I wouldn't read too much into it. You just happen to catch me off guard, that's all."

I reach up and grip the door handle, my eyes never leaving his, "Wow, and here's me thinking we were well on the way to becoming BFFs. Way to crush a girls dream, Professor."

Professor Saxton sighs and rubs the back of his neck in frustration. "I aim to please, Miss Valdez."

"So, I've heard."

He smirks and shakes his head, amused. "Have a good weekend, Miss Valdez."

I bite my lip and nod. "You too, Professor."

And with that, I open the door and walk out of his apartment, pulling the door shut behind me.

Well, shit, that escalated rather quickly.

I don't know how I'm going to face that man come Monday. But that's the least of my problems right now.

I'm fucking homeless.

"Rei Rei, I'm really starting to worry. Where are you? Please call me when you get this." I sigh and pinch the bridge of my nose while listening to the seventh voicemail from Paris. When I finally managed to charge my phone and turned it on, it was flooded with messages and missed calls from Paris, my Aunt Dani and of course, *Hunter.*

"Feliz cumpleaños, bebesita!" My eyes instantly water when I hear my aunt's voice over the voice message. She sounds just like my mum. "I'm so proud of you and the beautiful young woman you've become. I know your mother is watching over you with her eyes beaming with pride. I hope you're having lots of fun out there with your friends. I want all the deets! Grammy and I miss you and love you so much, mi amor. Call me!" She says with a chuckle and blows a kiss.

I brush away the tears that roll down my cheeks. I miss my family so much. Whenever I had a bad day, my Grammy would make me her special cinnamon and oat cookies to cheer me up. My Aunt D would lay my head in her lap and brush her fingers through my hair while she told me stories about what she and my mum would get up to when they were younger.

I'm the first in our family to make it to college. My mother and aunt didn't even finish secondary school. So it's a big deal. My Grandmother gushes about it to all her friends that her granddaughter got into a prestigious school in America. How can I give up and go home and risk disappointing her? I couldn't care less what anyone says or thinks about me, but my Grammy is a proud woman and hopelessly sensitive to what others think.

Even though she never admits it and will always put our happiness first, deep down, I know she'll be heartbroken to see me fail the way my mother did. I promised her and myself that I would be better, I wouldn't fall into the same trap as they all did and give up my hopes and dreams for a man.

How far do you expect to get if you up and quit each time you trip and fall? You shouldn't let the challenges you've experienced deter you.

I stare into the steaming cup of coffee and wrap my fingers around the mug while Professor Saxton's words from the night before whirl around my head.

I don't want to. I'm so close to the end, but I don't know where to begin picking up the pieces this time. Maybe I should have accepted his offer and taken the key to his friend's apartment.

No, I can't. I wouldn't feel comfortable living in someone else's space, and I'd never be able to afford a place like that on my wage. I have ten hours to find someplace to crash tonight, or I'll be sleeping at Zen's or worse under a bridge someplace in the freezing cold.

"There you are!" My eyes lift from the coffee cup I've been pensively gazing into when I hear my best friend's voice. Paris comes running over to me and throws her arms around me. "Jesus Rein, where the fuck have you been? I've been worried sick."

147

At what point were you 'worried sick', I wonder? Before or after you were done riding man-whore Colton's STD ridden knob. I don't voice my thoughts even though I'm dying too. I'm not her responsibility, I'm a big girl, and she's allowed to live her own life without being judged or having to burden my problems. I'm not that selfish. "Around," I utter monotonously with a shrug and trace my finger around the rim of the mug. Paris takes a seat opposite me, looking perfect as per usual. You wouldn't think she was stinking drunk the night before. Whereas I'm sat here looking like a donkey's rear end.

"We've been looking all over for you. I've called every hospital and police station in Chicago looking for you. I damn near had a meltdown when I saw your building had burnt down. I thought you were fucking dead. What happened? Why didn't you call me?" Paris questions hastily.

"I don't know what happened. When I got home last night, the building was engulfed in flames. And FYI, I did call you." I sigh and pull my hand away from her hold to sip my now tepid black coffee. "You were clearly too busy getting a dicking by Colton to answer."

P's face instantly falls, and her big hazel eyes fill with contrition. She sinks back into her seat and twirls a ring on her middle finger. "Rei, I'm so sorry."

I sigh and rub my forehead. "Don't be. There's nothing you could have done anyway."

"That's not the point. I should have been there for you. God Rein, I'm sorry, I'm such a shitty friend. You have every right to be upset with me. I abandoned you when you needed me most." Paris takes my hand again and squeezes gently.

"P, I'm not upset with you. It's fine, honestly. I'm a big girl, and I can take care of myself. Believe it or not, we are allowed to have our own lives. I don't need a minder to hold my hand twenty-four-seven." I say, giving her hand a reassuring squeeze.

"But I feel just terrible for leaving you all alone to deal with the devastation of losing your home."

Only I wasn't alone.

"You should call Hunter; he's beside himself looking for you."

I snort and shake my head. "I highly doubt that."

Paris frowns, "Did something happen, Rein? Did you two have a fight or something? Last I saw, you two were dancing hot and heavy on the dance floor, and then he tells me this morning you took off without a word?"

"Obviously, he neglected to tell you the part where I caught him in the elevator sucking faces and finger fucking Sydney."

Paris straightens, her eyes wide and brows knitted together tight. "Wait, whoa, he did what?"

"Yeah. The way they were going at it, it's clear he's been shagging her for a while now." I state irritably. "Fucking arsehole."

Paris shakes her head in disbelief. "I just can't believe it. I'd expect something like this from Sydney but, Hunter? He's never been into Syd. I know for a fact she's had the hots for him for a while, but Hunter never gave her the time of day."

I drop five dollars on the table and snatch up my phone as I stand. "Well, I assure you, P, he was giving her time and then some. She can have the rotten bastard. I was going to dump him anyway. If anything, she did me a damn favour."

Paris follows me through the café, and we walk out together. "You were going to break up with Hunter? Why? I thought you two were really into one another."

I fix Paris with a sidelong stare, and she shrugs apologetically. "I was never into Hunter, P. It was all your idea, remember? I never saw him as more than just a friend, but you were so persistent that we would be 'great' together. So remind me to never listen to you again."

"Oh, Rei. I truly thought Hunter would be good for you. He seemed to really care about you. How was I to know that he would end up being just another cheating scumbag." Paris justifies looping her arm through mine and resting her head on my shoulder as we walk together.

"I know your intentions were good, P. I'm not blaming you. If anything, I'm pissed off with myself because, deep down, I knew it didn't feel right. My heart wasn't in it, but I just kept holding on, hoping I would eventually start to feel something for him, but I didn't." I explain with a sigh. "It's time to accept the fact that I'm not cut out for the whole relationship thing. I've never been in love and don't plan to be. Not after witnessing what being in love did to my mother and aunt. Why would any sane person ever want to put themselves through such torture?"

"Oh, here we go, out comes the cynic." Paris drawls with a playful roll of her eyes.

"I'm not cynical. I'm realistic. I cannot fathom this obsession we mortals have with finding our one true love and envisaging a fairy tale romance like it even exists. Why do you think the movie ends when the prince gets the princess? What comes next?"

"Duh, they live happily ever after, of course."

I snort and shake my head incredulously. "There's no such thing as a happily ever after, P. There is not one couple on this earth that could convince me that they lived blissfully in love with no fights or obstacles throughout their relationship. Love is nothing but a farce. Sure, it feels incredible for all of five seconds and then eventually, that delirium you're both convinced will last forever subsides. Then reality takes over, and before you know it, you both become complacent and out searching for that same high with someone else." I explain wryly. Paris lifts her head off my shoulder and frowns.

"Sheesh, woman, you've just ruined every fairy tale I've ever loved in five seconds. Sounds to me like you're suffering from a severe case of philophobia, sugar tits." Paris drawls, nudging me playfully with her hip. "Perhaps we should look up some 'love doctors' to give you a good dosage of dicking to help you face your fear of falling in love." She adds with a giggle when I hit her with my purse.

"Unlike you, my happiness doesn't and never will be tied to a man or his manhood. However remarkable it may be." Paris laughs and loops her arms with mine again as we stroll down the high street.

"Mark my words. I'm going to find someone to rail the cynic right out of you one of these days, Rei Rei girl."

I roll my eyes in exasperation. "Not to sound crude, but I'll be happy if someone just railed me to a fucking orgasm. Is that really so much to ask?"

Paris giggles and rests her head on my shoulder again. "Oh, baby girl, your golden cock will find you. Just be patient."

I've honestly lost all hope.

I SPENT the afternoon trying to find someplace to spend the night. Paris, being Paris, wanted to drag me to a five-star hotel and pay for me to stay for a fortnight until I found a place. Still, I refused and was having none of her persisting.

When she saw I wasn't budging, she started insisting she could sneak me into her dorm room after hours. That was never an option I would consider for even a second with that snake living there. Even if I did, Sydney wouldn't hesitate for a second and would happily report me straight to the Dean and spin a web of lies that would likely get me kicked out of school. I'd rather freeze on the streets than ever give the stupid bitch the satisfaction.

In the end, I had to lie to get Paris off my case. I told her I arranged to spend the night with one of the girls I work with, and she begrudgingly dropped the subject.

I don't have a shift at Zen's till tomorrow night, and I've only got ninety-eight dollars to keep me going for two weeks. I'm regretting that four dollars I spent on the coffee now. "You know I would take you in without a second thought, but we live in a studio and with absolutely no privacy and a baby whose things take up ninety percent of the apartment." Clay states woefully while he leans against the bar.

I'm sitting opposite him on the bar with my head in my hands, using up every last bit of intellect I have left to come up with an idea that doesn't culminate with me sleeping on the streets. I shake my head and wave him off. "Hey, I'll talk to Ray tomorrow about giving you an advance. I'm sure he will agree, given the situation. The man is a total jackass, but he's not completely heartless."

I drop my hands from my head with a heavy sigh. "I'm not holding my breath. If my fate is reliant on Raymond Hooper, then I might as well get myself geared up to sleeping on the streets for the foreseeable future."

Clay drops the cloth in his hand on the bar and rests his elbows on it. "Rein, stop being stubborn, just let me pay for a hotel for you. At least for tonight?" I shake my head and skim through the listings of rooms to let on my phone.

I look up at him briefly. "Absolutely not. You're barely getting by yourself as it is with Leila and Jackson to provide for." I reply steadily and look at my phone again. "I'll be fine, don't worry about me."

Clay sighs and bows his head in frustration. "Kid, I *am* worried. Where the fuck are you planning to go?"

"I don't know yet, but I'll figure it out."

"No, fuck that. I'm clearing out the back room for you. You can stay here until you figure something out. I'm not having you sleeping on the street and freezing to death because you're too damn proud to accept help."

I scowl at him. "Pride has nothing to do with this, Clay."

Clay places his hands at his hips and glares at me morosely with those deep brown eyes of his. If I had been lucky enough to have a big brother, I would wish for him to be just like Clay. Instead, I just adore him and how protective he is of me. "Then what, kid? Who exactly are you trying to prove yourself to here? Chicago isn't exactly safe for a young girl to be roaming the streets."

I glare up at him. "A young girl? What am I fifteen? I'm a whole grown arse woman who can take care of herself. So why does everyone just assume I'm some helpless little damsel in need of saving?"

Clay rolls his eyes, "No one thinks you're a helpless damsel in need of saving. On the contrary, we care about you and want you to be safe. Why are you so affronted by that?"

"Why am I affronted? Maybe I don't appreciate being demeaned simply because I'm a woman. Newsflash, not every woman needs a knight in shining armour to come to her rescue. Some of us can stand on our own two feet perfectly fine." I argue haughtily, crossing my arms over my chest.

"Oh, Rein, for God's sake accepting help from people who care about you doesn't make you weak. No one has ever choked to death from swallowing their pride, and you won't either." Clay snaps agitatedly.

"On a long list of things that I'm willing to swallow, my pride isn't one of them, I'm afraid. Especially when it's all I have. I've got every intention of holding onto it." I retort and down the rest of the glass of Chablis I've been nursing the past two hours. Perks of working in a bar, you get to drink for free.

"You're senseless." Clay shakes his head perturbed and picks up the glass when I push it toward him. I don't understand why everyone has such an issue with my wanting to do things independently. I don't want to be obligated to anyone. Say I accept their help sooner or later; the day will come when they'll eventually throw it back in my face or hold it over my head.

Fuck that. It may be foolish and inane, but at least the risk of being left disappointed is slim to none when you rely on nobody but yourself.

I may not be able to control what life throws at me, but I sure as hell can control how I handle it. After all, moving forward is the only way to survive, right?

It's one in the morning, and I'm sitting on a bed in a chancy motel, with my back pressed against the headboard, and my knees pulled to my chest. My eyes scan the horrific place I'm forced into spending the night. This motel makes my old apartment look like a palace. This place is disgusting... actually disgusting is putting too mildly. It's simply ghastly.

As I sit on the very questionable bedspread, I wonder what illegal and horrid shit went down in this very room. The suspicious stains on the walls, the old tatty carpet with the large stain that looks alarmingly a lot like blood.

Fuck. I need to pee so badly, but I'm terrified of the kind of infections I am subjecting myself to simply by being in this room, let alone using the bathroom.

Only five more hours. I just need to bear it out five more hours, and it will be morning, and I can get the fuck out of here and sort something out.

I almost jump out of my skin when a door slamming shut shakes the walls of my room, and I can hear voices coming through the paper-thin walls from the room beside mine.

I sit still in the eerily dim lighting of the room, afraid to move or even breathe in fear someone will hear me, kick the flimsy door open and kill me just for kicks. If I have to be honest, I don't recall ever being this terrified in all my life. It feels like I'm trapped in one of those low budget movies where the heroine is a junkie or streetwalker and accidentally gets mixed up with the wrong kind of people and goes on the run, only to eventually wind-up dead in a seedy motel room by her pimp or drug dealer.

Fucking hell Rein, get a grip, will you?

"I'm going to ask you one more time." I hear an ireful voice warn from the other side of the wall. *"Where is the package?"*

"I don't know." A second voice fretfully responds, his voice juddering. *"I swear Zeke, I don't know, man, I don't know."* He whimpers.

Oh shit.

"You don't know, huh? So a package that was in your possession just goes missing, and you don't have a fucking clue where it went? I think we ought to jog your memory, Morris." A loud thump and a loud cry of pain send an ice-cold tremor through me.

"No, no, please! Zeke, I swear to you, I don't know where it went. I would never steal from you. Please, bro, just give me a few days, and I'll find it, I will."

I look back at the wall, my heart beating wildly up in my throat. Is this Zeke going to kill him? Holy shit, I was worried about roaming the treacherous streets of Chicago on my own, so I chose this shithole and somehow wound up an eyewitness to a drug deal gone wrong.

I jump when I hear an ear-shattering cry and the distinct sound of bones breaking. They're beating him. What the hell do I do? I pick up my phone and dial 911 but stop as I go to hit the call button. The phone shakes between my trembling fingers as I stare at the numbers. If I report them, who's to say they won't come after me? I don't know who these people are. But if I don't and this man dies, how will I live with myself?

Fucking hell, why me?! I gasp and leap off the bed when something hard hits the wall behind me, and it shakes threateningly. I back myself up against the wall by the window and sink to the floor, my head in my hands, my entire body shaking uncontrollably with trepidation.

God, please, please, this cannot happen; this can't happen to me.

CHAPTER *Thirteen*

Talon

"T*AY!*"

"Sir, please, stay back. We can't let you through."

"Get the fuck off me, that's my fiancée's car! TAYLOR!"

"Sir, please, I need you to stand back while the paramedics help your fiancée."

"Oh God, is she going to be okay? She's p-pregnant. Please, please God, let them both be okay."

"She's flat-lining. Hand me the paddles. All clear."

"Come on, baby, you can't leave me, not like this. Please, I need you. Come on."

"Charge to two hundred. All clear."

"Starting compressions."

"Charge to two-twenty. All clear."

"We've lost her."

"NO! Why are you stopping? She's not gone, she's not! TAYLOR!"

"Time of death, ten thirty-two."

"NO!" I jump, waking from my sleep and bolt upright on the sofa, my heart beating loudly in my ears and drenched in a cold sweat. While I sit there, disoriented, I take a couple of seconds to apprehend that I'm at home in my living room. After I lost Taylor, I had the same reoccurring nightmare, reliving the dreadful moment I lost her for months on end.

I thought it was over since I didn't have a nightmare in about six months. But I guess I was wrong. The terrors of losing Taylor and our baby will continually haunt me forever. I need to accept that I'll be living with this guilt for the rest of my life.

The buzzing of my phone on the coffee table beside me distracts me from my thoughts. It's an unknown number. Who the fuck is calling me at one-forty in the morning? I don't usually answer numbers I don't recognise, especially if it's hidden. I made that mistake in the past and realised it was students calling me at all hours in a drunken stupor, slurring and sputtering inappropriate comments. However, something inside my gut made me hit that green answer button.

"Hello."

"Mr Saxton?"

A heavy feeling falls deep into the pit of my stomach like a block of lead. "Speaking."

"I'm Detective Brown, and I'm calling from the Chicago Police department. Do you happen to know a Miss Rein Valdez?"

Oh, fuck. Something happened to Rein. I don't even remember when or how, but I was up on my feet, pacing the room restlessly.

"Yes, she's my student. Is she..." I fucking knew I shouldn't have let her go. What if she's been killed. "Is she okay?" I ask fretfully.

"Miss Valdez is fine." A wave of relief washes over me, and I close my eyes, exhaling slowly. "She's here at CPD. We couldn't find any listed contacts, and when we asked, she provided us with your number. Miss Valdez was an eyewitness to an assault, so we brought her in for questioning to take her statement. Unfortunately, despite our best effort to convince her, she wouldn't provide us with a residential address; therefore, we couldn't release her due to the nature of the case, her safety may be in jeopardy, and she's refusing protective custody."

Fucking Christ, Rein. What in the shit did you get yourself involved in.

"I understand, Detective. I can be there in twenty minutes to pick her up. Can I speak to her?"

"She's still being questioned at the moment."

I nod and shove my fingers through my hair. "All right. Thank you, Detective. I'll be there soon." I hang up and rush over to my bedroom to throw on a pair of grey jogging bottoms and a white t-shirt before I fled my apartment.

What am I going to do with this girl? The more I fight to stay away, the deeper I'm getting drawn in.

The hell was I thinking, letting her go off with nowhere to go. Of course, she's going to end up finding trouble. I should have never let her go... then again, who am I to stop her.

You're *the one she called when she needed someone.*

I didn't even know she had my number.

Thirty minutes later, I'm pacing back and forth in the waiting area at the police station. The officer at the desk eyeing me as I restlessly shift from one position to the next, waiting for Rein to be released. Finally, after what felt like forever—but in reality, it was only ten minutes—the wooden door opens, and an officer steps out of a room, Rein following closely behind. My heart clinches when I see her distraught state. She looks utterly exhausted, eyes rimmed red and puffy, face unusually pale and cheeks slightly sunken.

I take a step toward her when the officer hands her a piece of paper and says something to her, to which she responds with a nod, taking it from him, folding it and pushing it into her back pocket.

It wasn't until the police officer walked off that Rein raised her eyes and looked at me remorsefully. "I'm so sorry for disturbing you, Professor. I told them not to call you and try Paris or my friend Clay again instead, but they called you anyway."

I shake my head, "Don't worry about it. Are you okay?"

Rein shrugs, "Honestly, I don't know. My life is falling apart all around me, and I can't seem to put it together or control it." She admits, defeated and walks out of the police department when I hold the door open for her.

"What happened?" I question, walking beside her toward my car parked in the parking lot behind the precinct.

"I checked into a cheap Motel just to get my head down for the night and find someplace in the morning. But, of course, as my luck would have it, I got the room next door to some psychotic drug dealer whose deal went awry and was battering the shit out of some poor guy." Rein explains, wrapping her arms around herself to shield off the chill of the wind.

I wince and shrug off my jacket when I notice she's shivering, her teeth chattering. "You called the cops?" Rein looks up at me when I drape my coat over her shoulders.

Rein lowers her gaze briefly and chews on her bottom lip pensively. "I was going to, but I chickened out. I sat there, almost paralysed with fear and listened to that guy screaming in agony while they shattered his bones. If they could beat one of their own within an inch of their lives for simply losing a package, what would they do to me if they ever found out I was the one that called the cops on them? I'm a coward. They almost killed him, and I did nothing."

I frowned and held her upper arms, lowering my head to be at eye level with her. "You are no such thing. Protecting yourself doesn't make you a coward, Rein. Why should you risk your life for someone you don't even know? Do you think he would have done the same for you? Those who try to play the hero often find themselves six feet under. You absolutely did the right thing and kept your head down." I assert steadfastly, and she eventually nods. "Did anyone see you?"

"I don't think so. Detective Brown said they've been watching them for a while now. They only just missed them by minutes before they took off. He suggested I go into protective custody for a while until they catch them because, as it turns out, these men are dangerous and apparently wanted for a long list of crimes. I've told them all I overheard, which wasn't much, but I refuse to go into hiding at the off chance someone may or may not figure out that I was a witness." Rein explains tiredly.

"Are you absolutely certain no one saw you? It would be wise to consider it for your protection, Rein. You may not have been the one to call the police and report them, but these types of organisations take no prisoners, especially if they suspect you know something that could potentially incarcerate them." Rein watches me warily while I opened the car door and gestured for her to get in.

She shakes her head and does that thing where she narrows her eyes a little and slowly licks her lips.

"If that's true, then you're putting *yourself* at risk by being seen with me. Aren't you?" Well, she's got me there.

"I suppose I am," I admit, letting go of my hold on her arms.

Rein keeps her eyes on mine and wraps my jacket tighter around her body. She takes a step closer to me, and I watch her keenly. "Why are you always saving me, Professor?"

Christ, I wish I knew. A big part of me wishes I could go back to the time I wasn't even aware of her existence, but the harder I'm trying to convince myself to stay the fuck away and not give in to my urges, the more I'm finding myself wanting to be in her company. I open my mouth to speak, but she cuts me off. "And don't give me the spiel of how you'd do the same for all your other students because we both know that's not true."

Shit.

I thought I had this under control. Perhaps my apathy slipped away from me at some point, allowing her to get a glimpse of my attraction toward her. "Okay, why don't you tell me why you called *me?*"

Rein blanches. Her pouty mouth drops open while she stares up at me, startled. "I told them not to call you."

"And how do you have my number?"

She shifts from foot to foot, her eyes cast down. "I may have access to the faculty directory."

My brows go up with interest. She intentionally got my number from the faculty directory. How the hell did she get access when only the admin staff have access to that information? I should be angry as it was a clear breach of my privacy, but for some bizarre reason, I like the fact that she went out of her way to deviously get my number.

"How did you get access to the faculty directory?"

Rein bites her lip, "I was volunteering a couple of months ago, and Rosie from Admin had me update some information."

"You are aware that is a breach of a faculty member's privacy, right? That information isn't on there for you to take. They could expel you." I state sternly, crossing my arms over my chest and glowering at her.

"I know." She replies, taking a step closer to me when I lean against the car. "I never intended on using it."

"Then why take it?"

Rein shrugs and inches closer. My stomach goes all tight with antici-pation now that we're almost toe to toe. I should move. I need to move but, fuck me, I can't. I can't seem to take my eyes off her. "I know it's juvenile, but I kind of liked the thought of being the only one at that school to have your number." She declares brazenly, tucking her nose into the collar of my jacket while she gazes up at me through her lashes.

I chuckle with a shake of my head and rub my jaw awkwardly. "Seri-ously? The fact you can't comprehend how unsettling that sounds is honestly worrying to me. If I wanted you to have my number, I would have given it to you, wouldn't I?" I utter sharply.

"Say I did use it and texted you. Would you have replied?" I stare at her, jaw set tight and twitching. I need to be careful what I say here.

"That would depend entirely on the context of the text."

Rein's lips curl at the corners. She presses them together and takes her phone out of her pocket, and unlocks it. I watch her curiously while she swipes and then types something and smirks triumphantly.

A second later, my phone vibrates in my pocket. I pull it out and see a message from an unsaved number. I unlock my phone, open the messages app and tap on the message to open it. I almost choke on my saliva when I see a photo of Rein posing seductively in front of a full-length mirror in a pair of white heels, wearing a maroon, oversized shirt that barely covers her sexy arse and falling off one shoulder. The message at the bottom read, '*Now you have something personal of mine. We're even.*'

Fuck me dead.

I've never gotten a stiffy so fast in my life. Every last drop of blood rushes from my brain straight down to my cock, causing it to pulse with urgent need. I lift my eyes from the phone and hold her gaze. This is not the time to be fucking with me—it's five in the morning. I'm tired. I'm horny as hell. I will screw her like a savage till my name and the feel of my cock stretching her is all she can remember.

I lock my phone and push it back into my pocket before I reach over, grip her belt buckle and draw her into me till she's standing between my legs. Rein lets out a little gasp of surprise and cranes her neck to peer up at me with those striking eyes all wide and keen. "Listen to me, Snowflake. As much as I appreciate that photo..." I say gruffly and wet my lips, "You're a bright young woman. I know you can feel whatever this thing is between us. And yes, I am attracted to you, but as I've said before, Rein, nothing can ever happen. Our relationship can never go beyond Professor and student. Do you understand?"

Rein bites down on her bottom lip, her eyes flittering down to my mouth. I can see the desire glittering in her eyes, and I know she's thinking about kissing me, just as I am fucking bursting to have a taste of her. I get it, she's currently going through a shitty time and looking for some form of comfort, but as much as I would like to be, I can't be that for her—not without jeopardising everything we've both worked so hard for and risk putting her in an even worse situation.

"That's a real shame, Professor, because lately, you're all I've been thinking about." Rein affirms melodiously, her head tilting to the left; she gazes at me wantonly.

Bit by bit, I can feel my self-restraint slipping, especially with how she is eyeing me. "Rein, stop it. I've already broken one too many rules. I'm the last man you need to be getting tangled up with, trust me."

Rein's hands resting on my upper arms fall to her sides, and I hate that my body instantly craves her touch the way it does. "I'm a grown woman; let me decide who I choose to be tangled up with. It's not just me; I know you feel this is right."

I briefly close my eyes and count to ten to calm myself down before I do something stupid and spread her out on the hood of my car and gorge on her pussy for breakfast, lunch, dinner, and whatever other courses are in between.

Crikey, my dick is weeping. I can feel the warm liquid of my arousal suppurating and dampening my boxers. I force my eyes open and hold her gaze steadily. "It may feel right, but it's not. I'm your teacher. We both have too much riding on the line, Rein. My career, your scholarship, it's just too risky. You've got a lot going on, and I'm not even getting into the significant age gap between us." I explain.

Rein sighs and looks down at her feet disappointedly before she nods, "Seven years isn't a significant age gap, but you're right. I'm a mess." She replies and winces a little. "I completely understand your reluctance and would hate to put you in a position where you could face losing your career. I'm sorry, I'll delete your number, and we can forget this ever happened."

I won't be forgetting that picture in a rush. I can promise you that much for certain. I will delete it. I will.

The disappointment that sunk deep into my gut when she withdrew and put some space between us was just awful. I almost went back on my every word and reached to pull her back to me. "You don't have to be sorry, Snowflake. If we had met under different circumstances, believe me, I'd be all over you."

Rein smiles faintly and nods. We stare at one another wordlessly, but our eyes are speaking volumes. Fuck, I really want to kiss her.

"Uh, I should go. Thank you for yet again coming to my rescue. I honestly don't know how I'll ever repay you." I frown when she attempts to slide off my jacket and hand it back to me.

"Well, you can put that back on for starters because this time, I'm not letting you go off on your own with nowhere to go. You're taking Michael's apartment until you can find someplace to stay, *and* it's absolutely not up for discussion." I declare firmly when she tries to dispute. I opened the car door and gestured for her to get in. "You want to know how you can repay me? Please get in the car, so I can at least get a decent couple of hours sleep without stewing in anticipation whether or not my phone will ring again."

"I wasn't aware that I kept you up all night worrying about me, Professor," Rein utters. At the same time as she walks over and deliberately brushes past me while she slides into the passenger seat.

I suck in a deep breath and almost divulge that she's been keeping me up doing far more than just worrying, but I catch myself. I don't respond. Instead, I push the door shut and walk around the car, muttering profanities under my breath.

By the time we got back to my apartment complex, the sun was starting to rise. It has been the longest weekend, and I've burnt the fuck out. Thank God it's still Sunday, so I can catch up on some sleep before I prepare for my classes for the week.

"So, you should be all set here. There's a small supermarket adjacent to the third building should you need anything." I instruct as I walk to the door and open it. "If you need anything, drop me a message or give me a call."

Rein leans against the wall beside the door, a coquettish smile ghosting her plump lips. "So, I shouldn't delete your number then?"

I fight off the urge to smile. "You can keep it for *emergencies*." I assert, putting extra emphasis on emergencies just in case she gets the wrong impression and sends me more risqué pictures of herself. I don't think my poor, neglected norks would survive the torment; they're already unbearably full as it is.

"Of course, emergencies only, got it." Rein responds with a coy smile.

I linger, don't ask me why, but I'm unable to fucking move while we gaze at each other longingly. She's got me locked in her gaze.

"You'll make it impossible to stay away from you when you look at me like that, Professor." Rein jests, resting her head against the wall by the door.

I smile broadly and rub the back of my neck while I straighten from my leaning position. "Right back at ya, Miss Valdez. I'll see you."

Rein smiles and bites her bottom lip, "You sure will."

Goddamn, that smile of hers; it does things to me.

I've gone and got myself in a right quandary by admitting that I'm attracted to her. Regrettably, though, I've got a strong feeling shit is about to get a whole lot more complex if the sizzling chemistry between us is anything to go by.

I only hope I can scrape together enough strength to keep resisting her.

I'm a man of control. I've got this.

The ringing of my phone interrupts my thoughts as I lay in bed, staring up at the ceiling. Who does a bloke have to kill to get some shut-eye around here? I reach over and look at the number, unidentified. I push the green button and answer it. "Hello."

"Mr Saxton?"

"Speaking."

"This is Lieutenant Ryan, the firefighter you gave your card to Friday night." I lean up on my elbow. "You told me to give you a call if we come across the necklace in apartment 5b."

"You found it?"

"Yes, sir, it's a little charred but nothing a jeweller can't fix. If you drop by the fire department, you can pick it up from there." Lieutenant Ryan explains, and I smile.

"Perfect, I'll be there this afternoon to pick it up. Thank you, Lieutenant."

"Not a problem. She must be really special."

I stare at my reflection in the mirror opposite my bed. "Like you wouldn't believe."

CHAPTER Fourteen

Rein

"I AM THE WORST FRIEND IN THE WORLD!" PARIS WAILS AS SHE throws herself down on her bed.

I roll my eyes with a sigh, "P, don't be so dramatic. You are not the worse friend in the world. There's no rule that states we can't have our own lives. We're not joined at the hip, so don't sweat it." I explain, sitting beside her on the bed.

Paris pops one eye open and looks up at me. "You are a much better friend than I am, bitch tits. If I were going through the shit you are right now, and you were MIA, I'd be hella mad at you right now for not being there for me." She states and sits upright. "I'm truly sorry, my phone died, and I didn't have my charger with me."

"P, you don't have to explain yourself. It's okay; I'm fine, really." I assure her. "However, I do need something from you, though," I add with a sheepish smile, and Paris' ears perk up.

"Yes, *anything*."

I sigh, "Before I ask, I need you to promise me that you won't go all bananas on me because even considering asking you is making my arse sweat." Paris' face contorts to one of confusion and amusement all mixed up into one, but she nods in understanding.

"Okay, I promise. Tell me." She urges, her eyes all big and curious while she patiently waits for me to continue.

I inhale deeply, filling my lungs with air. My palms are sweating. "As you're aware, I lost everything in the fire, and all I own is literally on my back." Paris nods, a look of sympathy shadowing her pretty face. I detest when people look at me like that. I can feel it, I'm about to lose my nerve when my pride slowly starts to flare, but I swiftly force it back down. I have to do this. I have no other option. "I would never ask, but I need..." The words get lodged in my throat. Fuck, why is this so goddamn hard. "I, um, would you..." I scratch my temple, my face heating. This physically hurts.

"Hey," Paris takes my hand into hers and smiles warmly. "I got you, whatever you need, bae."

"I'm going to pay you back every single penny." I declare, shifting so I can face her properly.

"You know you don't have to pay me back, Rei, but I know you well enough to know that you would never accept the money unless I agree, so fine, you can pay me back whenever you're ready, there is absolutely no rush. I don't want you stressing or killing yourself."

I smile gratefully and throw my arms around her neck, hugging her tight. Paris laughs when we topple over on her bed. "You know what this means, don't you?"

I look over at her; she's grinning wickedly, displaying every single one of her pearly white teeth. *Oh, God.* "Shopping!" I groan when she jumps up off the bed and drags me up by the arm. "A whole day shopping with my best bitch, how exciting!"

"Yay." I drawl contemptuously while she pushes me toward the door to her dorm room.

FOUR HOURS, twenty stores, trying on an absurd number of outfits later, we finally find a spot to sit in a restaurant to have some late lunch. My feet are throbbing, and I'm in flats. How Paris prances around in those six-inch heels all day honestly baffles me. What are her feet made of exactly? Some sort of synthetic plastic? Or perhaps steel?

"So, I was thinking now we are out an all, we should hit the salon. I'm in despo need of a trim and treatment." I pull my menu down and look at her warily.

"We?" I utter warily. Paris nods, grinning giddily--she's practically bouncing in her seat. "I don't need a haircut; my hair is just fine," I state and look at the menu again. I scowl when it's suddenly plucked from my fingers. "Hey, I've not decided yet," I complain with a pout.

"You don't need a menu in this place; they're famous for their chicken, mushroom and avocado pasta. It's to die for, trust me." I shrug and nod. It does sound appealing, and Paris knows good food. "When was the last time you cut your hair?"

I frown, pick up a strand of my hair, and evaluate while I recall my last hair appointment. "Uh..."

"If you have to think about it, it's been too long, betch. We're going, and you're getting a shape up." She protests, holding up her silver starter knife and pointing it at me.

I relent and hold my hands up in surrender. "Okay, fine, *fine*, I'll get a haircut. Put the knife down, you psycho." Paris giggles and sets her knife down on the table.

"That's my betch." Paris chirps and gasps when two pornstar martinis are delivered to the table.

"Compliments from the gentlemen at the bar." The waiter announces, and we both turn to look at the two men sitting at the bar, swathed in expensive suits toasting their drinks to us.

"Ooh, they're cute." Paris purrs, nodding flirtatiously at one of them. This girl is impossible. "Should we invite them over?"

"No, absolutely not."

"Why not?" Paris questions after she takes a sip from her drink. "We're both single. You're getting over a breakup, and the best way to do that is to get under someone else, and that right there, my dear bestie, is definitely someone you want to be getting under." Paris states, her eager beaver eyes giving them a quick sweep.

I take a large sip of the martini and swallow. So much for not drinking again. At this rate, I'll end up a bloody alcoholic. "P, you know I don't like the idea of sleeping with random strangers. I've tried it and hated all five minutes of it."

Paris almost chokes on her drink and coughs. I hand her a napkin that she takes from me, and half groans and laughs while she gracefully dabs her mouth. "Right, I forgot about that little fiasco." She smirks, clearing her throat once she composes herself. "Take it from some-body who has been with an older man, unlike the self-centred boys of our generation, believe it or not, they're all about pleasing women and know exactly where everything is and how to work it."

While Paris rambles on and on about the benefits of sleeping with older men, my eyes wander over to the golden blond-haired gentleman at the bar in the navy-blue suit and find myself comparing him to Professor Saxton. The same sort of build, hair colour, only amiss is the icy blue eyes, the stubble—and of course the striking good looks. This guy has deep chestnut-coloured eyes and is clean-shaven, nice to look at, but he's no match to Talon Saxton.

"If we had met under different circumstances, believe me, I'd be all over you."

I know I need to stay away, but I can't help that I want him the way I do, and the fact he wants me just as bad is rousing the bad girl inside me.

I might not be able to have him physically, but no one said I couldn't have a little fun teasing and flirting with him.

"Rein? Heeeeello? Rein!" I snap out of my trance and look over at Paris, waving her hand in my face.

"Huh?"

"Juhccz, you two might want to get a room. There is some serious eye fucking going on across this restaurant. Oh, I got you, girl."

Oh crap, she thought I was flirting with the bar guy and is currently waving them over. I shift in my seat as they approach us at the table. "Ladies."

"Hello boys, I'm Paris, and this is my very attractive, very single friend, Rein. Please join us."

Oh boy.

FOUR ROUNDS of pornstar martinis and some heavy flirting with the attractive men—Mason and Dean from the restaurant who both work in The Loop—the finance district of Chicago as finance directors at Richmond and Co. They're both thirty years old, successful and are recently single.

Dean—the blond one I was supposedly 'eye fucking' gave me his number and said he would love to take me out for dinner. I took his card out of courtesy and told him I would call if I free up some time in my schedule. Paris, of course, took Mason's number and arranged to see him later that night. The girl is incorrigible; she moves quicker than a cat on a mouse.

After lunch, Paris begrudgingly dragged me to her hairdressers, where we had our hair done. I had a trim and added some layers. According to the stylist, my natural hair is sensational, and he would murder me if I ever tried to colour it.

With our hair freshly done, we went back to my new apartment.

"Yowza! This place is certainly an upgrade from the last shit hole you were residing in, Rein." I set my bags down on the sofa and set my keys down on the kitchen island. "Whose place is this again?"

"A regular punter that comes into the bar. He works on a contract basis and had to move to London for six months. He was looking to sublet or find someone to keep an eye on the place and offered it to me." I lie and pray she doesn't see straight through my lie. I cannot lie for shit, and she knows this. Thankfully she doesn't question it and smiles while she noses around the apartment.

"You little hoe bag, you were boinking him, weren't you?"

"No!" I exclaim, affronted by her accusation. "Even though that fleabag Hunter deserved it, I never stepped out on him. This guy is just a kind friend, helping out another friend, that's all there is to it."

"Bitch please, men will not do a damn thing for a woman just out of the kindness of their heart. There is always some underlying agenda or expectation at the end of it. Mark my words." Paris declares and picks up a picture frame with Michael's photo holding up a giant fish he just caught. I must admit he is a very attractive man. "Oh my god, he's effing hot! If you don't—what is that weird British word you Brits use for sex?"

I groan and bury my head in my arms. "Shag?"

"Yes! That's the one. If you don't shag him, I bloody will." She avers, showing me the picture of him.

I chuckle, amused, and shake my head. "My British lingo is rubbing off on you quite well, I see."

"I know, right? It's the bee's knees." So she claims, chuffed with herself for imitating what I assume is supposed to be a British accent.

I laugh and throw a sofa cushion at her. "I say this with a heart full of love, but you really stink at accents, bitch tits."

"Oh, hush it, you hussy. I've got my date with Mason in two hours, and I don't know what I'm wearing. So it's time to pop open that bottle of bubbles, get some tunes going and get me all dolled up." Paris chirps, pulling me along toward the bedroom. "Holy cow, the man has an *entire room* as a walk-in wardrobe. That's it. I am remodelling my bedroom the moment I get back home." She mutters while snapping photos of the lavish wardrobe and prattling on about colour tones and lights. I've seen her closet. It's stunning.

It sure is inconceivable how the other half lives.

Later that evening, after Paris got ready and left for her date with Mason, I had a long shower and curled up on the giant L-shaped, cream coloured sofa. Oh, sweet heavens, this is by far the comfiest sofa my arse has ever had the pleasure of sitting on. It almost feels like a bolstering hug. Although I would prefer the muscular arms of a certain, six-foot-something Professor to sink in to, nevertheless, this will just have to suffice.

While I'm watching but not actually taking in an episode of Gossip Girl, I hear a growl coming from somewhere, and the smell of fresh linen fills the entire apartment.

The hell is that? I lean up on my elbow and mute the tv, listening to see if I can identify the sound. I get up and follow the sound toward the utility room, where it gets louder. I push the door open and gasp loudly at the horrific scene before me. The washing machine is spilling over bubbles and shaking like some manic demon has possessed it.

"Oh my God!" I hurry over to the washing machine, almost slipping and falling over. I push the power button to switch the stupid machine off, but it seems I somehow manage to piss it off more because the soapsuds pour out faster. "No, no, no damn it, stop!" I pressed every button I could to turn it off, but nothing was working. "What is wrong with you, you demonic piece of shit! Where is your fucking plug? Do I need to exorcise you?!?" I exclaim as I frenziedly scoop up the suds with my hands and throw it in the sink. My foot slips when I spin too quickly, and I hit the floor with a thud and whimper, a dull ache shooting up my backside. "Ow!"

"God damn it! Why is my life such a disaster?" I rest my head back against the machine while it spits soap over my head. The doorbell chimes, and I stare at the door. Who on earth is that at this time? I grip the side of the machine and pull myself up, careful not to slip again.

Amazingly, I make it to the front door without breaking my neck and pull the door open, panting, and stare at the figure standing tall before me, holding a brown bag of... is that Chinese food? "Whoa. Uh, is this a bad time?"

I blink, "Professor?"

Professor Saxton's eyes grow large when he takes in the state of me standing before him in my matching pink Cami top and shorts covered in foam. I see the confusion and amusement all over his handsome face, and it makes me even angrier. "Are you throwing a foam party or something?"

I throw my hands up in the air, "Yes, yes, I am. Just the bloody demonic washing machine and me. We're having a grand old time in here. Please join us."

"What?" He utters, bewildered as he walks into the apartment. I close the door behind him and watch as he tugs his jacket off and sets the bag down before he turns and faces me.

Holy cheese balls. He sure is a treat for the eyes... and well, *other* places.

"The washing machine went bonkers on me and started spilling out all this soap all over the place," I complain heatedly whilst gesturing to myself. Professor Saxton presses his lips together and rubs his jaw, those blue eyes full of mirth. "Oh, you're entertained by my misery; that's just great." I huff and hurry back to the laundry room that is slowly filling up with more and more soapsuds. "How are you still foaming?!" I shout at the machine, and it grunts back at me.

"What the... whoa. Jesus, what did you do, Rein?" I glare back at the glorious bastard, absolutely seething. "How much detergent did you put in the machine?"

"Me? I didn't do a damn thing! I put in a couple of caps full and set the load on to wash, and it went absolutely ape shit, and well, as you can see, this is the result." I snap hotly and jump back when it starts the spin cycle again. "No, no, not again. Stop, stop." I whimper, pushing the buttons on the LCD screen.

Professor Saxton cracks up laughing and leans over me, pushes some magical button and the whole machine stops. I gape at the machine and turn my head to look back at him. "How the hell did you do that?" I pant.

"Believe it or not, there's an *off* button on the screen." He replies coolly, his lips curling into a gorgeous smile when I gape at him in astonishment.

"Of course there is because it didn't occur to me to push the damn off button while I was drowning in soap." I fume, placing my hands atop of my head and groaning in frustration. "Stop laughing! It's not funny. I am a walking, talking disaster. Like seriously, what more could possibly go wrong—ohh!" The words hadn't even left my mouth before I slip and we both go toppling to the floor in a heap, our limbs coiled like a pretzel. Professor Saxton lands on his back, and I fall on top of him. Our eyes open at the same time, and we stare at one another.

"Are you okay?" he pants, his eyes searching mine. I nod silently, unable to utter a word or look away. I can feel the warmth of his breath on my face, his firm pectoral muscles stiffening and flexing under my palms where they ended up pressed against his robust chest on our fall. I stare at his mouth, so invitingly close to mine, all it would take is a tilt of his head, and our lips would touch.

"Rein." My stomach clenches tight, and butterflies take flight in my stomach at the gruff undertone of his voice when he whispers my name. I can tell he's battling with himself to stay in control. His ocean blue eyes darken with desire, that chiseled jaw clenching and unclenching. We're both thinking the same thing. What if we give in to temptation, just for a moment and kiss? Who will ever know but the two of us? "We should probably get up." His voice is strained when he speaks, but he has yet to let go of his hold on me, a brawny arm still wrapped around my lower back, keeping me against him. Like a tidal wave, disappointment swamps me yet again. I close my eyes for a second and nod.

"We should," I sigh and shift to move off him. I place my hands on either side of his head, so I can lift myself off him, but my hand slips and I fall back on top of him.

Our lips touch ever so slightly, and we both go still, our breathing heavy, eyes closed, foreheads pressed together. I couldn't focus on anything but the impassioned electrical current thrumming through our bodies as my lips ghost over his.

CHAPTER Fifteen

Talon

I'M BEING TESTED. THIS IS A FUCKING TEST, ISN'T IT? IF IT IS, I am failing epically.

I'm aching in places I didn't even know were possible for this girl. It would be so easy for me to kiss her right now, just brush her soft lips apart with my own and glide my tongue over hers—our lips are practically touching anyway. I can almost taste her, and fuck, I want more —no, I *need* more.

I'm on the fringe of losing my bloody rationality. When that door opened, and she stood there soaking wet, her thin top clinging to her full breasts, nipples hard like bullets begging for attention, I damn near almost came apart.

I should have stayed home. Where it's safe, and I've got my impulses curbed. But no, there is something deep inside that doesn't want to let her be. If she's not causing absolute mayhem in my life, she's running amuck in my head, and for some bizarre reason, I have to be close to her to function nowadays. I cannot for the life of me talk an ounce of sense into my mind or body where she's concerned.

Maybe we just need to fuck and get it out of our systems. Diminish this intense chemistry once and for all. But, oh, sweet Jesus, her body feels so good pressed up against mine. I'm rock hard and aching to be buried inside her. I know she can feel the length of me pressed up against her hip, and at this point, I couldn't a give flying rat's arse.

The frustration I'm feeling right now is honestly too much to bear. I want to holler until my lungs implode. This is anomalous for me. I'm a man of control; I always have been. At least I was... until her.

My hand glides up her back, and I curl my fingers at the nape of her neck. "Rein, you need to get off." I almost growl, my lips brushing over hers as I speak. I squeeze her neck, and she moans breathily.

Oh fuck, fuck, that sexy little *moan*.

"Then get me off, Professor." I open my eyes and stare up into her fiery gaze. "Do you think *you* can do what no man has ever been able to?" My mouth goes dry. Fucking hell, what kind of morons have you been sleeping with that have left you unsatisfied. There's a hint of challenge in her eyes, and I'm never one to turn down a challenge.

Reaching up, I brush her hair away from her face and drag my nose over hers. "No, Snowflake, I don't think—I *know* I can get you off, and in so many ways, it will blow your mind."

"Put your words into action because I'm ready to have my mind blown, Professor." Rein purrs, rocking herself against my thigh; the heat between her legs seeps through my jeans, and I lose every single one of my cognitive functions.

"Christ, Rein." I breathe, gripping a handful of her ample bum. I grind up against her, and she gasps. "You think I haven't thought about it. Sinking my cock deep into your tight, dripping wet pussy is all I can think about. I'm constantly wondering what you taste like.

How you would feel wrapped around me. You've got me walking around with a constant hard-on. Believe me, if I had my way, I would have you spread out on my desk, fucking you first with my tongue, and then my fingers until you're a hot mess begging to be filled with my cock." I murmur lowly in her ear.

"Can't you see I'm already a hot mess for you, Professor? I have never wanted any other man the way that I want you." Rein whispers, her eyes lit up with desire and glittering like two of the most beautiful jewels I've ever seen.

"I want you too, but we can't. It's wrong and unethical, Rein. I'll be breaking every rule in the book and going against my own principles. If we get caught, this will go on my permanent record, my reputation will be tarnished, and I'll never be able to teach again." I explain, combing my fingers through her silky hair so I could see her pretty face.

Rein shifts and sits up, straddling me. "I know. God, I know, you're right. The last thing I want is to be the reason you lose everything, but how am I supposed to sit in your class day after day and not think about everything you just said you want to do to me?" Rein intones, her voice laced with frustration, mirroring my current state of dissatisfaction.

With a sigh, I sit up, placing my hands on her hips. "We need to forget everything that has happened this weekend, Rein. I never should have said what I did back there. I got caught up in the moment. Like I said, I've overstepped one too many boundaries with you this weekend, but come Monday, the moment I walk into that building, I'll go back to being your Professor, and that is all I can ever be."

"Just like that?" She questions, her brows furrowing. "You can just flip the switch and forget everything that has happened? It's that easy?"

I frown, "I never said it was easy, Rein; it's what needs to be done. Whatever this is between us has to stop. I can't give you what you want; even if I wanted to, I can't. You deserve to be with someone who can give you everything you desire, someone your own age who can take you out on dates, kiss you and hold your hand in public, not some sordid affair that solely depends on being fulfilled behind closed doors. It will probably be thrilling at first, but eventually, we'll both need more. I don't want to sneak around and hide my relationship like it's some dirty secret." I explain earnestly, and Rein sighs, closing her eyes for a moment. She nods and slowly slips off me.

"Someone my own age." She mutters under her breath, dark brows knitted together tightly. I stand up and observe her as she leans against the washing machine, her eyes cast down as though she's deep in thought.

"Rein."

Her eyes snap up to mine, and she shrugs, "I don't want someone my own age. I'm certainly not looking to jump into another relationship. In case you've forgotten, my last one didn't end all that well, and I'd rather spare myself the headache of killing myself trying to live up to someone's expectations of a perfect girlfriend." She gripes bitingly and wraps her arms around her torso.

"I don't know what kind of morons you've been dating, but relationships aren't great because there aren't any problems. They're great because both parties care enough about one another to want to fight to make it work. A *real* relationship is two imperfect people who refuse to give up on one another. It has nothing to do with perfection, nor should you ever change yourself for the sake of making someone else happy." I explain sombrely and veer my gaze from her penetrating one to glance around the laundry room. "Do you need a hand cleaning this up?"

Smooth Talon, way to change the subject. Idiot.

Rein glances around the room also and scratches her head. "Nah, I should be fine. How or where does one even begin to clean up this much soap?"

I chuckle and shrug, thankful the tension from moments ago slowly disappears. I'm trying my best not to stare at her wet body and the way her soaking clothes are clinging to her curves like a second skin.

I want to know how my name would sound flowing from those beautiful lips while I spread her pussy lips and tease her clit slowly, driving her wild.

Fuck. Now she's told me she's never been able to reach orgasm with a man... it will be all I'm going to be thinking about. "I mean, I'm no cleaning expert, but if I had to guess, it would likely involve a bucket and a mop?"

Rein turns her gaze to me and wrinkles her button nose. "Do we have any of those things?"

I shrug, "Michael had a maid, so I'm assuming there is a mop stashed away somewhere in the apartment."

Rein groans and straightens before she takes a step and almost slips again. I reach out and catch her before she falls. "Easy, are you going to be able to do this without breaking your neck?"

"Only one way of finding out." I let go of her, and she tiptoes out of the laundry room, clinging onto the walls for dear life. I bite back the urge to laugh as I watch her in delight while she tries to manoeuvre.

I ended up helping her clean up the mess. Although, I must admit, cleaning up soap, not as easy as one would think. It took us a good forty minutes to get the room back to its original state. "I am never doing laundry again." Rein declares, wringing out the mop. "On the plus side, I've never smelt cleaner."

I laugh when she lifts her arm and smells it. "Ah, I don't know about that; you always smell pretty great," I answer, and she smiles prettily. It always amazes me how quickly her cheeks go rosy whenever she gets a compliment. "You're not used to being complimented, are you?"

Rein pushes the mop bucket aside and licks her lips. "What makes you think that?"

I lean against the doorway, studying her closely. "Well, for starters, you go beet red and can't maintain eye contact."

"Well, your observations are correct, Professor. However, I do get a little flustered when I get complimented. It's not something I'm used to."

I scowl and straighten when she walks over to me. "Hard to believe. Your boyfriend didn't compliment you?"

Rein shrugs with a hefty sigh. "Every now and again, he'd say I was beautiful or when we were in bed during..." She stops and clears her throat, her cheeks burning red hot.

"Mm, that's a real shame because a girl like you should not only be commended but worshipped and absolutely more than 'every now and again," I affirm, looking down into her upturned face, my eyes searching hers.

"When you come across a guy like that, give him my number."

I smirk and take hold of her chin, taking a step closer. "He already has it."

"Well, then tell him to call me because I am well and truly long overdue for some worshipping." She fires back and nibbles on her bottom lip.

What am I doing? One minute I'm telling her we need to put a stop to whatever it is we are doing, and the next, I'm brazenly flirting with her. No wonder she's perplexed. I'm in a genuine dilemma. My mind is in a state of disarray, and I can't seem to figure out a way to get back to how things were before this weekend.

"I can tell you with absolute certainty he would take great pleasure in worshipping every single inch of your exquisite body," I murmur, trailing the back of my middle and index fingers down the side of her neck. Rein's eyes close, and she tilts her head back.

"My body is far from exquisite." She whispers breathily, her voice wavering ever so slightly as I drag my fingers sluggishly over her collarbone. Her skin is so smooth, like caramel, and I bet it would feel incredible against my tongue.

"You're absolutely right," I drawl, pressing my forehead to her temple, my lips brushing the shell of her ear as I speak in a low deep tone. "It's simply divine. Your curves, especially this one right here—" I trace my fingers under her top to the dip of her waist. "—is so incredibly sexy, specifically when you wear the crop top with the cherries printed on it. It short circuits my brain, and I can't focus for shit. I'm not even going to get into my fixation with your peachy bum."

Rein's breathing hastens, "No one has ever acclaimed my body in that manner before."

"Because the morons you've chosen to share your body with don't know how to appreciate the elegance and majestic features of a woman's body. Most men often have one trick that they assume works on every woman. That's why you've never been able to reach orgasm with those fools you've slept with, or maybe you've just never trusted them enough to completely give yourself up to them."

My fingers glide through her silky tresses, and I push her hair over her shoulder, exposing her neck. "You do smell good, like fresh laundry, but I definitely prefer *your* scent. I'm not particularly fond of smells that are too sweet but whatever it is you use reminds me of being a kid when my mum would bake cinnamon buns." I confess, running my nose along her neck, breathing her in. "You smell good enough to ravage."

"The body milk I use every morning is sweet orange and cinnamon." Rein clarifies with a breathy moan, her head falling back against my chest.

"I better go," I whisper in her ear, and an adorable groan of dismay emits from deep in her throat.

"Don't."

I close my eyes and press my molars together. "I have to Snowflake. If I stay a minute longer, I'm going to end up losing all control and doing something I know I'm going to regret later."

Rein turns to face me, her bottom lip between her teeth. Those stunning eyes meet mine when she steps closer. "I want you to stay." She proclaims, her hand slipping under my wet t-shirt, her fingers trailing over my torso, the muscles twitch and contract, her touch searing my skin. "I want to know what your skin feels like on mine." My heart rate spikes through the roof. I fist my hands by my side, my control quickly waning. "I need to know what your lips taste like. If your kiss is just as good and intense as it is in my dreams." She rasps, pushing up on her toes, her mouth a breath away from mine.

I swallow thickly. Lifting my left hand, I take her chin between my thumb and forefinger and tilt her head back, my eyes interlocking with hers. "I would kiss you so good and so deep you would forget whose air you're breathing," I vow thickly. Sweet Jesus, why do I keep doing this to myself? I want to kiss her so badly it's fucking killing me.

"So, kiss me, Professor. Steal every last drop of oxygen from my lungs," Rein whispers, her fingers dancing up my chest, nails lightly dragging along my skin, leaving a trail of fire in its wake. "Kiss me until I can no longer remember anyone that's ever kissed me before you."

"Fuck, Rein, you have no idea how much I want to. I'm fighting so hard to do the right thing and walk away and not take advantage of what you're offering, but when you say things like that, it makes me want to risk it all and fuck you in every square inch of this apartment." I growl avidly, brushing the pad of my thumb over her bottom lip.

Rein keeps her gaze on mine and parts her lips. Her tongue darts out, and she sensually runs her tongue over my thumb, wrapping her lips around it and sucks gently. "Fucking Christ." I lose my breath, and my head whirls when all the blood goes rushing straight to my dick while I stare fixedly at her mouth swathed around my thumb.

"Snowflake, stop, stop," I plead, pressing my forehead to hers. I'm hanging on by a thread that's fraying more and more the longer I'm close to her. "I need to go." I scrape up what's left of my control and break away from her. To say it scalded me from the inside out like a mother was an understatement.

I grab my jacket, hanging on the chair, and hightail it out of there like someone lit a firecracker up my arse. I almost rip the door open and yank it shut behind me before I lean against it, my eyes closed and heart-pounding like I'd been running a marathon.

I have got to get my shit together and stay the hell away from her long enough to gain some perspective, or we're going to both end up rescinding our futures.

THAT NIGHT, I didn't get a wink of sleep. Even after I whacked off once in the shower and twice in bed, I still couldn't relax enough to get some shuteye. I should delete this photo of her on my phone, but every time I try, something stops me. Just looking at the picture, I'm rock hard again, and my dick isn't even dry from when I blew my load a few moments ago.

I think I'm besotted with her. That's the only logical explanation I can come up with for my behaviour. This isn't me. Either I chew over my morals and break every oath I took as a professor and have a secret affair with my student, or I shut her the fuck out and be a cold-hearted bastard until she hates me enough to give up hope of us ever being a thing.

The next morning, I went out for a run before work to clear my head. It didn't work. All I could think about was her. When I finally made it to the school, I kept my head down and hurried to my office before I saw her. My class with her isn't until later, so I'm safe... for now.

While I'm preparing for class, I hear a knock on my office door. "Come in," I utter, typing on my computer. "Professor." My fingers flying over the keyboard halt, and an aberrant heat surges through my body when I hear her voice.

Oh, bloody hell.

"May I come in?"

My eyes snap up to her, and my mouth instantly goes dry at the vision of her standing at the entrance of my office wearing a pair of tight, black leather trousers, a white crop top and a plaid, oversized, drop shoulder jacket.

I clear my throat and shift in my seat, readjusting myself in my trousers that were feeling a little snug upfront. "Please, come in, Miss Valdez. What can I do for you?"

Rein walks in and closes the door behind her softly. I let my eyes wander over the length of her body, her bum looking appetising in those leather pants. "Uh, I was up all night last night, thinking about our...." She stops and looks back at the door and then turns to look at me again, "...situation," she lowers her tone an octave. She takes a step toward my desk, pulling out a folded-up piece of paper from the binder she's carrying under her arm.

"Okay." Rein exhales, and I can sense her hesitancy as she drops the piece of paper on my desk. "What is this?" I question, reaching over to pick it up and unfold it.

"I'm considering transferring out of your class."

CHAPTER Sixteen

Rein

Professor Saxton glowers at me, his brows fused snugly, his facial expression grim. "You what?" He intones, resting his forearms on his desk and leaning toward me.

"I'm considering transferring out of your class," I reply, hooking my thumbs into the belt loops at the back of my jeans.

"Rein if this decision is because of this weekend..." He trails off apprehensively.

I shake my head and sigh.

Unable to hold his gaze, I lower it to the mahogany and gold desk plaque with his name, **Prof. T. Saxton. BA (Hons), MA, PhD** engraved on it. "Shit, it is, isn't it? I've gone and made you feel uncomfortable."

I shake my head, "No, not at all. It's not that. Look, Professor, you were right with everything you said. There is no point in us repeating the same things again and again, which at the moment, it feels like that's all we're doing, going back and forth. A part of me wishes things weren't said yesterday, but it's too late for that now, we're in the situation we are in and we can't change that. Given how intense things are between us now, I'll always be apprehensive our eyes will linger on each other a little too long and someone will suspect something is going on between us. I can't put your career in jeopardy. Me transferring classes is the best option for us both, that way we see less of each other."

Professor Saxton stands up and walks around his desk. "This is exactly what I was worried about. I understand where you're coming from, the situation isn't ideal for either of us, but from an academic point of view, I assure you it's absolutely the wrong move. What reason will you give for wanting a transfer when I'm the top professor in this field and your grades are exceptional? This class is key for you to be able to get your degree and apply for your masters next year. Compromising your education for something so trivial isn't a decision you should make on whim, Rein. You're in the middle of your semester, your end of year exams will start soon, it would be unwise to transfer." Professor Saxton rationalises and holds up the paper. "I'm not signing off on this."

I blink, "But—"

"No buts." He interjects firmly and takes a step closer to me. I crane my neck to look up at him. "I know things feel complicated right now, but I believe we're both mature enough to put what happened this weekend behind us and move forward."

I lick my lips and feel the tightness in my stomach ease a little bit. "And if we can't?"

Professor Saxton sighs, his cerulean gaze scanning my face and lingering at my lips before he drags them back up again. "We have too. Both our futures depend on it."

A deep sadness fills me at his declaration. I nod dejectedly and avoid looking at him. "I better go. My first class of the day is in five minutes."

Professor Saxton nods also, pushing his hands into the pockets of his black trousers. The crisp black suit he's wearing today makes his eyes stand out more. "What?"

I blink and snap out of my trance. *Damn it, I was totally just staring at him like a lovesick teen.* "Nothing,"

His lip curls into a knowing smile, one that tells me he's not buying a word of what I'm selling. "The zealous look radiating in your eyes tells a different story, Miss Valdez."

I roll my eyes in exasperation, "Oh, we're back to Miss Valdez now, are we? What happened to Snowflake?"

A slow, sexy smile graces his face making him look even more attractive. I groan inwardly when my lady parts throb in appreciation. This man literally gives my vagina a heartbeat with one smile.

God, why am I such a melt?

"It wouldn't be appropriate for me to refer to you as Snowflake on school grounds, would it now, Miss Valdez?" He voices playfully and gestures to the door with his brows. "You better hurry to your class. Professor Henderson is a real stickler for punctuality,"

"No one holds a candle to you, Professor. I haven't forgotten the time you kicked me out of your class for being a *minute* late." I utter as I turn and walk to the door. I smile when I hear him chuckle behind.

"Your time is no more valuable than mine, Miss Valdez." He calls out as I exit his office. I shoot him a distasteful look and he just grins back at me. Beautiful smug bastard.

MY FIRST TWO classes for the morning were composition painting and photography, which thankfully went by quite fast. My apartment before was only a five-minute walk to campus, but now I need to trek a mile and a half to school from my new place which doesn't leave me a whole lot of time to grab a coffee on my way in. My next class after break is business, so, I need my caffeine fix in order to focus on Mr. Carlton's tedious voice droning on and on. One plus is that Paris is in that class with me, oh and Hunter too. Not seen or heard from him since that night I caught him cheating. Can't say I'm looking forward to it, if I'm completely honest.

"Rein!" Ah speak of the devil, and he shall appear. I ignore him and keep walking. "Rein, hold up."

I look down and begrudgingly stop walking when I feel his fingers wrap around my upper arm. I fix him with a glare and yank my arm free of his hold. "Oh, look who finally managed to pull his tongue out of Sydney's arse long enough to face me."

Hunter heaves a heavy sigh and shoves a hand through his dishevelled hair. His brown eyes scan the cafeteria before they settle on me again. "Rein, baby, come on you know I have never had any interest in Syd. I was so fucking drunk I couldn't tell my ass from my elbow that night. I thought she was—"

I hold up my hand to cut him off. "Don't you fucking dare say you thought she was me, because there are absolutely no similarities between that skank and me. Also, you and I both know you weren't *that* drunk. And from what I witnessed, you seemed to be plenty interested in Sydney what with you slobbering all over each other so don't waste your breath lying. How long have you been fucking her behind my back Hunter? How long?!"

Hunter rubs the back of his neck, his eyes full of remorse. "It was only a couple of times. It was a mistake, it meant nothing; she means nothing. You're the one I want, baby—" Hunter declares, reaching for me, but I bat his hand away and slap him hard across the face. Everyone in the cafeteria stops and watches us.

"A mistake?" I gripe hotly. "I had a feeling something wasn't right; I should have trusted my gut a lot sooner, but I foolishly trusted you and didn't for one second consider you would ever do something like this. Putting aside our relationship, it's the fact you would betray my trust as my friend, that's what hurt, Hunter." I tell him with a shake of my head. "Don't feel too bad though, I was going to break up with you anyway, so you did me a favour. I wish you and Sydney all the best." I utter icily before turning and walk off to my class.

Stupid prick.

When I got to class, I just about managed to set my cup of coffee in the cup holder and books down on the table before Paris came scurrying over to me. "Oh my gosh, Rein, I just heard about your exchange with Hunter. Are you okay?"

Well, that didn't take long. Then again, the golden boy of the school getting slapped across the face in the middle of the cafeteria isn't exactly an everyday occurrence here at Oakhill.

"Yes, I'm great." I utter curtly and take my seat. Paris tilts her head to the side and scans my face for any sign of distress. I lift my eyes and look at her. "I'm fine, P."

"What did he say? Did he apologise?"

I shake my head, "No, just as I expected, he came prepared with a fuck-load of lies and excuses. He even had the audacity to lie and say he was drunk and thought Sydney was me." I iterate with disgust.

Paris gasps, "Ugh, that disgusting pig! No wonder you slapped him, good, I would have kicked him right in the nutsack. The cheek of him, you've been caught, at least man up and own up to your mistake."

"It wasn't a mistake P, they've been sleeping together for a while, which I suspected anyway. He's not the guy I thought he was, but better I found out sooner rather than later. Sydney wants him that bad, she's welcome to him." I sigh and take a sip of my coffee.

"We had a fight after I confronted her last night when I got back from my date with Miles." Paris voices, placing her elbow on the table and resting her chin in her hand. "She's claiming Hunter was always interested in her and when you showed up, he dropped her to pursue you. She said she only took back what was rightfully hers and you deserved it. She honestly makes me sick; I can't believe I was friends with her for so long. It's one thing not liking someone, but to deliberately go out of your way to pursue another girl's boyfriend is repulsive. As a woman, it's immoral, we should be looking out for one another, we shouldn't be tearing each other down." Paris avows sadly. "I don't want a vile person like that in my life."

"P, you know you don't have to burn bridges with her because of me. You guys have been friends a long time; I don't want to be the reason your friendship falls apart with her."

Paris takes my hand in hers and smiles warmly. "Rei, do you know what I noticed after becoming friends with you? I've been friends with all the wrong type of people. I would rather have one good and honest friend in my life than a handful of Sydney's. Some people are filled with such darkness that they wouldn't even hesitate to burn you just to see light. Sydney is one of those people and I don't want that kind of toxicity in my life. I want to surround myself with good people, people I can trust, and I know would have my back." She explains, reaching over to brush her fingers through my hair affectionately. Her words warm me through and through and I smile, my eyes watering.

"You're an incredible friend, P. I'm so glad I met you and I'm so blessed to have you in my life." I affirm earnestly and she smiles brightly.

"Well, I'm not going anywhere betch, to hell with the Hunters and Sydneys of the world. Hop aboard the sista ship." She beams holding up her cup of iced coffee.

I chuckle and hold up my latte, "Aye, aye captain."

"That's el capitana to you, sugar tits." Paris giggles when Mr Carlton enters and shushes her.

"Good morning class, today we will be taking a look into business ethics..." I groan inwardly and sink into my seat. No amount of coffee will be enough to keep me alert during this class.

Minutes drag on and feel like days while I wait for the class to end. I have Professor Saxton's class next and my nerves bunch up in my stomach with the thought of seeing him.

We've agreed to forget everything that happened and all that was said over the weekend, but I can't stop thinking about him and all the things he said to me. How could I? It's not like there's a switch I can flip and erase my thoughts and desires. Oh, how I wish there were.

"All right class that's all for today. I look forward to reading your papers next week. Enjoy your Thanksgiving break."

Oh shit, I completely forgot about the Thanksgiving break. I always get so depressed this time of year because everyone gets to go home to their families, eat great food and I'm stuck here missing mine terribly. We FaceTime but it's not the same as being home. We don't celebrate Thanksgiving in the U.K. but since I moved to the U.S., I've sort of become accustomed to it. I just feel so lonely especially around the holidays.

"Oh joy, four whole days listening to my parents clucking over one another incessantly, putting on their little show to convince my brother and I they can tolerate one another." Paris complains, slamming her book shut. "I wish they would just accept that the marriage is over and divorce already. It's always so awkward this time of year."

I stand up and throw my empty coffee cup in the bin before we walk out of the class. "At least they love you and your brother enough to want to stay together and keep fighting to make it work." I tell her frankly and she looks at me sideways.

"Unfortunately, some people just aren't meant to be together, and as much as it sucks to admit it, my parents are those people. It's clear as day there isn't an ounce of love between them anymore so why waste time trying to fix something that's already broken. Rob and I aren't kids anymore, we'd rather they split and be happy than live together and be miserable for the rest of their lives, ya know?"

I nod in understand and hook my arm with hers as we walk through the corridor. "And that, my dear bestie, is precisely why I always say love is nothing but a farce." Paris laughs.

"Careful sugar tits, you do know what they say about those who talk big?"

I frown and give her a questioning look. "I don't believe I do."

"They fall the hardest," She sings melodiously and giggles when I stare at her blankly before I burst into fits of laughter.

"Oh please, you need to stop watching those ridiculous hallmark movies and take a look at the world we really live in, P. There is no such thing as true love. It's all a bunch of made-up bollocks, like Santa and the fucking tooth fairy. There is no happily ever after." I assert sardonically. Paris rolls her eyes and playfully hits my arm with her book.

"Stop being such a kill joy. Maybe I like being a hopeless romantic. I'm happy waiting for my Prince Charming to sweep me off my feet and like Aladdin promise to show me the world."

I gasp, "Oh my god, can you see my eyes?" Paris stops and looks into my eyes.

"Yes, why?"

I place my hand on my chest and exhale rather dramatically. "Oh, thank God, because I rolled them so hard, I thought they fell out of their sockets."

"Bitch."

I laugh when Paris shoves me and I almost fall over until I hit something solid and a pair of arms go around my waist, steadying me before I fell. The first thing I see when I slowly lift my eyes are a familiar pair of blue eyes. Professor Saxton stares down into my face.

Oh, fuck me sideways.

"Careful, Miss Valdez." He drawls, blue eyes narrowed. "Are you all right?"

My mouth opens and closes like a fish while my brain scrambles to find words. I quickly straighten and step away from him. I clear my throat, my cheeks burning. "Yes, thank you." Why is this man always saving me?

"Oh shoot. I'm so sorry, Professor. That was totally my fault." Paris jumps in, her hand over her mouth. She gapes at him apologetically.

Professor Saxton's eyes veer from me to Paris and he nods. "No problem, maybe bear in mind that other people also use this corridor, it's not a playground, girls."

Paris smiles coyly and tucks a strand of her honey blonde hair behind her ear coquettishly. "Yes, Professor." She whirrs while I stand there like a timorous mute. Professor Saxton nods, his eyes glide over to me once more. "Get to class." He orders frostily and turns to continue walking down the corridor.

"Oh my God, Rei. You literally just fell into Professor Hottie's arms, you fucking lucky bitch." Paris gushes like an over excited schoolgirl. "How did it feel? Oh gosh, look at you, you're all red." She giggles. I blink and touch my face. My cheeks are burning red hot, I can only assume my face bears a resemblance to an overcooked tomato.

"I can't believe you pushed me into him. What the hell P?! I'm going to kill you." I exclaim stormily.

Paris giggles and holds her hands up, "I didn't see him there, I swear." I roll my eyes and pick up the book I dropped on the floor. "Did you see the way he looked at you, though? Bae, I would have fainted, I almost did when he said, 'girls' in that sexy Australian accent."

"Yes, I did see the venomous glare he shot me. Thanks for that, bitch." I drawl sarcastically. "I better go before he locks me out of his class again for being late."

"I'm so jealous, while you get to sit there and stare at that luscious specimen of a man I have to go and look at five foot five, balding and garlic breath, Mr Morris."

Even though I was angry with her, I couldn't help but laugh. "Mr Morris is a dish; I don't know what you're talking about. That balding spot on the crown of his head really gets me hot,"

Paris cackles. "Oh hush, you little minx. Get on outta here. Oh, and snap me some pictures of him, specifically his tush, so I can pretend perv while I'm bored to death in old fart Morris' class."

I throw my head back and laugh heartily. "I am not going to do that, you can stare at Mr Morris' saggy arse instead, that's what you deserve for pushing me, you tart."

"What if you sneak me into your class?" She offers, grinning cheekily.

"I'm leaving."

"I hate you."

"I know, I love you right back." I throw over my shoulder and I half speed walk, half jog down the corridor toward the lecture hall. Just as

I reach the door, I see Professor Saxton's hand on the handle about to close it. Our eyes clash. He stares at me, and I hold his piercing gaze. The stormy look in his eyes sends a shiver cascading down my spine. I can see his peeved off, so I soften my gaze and peer up at him through my lashes, feinting innocence. Those perfect lips twitch ever so slightly, and he exhales deeply, stepping aside to let me by. "Cutting it fine, Miss Valdez."

"I'm sorry, Professor." I scurry to my seat, and he walks down the steps toward the front of the class, his posture stiff.

"I don't need to keep reminding you all the importance of punctuality. I said this on my very first day and I'm saying it one last time. I will not tolerate tardiness and laziness in my classes. If you can't be bothered to get yourself to class on time or commit one hundred percent to your work, then please save yourself and me the headache and quit." He turns and scans the room. "You all know where the door is. I expect you all to be here five minutes before class is set to commence, ready to start at eleven-forty-five. Is that clear? Is there any part of that anyone didn't understand?" He expresses sternly, his eyes zeroing in on me making me squirm in my seat.

Not going to lie, I can feel myself getting moist between the legs. There is something about the way he looks when he is angry that makes him ten times sexier than usual.

"Now, if *everybody* is settled, we can start." By everybody he means me, that was a gibe at me. Jeez, he's an even bigger arsehole than usual.

Professor Saxton's classes always fly by quicker than any of my others. Not because of him... entirely, but because I genuinely enjoy this class. I love learning about the history of art and how it originated and evolved over time.

The way Professor Saxton speaks so passionately about art truly astounds me. You can't help but be enthralled. I'm always disappointed when his class ends. "That's all we have time for today. I'm not giving you any homework this week because I want you to take the Thanksgiving weekend off and enjoy it. However, I do want you back refreshed and ready to delve into a hefty corpus of assignments upon your return. Remember, finals week is around the corner, and we have a lot to cover, so when I say relax, I don't mean drugs and alcohol. I want you all bright eyed and bushy tailed come Monday morning. Off you go, have a great Thanksgiving."

The class empties as I finish up writing the last of my work. I have a quick read through of what I wrote and gather up my books. I sneak a look over at Professor Saxton also gathering up papers on his desk, his back to me.

With a lust filled sigh I turn to walk up the steps toward the door. "Miss Valdez, can I speak to you for a moment?" I pause just before I get to the door, my heart racing up in my throat. "Please close the door."

A shaky breath escapes me as I grip the handle and close the door quietly and walk down the steps toward him. Professor Saxton is leaning against his desk, his hands gripping the edge of the table, watching me intently. "Yes Professor?"

"Why were you late to class?" He demands, his tone clipped.

I bite my lip, "I'm sorry, Paris was distracting me, and time just got away from me. It won't happen again." I answer curtly, avoiding looking at him.

"Be sure that it doesn't."

"Don't worry Professor, I heard your little rant loud and clear and made a mental note." I sneer and spin on my heel to march on out of there, but he grabs hold of my arm, stopping me.

"Come back here, I'm not done with you yet." I glance down at his fingers wrapped around my forearm and slowly drag my eyes up to look at him. My annoyance flaring.

"No? Did you want to make a couple more digs at me and perhaps humiliate me some more in front of the entire class because in case you've not noticed, it's just us. It may not give you the same satisfaction." I throw back stormily, pull my arm out of his hold and cross them over my chest.

Professor Saxton wets his lips and glowers at me, "Rein, my intention wasn't to humiliate you."

"Well, you did. So, congratulations Professor, it seems we've reverted right back to how things used to be. Now if you'll excuse me, I don't want to miss my lunch."

"Rein, stop." I sigh deeply and turn to face him again. "What did you expect? That I would show you more leniency or treat you differently."

"No, but I didn't expect you to turn into an even bigger arsehole than you already were." His brows go up in surprise and I realise I just called my professor an arsehole. Shit, I regretted it the moment the words left my mouth.

"An arsehole?" He intones, his eyes darken and his tone austere. I open my mouth to apologise but he shakes his head and the ringing of his phone interrupts whatever he was about to say. He looks down at his screen and then at me. "I have to take this, but I'd like to see you in my office at the end of the day."

"Professor—"

"Go, Miss Valdez." He snaps. I nod sullenly and skitter out of the classroom with my tail tucked between my legs. Well, now I'm just as much an arsehole as he was.

The rest of my day as you can imagine went by terribly. I couldn't focus on shit, dreading every minute that got closer to the end of the day. I got glimpses of Professor Saxton in between classes in the corridor but he wouldn't even make eye contact with me.

So, here I am walking at snail's pace toward his office, my hands clammy and stomach flip flopping like I'm on a rollercoaster ride. I fill my cheeks with air and blow it out slowly as I lift my hand and knock on the door.

"Come in." I turn the knob and push the door open hesitantly. Professor Saxton's eyes flicker up from his computer screen to look at me while I linger in the doorway.

"You wanted to see me?" He leans back in his chair and laces his fingers together.

"Take a seat."

"I'm fine standing." I utter cagily standing a couple feet from his giant desk.

Professor Saxton exhales slowly and stands from his chair. I watch him as he moves toward me. "Before you say anything, I just want to apologise for my comment earlier. I was out of line, after everything you've done for me, I shouldn't have spoken to you like that." Professor Saxton nods and leans against his desk, arms crossed over his chest, staring at me indignantly.

"No, you shouldn't have. Despite what's happened between us, while on these premises I'm still your professor and I will not tolerate being spoken to in that manner, do you understand me?" He proclaims grimly. I chew my bottom lip and nod, lowering my gaze to the ground. I feel like a child being scolded by her parent for getting caught with her hand in the cookie jar.

"I understand. It won't happen again."

"Be sure that it doesn't." With one final nod I spin on my heel to leave. "I didn't say you could leave." I stop and stare at the door, my back to him. What more could he possibly have to say? I turn and face him again, this time holding his gaze. "Come here." He beckons me with a nod of his head.

Before I could muster up a single thought, my feet were already moving, like a magical force is gravitating me toward him. He straightens to his full height, and I tilt my head back to look up at him. The anger in his eyes from before simmers and desire takes its place. He's looking at me the way he was at my place last night. Like he's starving and the only thing that will gratify his hunger is me.

"You've managed to royally fuck me off today, I hope you know that." He states gruffly, licking his lips and all I could do is look at him. "If you were mine, I would have you face down on this desk, my fingers tangled in your hair, screaming my name until I fucked this annoyance out of my system."

Okay. Not what I expected to hear. I gulp and squeeze my thighs together when my clit starts to throb. "I'll make a mental note to piss you off more often then."

Professor Saxton takes hold of my chin, his eyes fixed to my lips. "Don't play games with me, Rein. As I'm sure you've already become aware, I have an abundance of control of which I can and will exhaust every ounce of..." he speaks softly, the words rolling off that velvet tongue of his in a very seductive manner making me ache in places I didn't even know existed. "...on you." Oh, okay, so we're back to this again. I can play this game all day long.

I keep my eyes firmly on his, "And when do you suppose you will put this plan into action then, Professor." I question, curling my fingers around his tie and drawing him closer. "Because I'm only getting wetter." I whisper, staring ravenously at his lips.

"Rein," he growls, pressing his forehead to mine.

"Professor," I moan breathily, ghosting my lips over his. "It's clear we can't fight whatever this is between us and I don't want to anymore." Professor Saxton grips my hips tight and draws me closer until I'm pressed up against him. Fuck it, I can't take it anymore, I'm burning for this man, let the chips fall where they may. Before I lose my nerve, I push up on my tiptoes and press my lips to his.

CHAPTER Seventeen

Talon

I'M FUCKED, WELL AND TRULY. I'VE GONE AND FUCKED IT ALL.

The moment I felt Rein's lips on mine I knew I was done for. I should have stopped her, pulled away, but I couldn't, nor did any part of me want to. There is no going back now, definitely not after I've gotten a taste of her.

I freeze the second her lips descend upon mine and the control I've been desperately clinging too just drains away. In that moment it didn't register that I was on school grounds, in my office, with the door unlocked. All I could think about was the feel of her lips on mine and how damn good it felt.

God help me.

My lips part and I run my tongue along her bottom lip until she opens for me with a moan—a moan that causes every hair on my body to rise. As our kiss deepens everything gets hazy fast, I press her up against the wall beside the door and lock it as my mouth devours hers.

Oh, how I wish she was a terrible kisser, but she's anything but. Just as I imagined she would be, her kisses are mind blowing and her taste even better. The kiss sent shockwaves of electricity from my toes all the way up my spine.

My lungs burn in protest when they slowly run out of oxygen, but I didn't care, I could survive on sips of air, what I couldn't stand, was the thought of not hearing her little moans, or the way her tongue brushes mine teasingly making my head spin with fevered desire.

"I want to fuck you so bad." I groan zealously, biting and tugging her bottom lip. Rein mewls in response, rocking herself against my erection when I lift her into my arms and she wraps her legs around me tight.

"And I'm so ready for that, Professor."

I groan audibly and press my molars together. "Please stop calling me that. It's not exactly ethical what with you dry humping my dick and all. The last thing I want or need right now is to be reminded of what an immoral bastard I am."

Rein pulls back and looks at me, her face flushed, lips swollen and panting. "Look, let's be straight with each other. I stopped being your student and you my professor after this weekend and you know it. We both put up a good fight and resisted for as long as we could, but somethings are just inevitable." I close my eyes and shake my head. "Talon." My eyes snap up to hers when I hear her say my name and just as quickly as it came, the guilt I felt disappears and she fires me up all over again.

Oh, to hell with it. If I'm going to burn for this, I may as well make it worthwhile. I draw her mouth to mine and kiss her hard and deep. I grab handfuls of her arse and squeeze appreciatively, grinding her searing pussy over my rock-hard erection which is aching and threatening to bust through my trousers at any given moment. "Uhh, Talon..."

Fuck, I love that sound. I tangle my fingers in her hair and tilt her head back, exposing her neck so I could drag my lips down to the base of her throat and suck. Rein bucks her hips and whimpers. "Shh, quiet Snowflake."

"Talon, please, I want you."

I pull back and press my forehead to hers. "I know you do; I can feel the heat between your legs and I want nothing more than to choke your ravenous little pussy with my dick until you're a weeping mess for me." I push my thumb in her mouth and she sucks it. "But not here, not yet." I whisper, dragging my thumb over her bottom lip.

"What?" Rein whimpers in discontent. "Let's just go back to yours."

I smile and bite my lip, "When was the last time you got off?"

Rein licks her lips and sighs, "Last night."

"And what's your preferred method of masturbation?" I question and she stares at me silently. "Rein, answer me."

Rein sighs, her cheeks burning. "Vibrator."

I nod in understanding, "Three days, no touching yourself and no getting off." Rein gapes at me.

"You've got to be joking." She sputters wide eyed.

I stare at her sombrely and she groans. "Do I look like I'm joking?"

Rein scans my face, and she shakes her head disappointed. "Would you mind explaining why?"

"Certainly, the reason you can't reach orgasm with a partner is because you've become too dependent on getting off with your vibrator. It's a psychological barrier per se, we're going to break that barrier. So, if you want to orgasm you need to refrain for a couple of days." I explain, leaning in to kiss her pouting lips. "I want you to be absolutely wild with desire for me."

209

Rein softens her gaze, and she smiles teasingly. "I already am wild with desire for you."

I gaze deep into her eyes, "Not as much as I need you to be. I want you to be so hot and bothered that all day every day all you can think about is my tongue lapping at your clit until you fall apart. Snowflake, I'm going to make you so unbelievably horny you're going to be begging for me to fuck you." Rein moans and rocks herself against me again. "So, are you going to be a good girl and play by the rules?"

Rein exhales and opens her eyes, "Fine, but the same rules apply to you."

I grin and wet my lips, "I don't have a problem reaching orgasm, Snowflake."

"I don't care, if I'm going to suffer, so will you." I laugh and nod in agreement.

"That's fair, it will be worth the wait."

"It damn well better be." She sulks.

I draw her mouth to mine and kiss her deeply before pulling away and setting her back down on her feet. "Fix yourself up before you leave." I murmur cleaning up the smeared pink lipstick around her mouth with my thumb.

Rein smiles and walks over to the full-length mirror on the wall and straightens herself up while I readjust myself in my trousers. It's going to be a major bitch trying to get rid of this without wanking. Thank heavens it's the end of the day. I sit back in my chair and observe Rein fixing her hair. Those gorgeous eyes of hers find mine and she smirks.

"Do I look presentable enough?"

My eyes roam over the length of her and I nod wordlessly. Rein wanders over to my desk, her fingers trailing along the edge as she saunters toward me. "I suppose I better go then."

"I suppose you better." I take hold of her hand and brush a kiss in the centre of her palm. "I'll see you, Snowflake."

"Sooner rather than later, I hope?"

I smile up at her, her hand still pressed against my lips. Rein steps closer, her fingers brushing through my hair. "We need to be careful."

"We will be." She avows tranquilly. We share a look, neither of us able to look away. Rein smiles and turns to walk away but I tighten my hold on her hand before it can slip out of mine and she turns to look back at me questioningly.

"Forgetting something?" I query. She frowns a little and lets out an adorable squeak when I pull her closer and hungrily snatch her lips with mine, kissing her deeply.

"Go." I whisper against her lips, smiling. Rein sighs and rubs my jaw affectionately, her eyes never leaving mine.

"You make it hard to."

"I'll call you later."

Rein nods and walks off toward the door, stopping to pick up her book and bag before she leaves my office. I stare at the door she just walked out of and rake my fingers through my hair with an audible groan.

I'm a bad man. But then again, the heart wants what it wants, and it just won't listen to reason.

You mean your knob wants what it wants.

Okay fine, maybe I am thinking with my knob, but Jesus, I tried to resist her—I sodding tried. I've been clutching onto my control for dear life with this girl, but it seems I've lost the battle within myself and I'm hurtling head first into the fiery pit.

Am I proud of myself? Absolutely not. I can practically see my past self shaking his head at me in disgust. When I envisioned my future as a professor, the thought of consorting with a student didn't even cross my mind, not for a second. However, I must admit that a small part of me is just a little satisfied to surrender to my desires after fighting it for so long. As wrong as it is, it feels good. It's been a long time since I felt this... *alive*.

JT would have a field day if he got wind of this—not that he will ever find out— but he's been on my case about getting back in the saddle for over two years.

My phone vibrates on my desk disrupting my thoughts. I stare at the name on the screen and swallow thickly before answering it with a sigh. "Kev, talk to me."

———

ON MY DRIVE home I stop at the graveyard as I do every most Mondays. A bouquet of white roses gripped tightly in my left hand as I hesitantly walk toward my fiancée's grave.

"Hi sweetheart." I sigh, picking off the dried leaves and wilted roses I left last week from her grave. I perch down and slide the fresh roses into the memorial vase. "Looks like I beat your mum to it again this week, huh?" I smile sadly and look at her beautiful face engraved on the gravestone. "She'll be pissed at me again for wasting money on a bouquet of flowers instead of planting them in your garden, but in my defence, I can't stand to see your grave so bare, especially when I know how much you love flowers—even if the real ones die and the fake ones get stolen." I bite my lip and shake my head, my eyes burning as tears gather in my eyes blurring my vision. "I miss you sweetheart, so fucking much." I whisper woefully, wiping away the tear that rolls down my cheek.

"I shouldn't even be saying that to you after what I did today and I know you're probably just as disappointed in me as I am with myself right now, but I fucked up, Tay, I fucked up big time." I admit pinching the bridge of my nose. "I've been holding onto you for three years, terrified of moving on and somehow betraying you and it's been fine, I've been coping. But then she came along—she made me realise how lonely and withdrawn I've been from everyone and everything around me." I utter, picking at a blade of grass. "There was something about her, I felt this unfathomable connection the moment my eyes met hers and when our hands accidentally touched there was this spark, it was almost like an electric shock that brought me back to myself. Rein somehow awakened a part of me I thought I lost the night I lost you."

Lifting my gaze, I look at her photo, my heart clenching tight in my chest. "I'm scared Tay, this girl is wrong for me in so many ways and I'm risking everything for something that doesn't even have a future and I tried so hard to fight it, but when I'm with her, I feel like the old me again." I defend pitiably. "I feel like the version of myself when I was with you. I can almost hear your disapproval of my decisions and I want you to know that I'm not proud of myself, but I hope you'll find a way to understand." A quivering breath escapes me slowly and I close my eyes. "I love you sweetheart; I will always love you." I kiss my fingers and press it to her angelic face. "Both of you." I brush my fingers over the words 'and Baby Saxton'.

As much as I know Taylor would never agree with my decision of risking my career, especially when she knew how hard I worked to get to where I am, I knew she would want me to be happy—and right now my only way to some form of happiness is Rein. I need to heal, and I believe she'll be the one to help me do just that.

"Hello?"

"What are you doing right now?"

"Do you want the honest version or the sexy version?"

I grin, "Both."

"All right." Rein sighs softly, "Honest, sitting in my oversized sweatshirt."

"And sexy?"

"I'm not wearing underwear."

"Damn, that's a good combination." I groan throatily and smile when I hear her melodious laughter.

"Try telling that to my vajayjay." Rein complains with a breathy sigh.

I lay back on my bed and stare up at the ceiling, my brows drawn together in confusion. The hell is a vajayjay? "Your what?"

"You know... my lady bits, my flower garden. My vagine?"

I laugh, folding my arm behind my head, "Oh dear God, it just gets worse and worse."

Rein giggles, "Goodness sake, my pussy. You happy now?"

"Much. There is absolutely nothing sexy about any of those words used to describe the elegance of a woman's pussy." I explain, closing my eyes and picturing her legs wrapped around my head.

"You're right, nothing screams elegance like the word pussy." She drawls sarcastically. "Or cunt for that matter."

"Sounds better than vajayjay. Be honest, if I was there with you right now and whispered, 'I want to devour your vajayjay' in your ear, would that seriously turn you on?"

Rein chuckles, "No, I would probably either die of second-hand embarrassment or laughing—or possibly both."

"And if I whispered that I was aching to gorge on your pussy and drink up every last drop of delectable girl cum that trickles from that tight little cunt." I voice gruffly and feel myself grow hard when her breathing hastens.

"Okay, point taken." Rein replies, her voice a breathy whisper. "And I would like to point out that you wouldn't have to utter a single word to turn me on." Rein declares sensually.

I bite down on my lower lip and smile, "No?"

"Not one." She murmurs, "The thought of you alone is enough."

"You're desperately making me want to come over there and do unspeakable things to you." I drawl hoarsely, brushing my index finger up and over the length of my raging erection pitching a tent in my boxers.

"Maybe you should come and fix this relentless trickle you've managed to cause between my legs, because I'm making a real mess over here." Rein groans lasciviously.

"Don't tempt me, Snowflake. I'm so hard I might actually take you up on your offer, and what I have in mind for you is definitely going to require more than one night."

"What if I told you I was outside your door right now?"

My eyes fly open, and I lean up on my elbow, "Are you?"

"Maybe."

I sit up in such a rush I make myself dizzy. I throw my legs over the side of the bed and get up, making a beeline for the front door. "Rein, don't screw with me." I yank the door open so hard I was worried it would fall off its hinges. I look around the empty hallway and my stomach sinks in displeasure. "Fuck."

"Disappointed, Professor?" I close the door and press my forehead against it, counting slowly to ten to calm myself before I lose what will I have left and run over to her apartment in my boxers and fuck the wits out of her. She's making me crazy.

"That wasn't funny, Rein."

"I'm not laughing, Professor." I open my eyes when I hear a soft knock on the door and my heart kickstarts again. My head lifts off the door, I straighten, grip the door handle and pull it open. Fuck, there she stood, looking like the star of my every wet dream. Clad in an over-sized hoodie *only* and a pair of trainers. Her eyes wide and burning with desire, cheeks flushed, she's biting down on her bottom lip while she holds the phone to her ear. "Hungry?"

I slowly lower the phone, my eyes fixed on hers. "Like you wouldn't believe." I curl my fingers at the nape of her neck and draw her to me, sealing our mouths together in a passionate kiss fuelled by frenzied need. I kick the door shut and press her into it all in one move. My tongue teasingly glides over hers, making her moan into my mouth lasciviously. I'm not going to fuck her, not yet... she's not ready just yet.

"Talon," She whimpers, clinging to my shoulders when I lick down her throat and bite the base of her neck, sucking her flesh into my mouth.

"You're so disobedient," I growl, cupping handfuls of her arse and squeezing appreciatively. Rein responds by grinding herself against my thigh wantonly and raking her fingernails down my back making me hiss, the sting only spurring my already insatiable need for her.

"I'm also soaking wet and aching for you." Rein moans urgently into mouth. I bite and tug on her bottom lip while I drag my fingers up her bare thigh touching her everywhere but the places she so desperately needs. If I get a feel of how wet she is I know I won't be able to resist her. My mouth is already watering at the thought of her being so wet for me. I'll fall to my knees, wrap those legs around my head and lap at her like the starved man I am.

"I bet you are Snowflake, but we're not fucking yet. You're not where I need you to be." I whisper against her lips, gliding my fingers around her inner thigh just missing her pussy and she whimpers in frustration.

"Talon, come on, I've not been this randy in my life, *ever*. I honestly think I've hit my limit."

I smile and suck at her pulse point hard, "You're not even close, Snowflake. Two more days and I'm going to take care of your every need. I'm going to fuck you so good you'll need days to recover."

Rein pulls her head back and gives me a deadpan look, "I'm not an easy girl to please, Professor. I sure hope you can deliver, because I've heard all these promises before and was still left disappointed." She states matter-of-factly and raises a brow while her arms snake around my neck.

"There's an old saying, never send a boy to do a man's job." I reply with a smirk. Rein's lips curl into a pretty smile and she rolls her eyes.

"I don't like to be proven wrong; however, this is one instance I will be more than satisfied to be disproven."

I brush my nose over hers, smiling. "And I'll happily abide." I press my lips to hers chastely and pull away, putting some space between us. Man, the fact she's completely naked under that over-sized hoodie is making me go troppo. Rein watches me closely, her teeth sunken into her plump lower lip. "Come sit with me."

Rein nods, pushes off the door where she was leant against it and saunters past me toward the living room. My eyes follow her as she moves around the living room and stops in front of the floor to ceiling window overlooking the city.

I stroll over to stand behind her, "It's snowing." She announces, staring out of the window. I nod and draw her back against me, peppering affectionate kisses along her shoulder toward her neck. "What are you plans for Thanksgiving?" I ask, nipping at her earlobe gently.

Rein sighs, her eyes closing, she rests her head back against my shoulder, tilting her head to the side to give me more room to kiss and nip at her neck. "I don't have any. I was supposed to work, but Ray decided he wants to close for the Thanksgiving weekend this year and have the floor replaced in the bar." She explains with a sigh. "So, I suppose I'll be home, sprawled out in my sweats, like a true couch potato, eating my feelings as a means to comfort myself for missing my family during the holidays."

I pull my head back and look at her with a frown, I turn her so she's facing me. "Rein, you can't spend Thanksgiving alone."

Rein shrugs and peers up at me, "Well, I don't really have much choice in the matter, I was looking forward to working. Paris begged me to go with her on her family trip to Aspen, but I would literally have a better time watching grass grow. I made the stupid mistake of going last year, it was one of the worst decisions I have ever made. I've never met a more dysfunctional family in my life and my family aren't exactly sound." She explains with a shake of her head. "What are your plans?"

I smile warmly and tuck a strand of her hair behind her ear. "I'm heading home to Ohio on Thursday. My folks live in Cincinnati."

Rein smiles, but it doesn't quite reach her eyes. "I thought your parents lived in Australia."

I shake my head and pull her toward the sofa so we could sit. Rein toes her shoes off and curls up on the sofa, facing me. "Nah, we moved to the states when I was a kid. My pops lost his job out there and got offered a job here in the states so we up and moved. I've not been back to Australia for some years." I explain, brushing my fingers through her hair.

"Don't you miss it?"

I nod, "Of course. I was only fifteen when we moved. One day I was surfing on the beach and the next I'm packing up my life and moving halfway across the world. My whole life changed overnight. Our home, family. I left behind some great friends, even my girlfriend Haley."

Rein smiles warmly, watching me rivetedly while I tell her about my life in Australia. "Would you ever move back?"

I nod without hesitation, "In a heartbeat. Life is just different out there. Don't get me wrong, I love the states. I've got a good life here too, made some incredible lifelong friends, but my heart will always be in Australia." I declare, playing with her silky soft hair, my eyes lingering on hers.

Rein nods grinning prettily, "Be honest, how many times have you Facebook stalked your childhood girlfriend?"

I laugh out loud, "I don't need to stalk her on social media, we're still in touch." Rein's eyes go round with surprise.

"Thirteen years later and give or take ten thousand miles apart and you've still managed to stay in touch with your childhood sweetheart. That's real impressive, she must have been really special."

I nod wetting my lips, "She is really special, we grew up together, so we knew each other pretty well before we decided to date." I explain pulling my hand back from her hair and caress her jaw.

"So she was your first love."

I shake my head pensively as I think back to my younger years. "No, she wasn't my first love. My first crush sure, but not first love." No, Tay was my first real love. "She's married now with two beautiful kids." Rein's eyes close when I brush my thumb along her lower lip. I smile watching her. "Come to Cincinnati with me."

Her eyes flicker open, and she gapes at me bemused. "What?"

"For Thanksgiving." Probably not the wisest idea, but if this is the only way I can get a couple of days away with her where we don't have to sneak around then I'm all for it. Usually, I wouldn't dream of taking a girl I'm casually seeing to meet my folks, but I don't like the idea of her being all alone for Thanksgiving, plus seeing me with a girl would get my mum off my back. Perhaps I'll skip the part that Rein happens to be my student and introduce her as a friend.

"You're not serious?" Rein questions warily, looking at me like a deer caught in headlights.

"Do I look like I'm joking?"

Rein blinks and straightens. "You want me to spend Thanksgiving with you and your parents?"

I nod, resisting the urge to laugh at the stunned look on her face. "It's not a big deal, my folks are easy going people. My mother will love you."

"Thank you for the offer, Talon, but I honestly don't think that's a good idea. Wouldn't your parents wonder why you're bringing your student home to meet them?"

I shrug and pull her close to me, "We won't tell them you're my student. I'll introduce you as a friend."

"A friend?" Rein intoned dubiously. "Friends don't look at one another the way we do. They will have us sussed in five seconds flat."

I chuckle and tug her into my lap, she straddles me and rests her hands on my chest. "Well, you'll need to stop looking at me like you're famished and ready to devour me at any given moment."

"Kind of hard to do that when you refuse to put out and insist on making me even randier than I already am." She opposes boldly making me laugh out loud.

"You'll thank me when your legs are shaking from the best orgasm of your life." I affirm gazing into her eyes. "Can I ask you something?" Rein nods.

"Sure."

"Why the contacts? Do you need them to see?" I question, brushing her hair away so I could see her pretty face.

"No, I don't need them to see, I have twenty/twenty vision, but I've always hated my eyes." She admits morosely veering her gaze from mine. "I was born with a rare eye condition called heterochromia and growing up kids at my school would call me a freak for having different coloured eyes. Clearly, they didn't understand that it was a condition. The older I got, the more uncomfortable it made me when people stared at my one eye, so I started wearing contacts."

"Believe it or not your eyes were first thing that attracted me to you. My first day on campus you came crashing into me and spilt your coffee all over me before class, when you looked up at me with eyes full of fury, I was truly captivated." I declare evenly and smirk when her cheeks start to redden. "It's a real crime to veil something so exquisite."

"Unfortunately, we don't all see things the same way, isn't that what you taught us. Beauty is in the eye of the beholder and all that. What's exquisite to you might be hideous to someone else." Rein replies with shrug, her eyes still cast down staring at her hands, as though she's suddenly too self-conscious to even look to me.

"Snowflake," I tuck my finger under her chin and tilt her head up a little so she could look at me. "What matters is how *you* see yourself, sod what anyone else thinks. Never allow yourself to be defined by someone else's opinion of you." Rein holds my gaze, her eyes hot on mine, she bites her lip. "What?"

She smiles sultrily and leans in closer, "Have I ever mentioned how incredibly sexy your accent is?" She murmurs tilting my head back and kissing my neck.

I grin languidly, closing my eyes I rest my head back against the sofa while she licks and sucks the flesh just behind my ear. "I don't believe you have, Miss Valdez."

"Keep talking to me, Professor..." She breathes, dipping her tongue in my ear.

I groan, "Crikey."

CHAPTER *Eighteen*

Rein

Two days later.

Adonis:

"You're coming."

Me:

"I am not."

Adonis:

"Snowflake, you're coming. I'll be there at seven to pick you up. I already told my folks, they're expecting you."

Me:

"Just tell them I'm sick and can't make it."

Adonis:

"Are you asking me to break my mother's heart? You're a savage."

For a moment I forget I'm in class and I giggle, the entire class including Professor Tippett turn to look at me. I clear my throat and sink further into my seat.

Me:

"Don't be so dramatic, she doesn't even know me, I highly doubt she will care."

I send the text and go to put my phone down and see another message pop up on my screen. Talon sent me a screen shot of the conversation he was having with his mother over WhatsApp. She's asking him question after question about what I like to eat, if I have any allergies, if I'll be comfortable around their dog Rocky and if not, they can let someone named Tim Tam take care of him till I leave.

Adonis:

"Does that sound like someone who doesn't care? She's even looking up recipes for trifle just for you."

Guilt floods me and I heave a sigh, typing out a message.

Me:

"I do love a good trifle.
Fine! I'll come, but don't be fooled, I'm only going for the trifle... and Rocky, because I love dogs so don't go thinking I'm going for you because you'll be sorely disappointed, Professor Hottie."

Adonis:

"Will you stop calling me that."

All our classes on Wednesday finished early due to it being Thanksgiving, the teachers were in good spirits, students were bouncing along the corridors excited for the long weekend. Me? I was nervous, more nervous than I can ever recall being. Four days with Talon and his family and let's not forget the four-and-a-half-hour drive there and back. What on earth have I gone and gotten myself into? Why did I agree to go and meet my professor's—who I am currently having a secret affair with—parents pretending to be his 'friend'.

There isn't a snowball's chance in hell that they will believe Talon and I are just friends. If the insatiable way we look at one another doesn't give us away then the intense chemistry between us will for damn sure.

My hands and knees are shaking, my stomach full of anxious butterflies fluttering around in a frenzy. Fucking hell, I'm a big bag of nerves. The black Mustang pulls up alongside the sidewalk and my heart rate accelerates when Talon steps out of the car looking delectable as always, dressed in all black, a pair of black jeans and a tight fitted Versace t-shirt paired stylishly with a Boda Skins leather jacket and tan boots.

Why does he have to be so fucking gorgeous all the freaking time. "Ready Snowflake?" He drawls, smirking at me knowingly when he catches me gawping at him. I nod, watching him closely while he takes my bag and walks around to the boot of the car.

"Are you absolutely sure this is a good idea? It's not too late, I can go back upstairs, and you can be on your merry little way." I declare warily and he chuckles pushing the boot shut and strolling over to me.

"Relax Rein, it's going to be a pleasant, stress-free weekend. I would have thought you would be more excited to be away from the city where we don't have to look over our shoulder and worry who will see us together." He states, his blue eyes narrowing a little while he observes me.

"It would be a different story if it were just the two of us going off someplace, but you're taking me home to meet your parents. Given our situation you have to admit it's a little... odd." I admit apprehensively. Talon takes a step closer to me, rubbing the back of his neck, his heated gaze on mine making me even more anxious.

"You're allowing your mind to get ahead of yourself. This isn't some romantic thing; you're not my girlfriend and I'm not asking you to be.

It's just two friends going to another friend's house to have Thanksgiving dinner. That is all."

I stare up at him wordlessly and he smiles broadly flashing his perfect pearly white gnashers. "Okay, fine."

"I have something for you, I was going to wait till we got to Cincinnati to give it to you but maybe it will help you relax a little. Close your eyes." He instructs, a wicked glint in his cobalt gaze. I hesitate, but he nods encouragingly so I close my eyes. I jump a little when I feel him behind me all of a sudden. Something cold goes around my neck and I open my eyes, my hand reaching up to touch whatever it was. I gasp when I look down and see it's the necklace my mother got me— the necklace I thought I lost in the fire. I spin and look up at him, tears filling my eyes almost instantly.

"My necklace," I whisper, taken aback, "How did you..."

Talon shrugs casually, "I may have told the fire fighter that night of the fire to have a look around your apartment to see if they can find your necklace. They called some days ago saying they found it, so I went and picked it up. It was a little damaged, so I took it to a jeweller, and they cleaned it up and restored it. I picked it up this morning." I wasn't sure what emotion to focus on. I was beyond relieved, grateful and so overwhelmed. All I wanted to do was jump into his arms and kiss him until we're both breathless, but I couldn't, considering we were standing in the middle of the street.

"I can't believe you did all that for me."

"It's not a big deal. I saw how devastated you were that night about losing the only thing you had left of your mum. It may seem insignificant to me and everyone else but it's clear it means everything to you, so I just wanted to make sure you got it back. You've lost enough as it is." Talon explains leaning against the driver side door.

My eyes scan the area, contemplating whether I should kiss him or not. I desperately wanted to but feared someone might see us. "It's a very big deal to me. I honestly don't know what to say or how to thank you, Talon. You've just given me the world and a part of me wishes that you waited till we were away from the city to give this to me because right now all I want to do is kiss you." I admit all in one breath. Talon smiles, his heated gaze finds mine and he nods.

"How about you jump in then and we get out of this town so you can satisfy that particular need as soon as fucking possible?"

I grin brightly, and without wasting another second, we get into the car and start our four-and half-hour journey to Cincinnati.

It took forty minutes to get out of the city and onto the I90. I sink into the plush leather seats, observing Talon while he drives, one hand on the steering wheel and the other resting on his thigh. This might just be a weird new quirk of mine, but the way he's driving, so calm, cool and confident is really turning me on.

The song playing isn't really helping either. Dirty Mind by Boy Epic. Which happens to be very fitting considering the lewd thoughts going through my mind right now. I'm picturing all sort of scenarios. Talon senses me watching him and he gives me a side long stare, his blue eyes twinkling with mischief. "What's on your mind, Snowflake?"

I bite my lip, keeping my eyes on him. "You are."

Talon reaches over, laces his fingers with mine and brushes a kiss over my knuckles. "Tell me what you're thinking."

"I'm wondering what that mouth can do."

Talon flashes me a panty melting smile and I swear to all that is good and pure I felt my vagina clench when my clit pulses with need and my lace thong dampens. I press my thighs together. Thank heavens I'm in a skirt.

Talon licks his lips, his eyes on the road, he places my hand on his thigh and plays with my fingers. "You'll find out soon enough."

I think it's high time I give him a little taste of his own medicine. It's my turn to torture him a little bit. I pull my hand away from his and stroke his thigh, my fingers slowly and teasingly inching up his inner thigh toward his crotch. I hear him suck in a deep breath, his head falling back against the headrest when my finger dances over his testicles through the thick fabric of his denim jeans.

I notice the bulge in his jeans instantly and my stomach burns with nerves. He makes no move to stop me when I trail my finger over the length of his erection. I don't need to see it to know he's well-endowed. I've felt it when I was practically dry humping him on the sofa.

I lean over the middle panel in his car and whisper in his ear, "I've been dreaming of the taste of you, Professor."

Talon bites his lip, his eyes growing heavy with desire. He grips the steering wheel, his jaw clenching. "Not as much as I have, believe me, Snowflake." He rasps, biting down on his bottom lip and rocking his hips up into my touch. "The indecent thoughts I have of you keep me up most nights."

"Like what?" I nip at his ear gently and he groans, cursing under his breath.

"Sit back." He orders gruffly. I draw back a little and he turns to look at me, his cobalt gaze dark with lust. "Take off your underwear and give them to me."

I swallow thickly and sink back into the seat before I raise my hips off the seat, slide my underwear off and drop them in his hand. I felt my jaw drop when he brings them to his nose and inhales deeply.

Fucking hell

My insides were burning—no, they were scorching. "Christ, the scent of you alone is enough to drive me crazy." He almost growls. "Touch yourself."

I stare at him, stunned, my cheeks aflame. "Now? In the middle of the highway?"

"Yes, now," he nods, his eyes darting between me and the road. "Touch yourself for me, Snowflake."

I exhale, my fingers tremble as they glide up my thighs. I thought he didn't want me touching myself.

I've never let anyone watch me pleasure myself before, this is completely new to me, but this is the affect this man has on me. I'm willing to push myself beyond my comfort zone.

My heart starts to race at an abnormal pace. I close my eyes and lazily drag a single digit through my slick folds and gasp. I'm surprised to find how wet I actually am. My head falls back against the head rest when my finger makes contact with my swollen and sensitive nub. "Mm."

"That's a good girl. Open your eyes and look at me, Rein. I want those beautiful eyes on me." I lift my gaze up to look at him through my lashes while I caress myself with slow teasing circles. My fingers start to get hastier as the pressure builds and my body starts to tremble as I near my release. "Ahh, yes, yes. Talon..." I whimper.

Talon looks at me briefly and swallows hard, his Adam's apple jumping up in his throat. "Rein, don't you dare come. That pleasure is going to be all mine when I pull this car over, spread you out on top of it and feast on that succulent pussy of yours till you're enraptured with pleasure." Talon demands thickly, reaching over and caressing my thigh. "So, you be a good girl and you keep that pussy nice and wet for me Snowflake, because you're making me fucking thirsty and there's only one way I'm quenching this thirst."

Oh, sweet God, I am freaking delirious with voracity for this man. "Jesus, Talon, I can't, I don't think I can hold back." I pant, biting down on my bottom lip to keep from going over. "I'm so close." I moan breathily and whimper when my hand is suddenly pulled away from between my legs, leaving me pulsing with need and dissatisfied when I feel my *almost* climax start to ebb away.

Talon wraps his mouth around my fingers and sucks them clean with a guttural moan sending me into a whole new state of delirium. "You need to pull over, right now. I don't care where, just pull the car over and fuck me, in it, on top of it, fuck me through the damn thing, I don't care."

Talon smiles, "Yeah?"

I gaze up at him and take his hand, pressing it between my legs. I moan when he stokes me and sucks in a sharp breath. "I hope that's wet enough for you, because I'm sure I've soaked through your seat."

Talon caresses my pussy and glances over at me lecherously. "Good, I hope you have. That way every time I get in my car it will be a pleasant reminder of what I'm about to do to you." The car rolls to a stop and I look around, in my haze I hadn't noticed we came off the highway and we're currently in the middle of nowhere. No cars, not a soul in sight, just the two of us.

"Where are we?"

Talon takes his seatbelt off and I do the same. "Away from prying eyes and a place you can scream as loud as you want, because believe me Snowflake, you're going to need too."

I give him a sceptical look, "Is this the part where I find out you're actually a serial killer?"

Talon grins, "Yes, they call me the killer of pussy. Come here." He curls his fingers at my neck and draws my mouth hungrily to his. I melt the moment our lips meet, and we kiss like two feral animals in heat.

After a minute or two Talon groans and pulls back panting. "Out of the car." He orders hoarsely, dragging his thumb along my bottom lip. I nod and push the car door open and scramble out of the car. The sun was setting around us leaving the sky a picturesque fusion of oranges, purples, and a deep blue.

Talon strolls over to me, taking my face in his large hands he brushes a kiss over my lips. I part mine when he licks along my bottom lip silently requesting access which I eagerly grant him. Our tongues glide over one another sensually. Talon skilfully sucks mine and I moan into his mouth. In the hazy state of my mind I hadn't realised I was being backed up against the car until I felt the cold metal of the hood pressed up against the back of my legs and heat of his body covering my front. Talon effortlessly lifts me and lays me down on the hood of his car. I open my eyes and gaze up at him when he draws back a little, his large hands skimming up my legs until they disappear under my or rather Paris' black leather mini skirt.

I keep my eyes on Talon's, my heart beating like it's going crazy in my chest when he pushes my knees apart, spreading me out, fully exposing my bare pussy. I watch as he lowers his gaze, waiting with bated breath to see his reaction when he sees it for the first time. His gaze lingers for the longest moment, and he licks his lips avidly. When he finally lifts his gaze to look up at me, he smiles knowingly. "I think we may have a little problem, Miss Valdez." Oh God, what is it. Do I have an unattractive looking vagina or something?

I lift my head, my brows fusing. "Problem? What problem?"

Talon bites his bottom lip before he presses a kiss to my inner thigh. The fervour that is glowing in the depths of his blue eyes tells me the opposite of his words. He's not put off at all, if anything he looks even more aroused. "There is no way I'm going to satisfy my appetite with just one taste of a flawless pussy like this." He groans, dragging his middle finger through my folds. "It's so much better than what I could have ever pictured." A flood of relief rushes through me and I instantly feel my body relax.

I smile and brush my fingers through his hair, "Lucky for you Professor, I happen to be quite insatiable and have no problem with satiating your appetite—ohh." I gasp when his finger slides into me and my head falls back. "Fuck."

"You're so tight." He hisses sliding his finger out and smearing my liquid arousal over my folds, "Do you hear how wet you are for me, Snowflake? That squelching sound is like music to my ears." He whispers removing his finger and replacing it with his tongue. That long, deliberate lick from my entrance through my folds right up to my clit made me quake visibly.

Talon moans, the deep vibrations of his vocal cords hums right through me heightening my pleasure. His lips close around my clit, and he sucks teasingly then flicks his tongue again and again making the muscles in my stomach contract with each flick of his dexterous tongue. My fingers curl in his hair and I rock my hips up against his mouth. My moans of pleasure get louder as the pressure builds and builds and my body heats up. It's at this point I get stuck and can never go over. Talon opens his eyes and looks up at me when he feels my body tense. Our eyes lock and I hold his feral gaze. My entire body tingles delightfully from my head all the way to my toes.

"Ahh, yes, yes, fuck, Talon." I whimper, panting, when he slides two fingers deep into me and sucks my clit hard. My hips lift off the car, with every relentless thrust of his fingers. The pressure becomes too much, and I try to scoot away, but he keeps me in place.

"You're right there, Snowflake, give it to me, c'mon. Let it go and come all over my mouth. I can do this all-day baby, all fucking night until you come." Talon urges, his thrusts getting faster. I feel around for something to grab onto as I thrash in his arms. Once I pushed through the immense pressure, it felt as though something else entirely overtook my body.

"Ohhh, yes, yes, I'm gonna... come... Talon!" He was right. I did need to scream, and I did. I couldn't even put into words how good whatever he was doing to me felt. The slow intense build up in my groin, followed by red hot release fires rapidly through me as I climax *hard*. My entire body shook uncontrollably with pleasure, so much so that I forgot I had to breathe.

"Ohhh, God, Uhhh fuck." I whimper, collapsing back onto the car, gasping desperately to catch my breath. It wasn't till my body stopped shaking that I realised when I climaxed, I squirted. Something I never knew I was capable of. My inner thighs, the hood of his car and his t-shirt soaked. "Holy shit." I pant, biting down on my lip while Talon kisses my thigh. "Did I just..."

"Squirt all over me? Hell yes." Talon grins and leans over to kiss me. "You damn near drowned me in it and I fucking loved it, you tasty little thing." He adds with a sexy grin, grabbing my ankle he yanks me down. My bum slides down the hood of the car and he pulls me upright, his fingers curling at my throat while his mouth descends upon mine hot and hard.

"I had no idea my body was capable of doing that or feeling such intense pleasure." I moan breathlessly, wrapping my legs around his waist. "If that's what sex is supposed to feel like, I don't know what the hell I've been having, because it was never like that with anyone."

Talon presses his forehead to mine, his thumb caressing my jaw. "It's all about knowing how the female body works and pressing the right buttons. You'd be surprised what your body is capable of, Snowflake and I plan to show you just what you've been missing."

"I look forward to it, Professor," I purr while unbuckling his belt and popping his button open. "But for now, I'd like to satisfy *my* cravings." Talon watches me with hooded eyes and bites his lip.

I drop a chaste kiss on his lips, my fingers unfastening his jeans. I turn him so he's leant back against the hood of his car. As I kneel in front of him, he presses his palms down against the car, observing me as I tug down his boxers freeing his hefty dick from its confines.

Whoa. I knew he was well endowed when I felt it pressed up against me, but that sure is impressive and probably the most attractive penis I have ever seen. Hunter's was a little smaller and not so girthy and his one curved slightly at the end always reminded me of a banana. Licking my lips, I stare at it in awe like a kid in a sweet shop while Talon waits patiently, studying me fixedly.

I couldn't wait anymore; I was dying for a taste and that drop of sheen pre-cum is just begging to be licked off. I wrap my fingers around him and stroke base to crown. Talon hisses, his eyes closing, head lolling back when my tongue licks up the pre-cum and I moan insatiably, the salty taste excites my taste buds.

"Oh fuck," Talon groans, his left-hand curling in my hair when I suck him deep into my mouth. "Christ, that mouth..." He growls, thrusting himself into my mouth. I tighten my grip on his dick and twist, pumping him and suck at the same time, releasing more of that delicious pre-cum. "Yes, Snowflake. Fuck, just like that, right to the back of your throat. Shit, you're going to make me cum so hard."

I moan, sucking him deeper and harder, swirling my tongue around the crown and flick it against the ridge, making his hips jerk as he nears his release. The sexy sounds and heavy breathing that was emanating from him was driving me wild. The throbbing of his cock and his hasty breathing tells me he's close. The fingers tangled in my hair tightens and he pushes himself deeper and shatters with a carnal growl, spilling his hot seed down my throat, each spurt causing his hips to tremble with pure gratification. Goddamn, he's a freaking sight when he climaxes, no whimpering or overdramatizing his pleasure. Only deep throaty growls and heavy breathing.

"Ohh, Rein, *fuck baby*," he moans, sated, his thumb brushing across my bottom lip when I sit back and peer up at him. "Come here." He pulls me up and draws me between his legs, snatching my lips and kissing me till we're both starving for air. "I could fuck you right here and now, but I don't want our first time to be on top of a car. A quick fuck won't suffice, it won't appease this burning need I have for you. I would like to spend the night fucking you raw, if that's all right with you."

I resist the urge to moan out loud. Is this guy for real? Leave it to him to be such a gentleman and so yet so uncouth. "That is more than all right with me, Professor." I reply with a teasing smile. Talon's sneaky hands disappear under my skirt, and he cups my bum cheeks in his large hands and squeezes. "We're going to have to wait till we get back home though, aren't we?" I sigh with a playful pout. A slow smile graces his handsome face, and he stares at my mouth. "I can fuck you in my old bedroom if you prefer with my folks next door?"

My jaw drops. I stare at him dumbfounded. "You wouldn't?" He grins wolfishly. "You're a bad, Professor."

Talon laughs and pulls me closer, burying his face into the crook of my neck. "I think we've already established that, my dick is still wet with your spit, Snowflake."

"I didn't mean it in that context, you're actually an incredible teacher. It's just unfortunate for *you* that you're so hot and so many girls—and some boys—want to do very sinful things to you."

Talon shudders with a roll of his eyes, "I've heard some of the things floating about school and have had one too many worn panties delivered to my office over the years."

I smile and bite my lip, "You didn't happen to come across a red lace thong with crystals as the straps, did you?" Talon frowns and pulls his head back, his eyes scanning my face.

"Those were yours?" He drawls dryly and when I press my lips together, he narrows his eyes. "You seriously sent me a pair of used underwear?"

"It wasn't used, they were clean. I'm not that crude nor brave. It was also Paris that sent it without my knowledge. She thought it would be funny."

Talon sighs, his brows knitted together tightly. "Well, I assure you, I did not find it at all funny. It got so bad at one point I was contemplating leaving. I had my resignation all typed up."

"You did?" I ask surprised. "What made you change your mind?"

"I love my job." He affirms, brushing a strand of my hair away from my face and tucking it gently behind my ear. "Not many people are lucky enough to do what they love and the fact I got accepted into such a notable position at my age was enough reason for me to fight to stay."

"Well, I'm really pleased you decided to stay. Putting aside all of this, you truly are an exceptional teacher and talented artist, Talon." He smiles, but it doesn't reach his eyes. I can see the guilt as clear as day projecting deep in those baby blue eyes, and it makes my stomach sink. I'm no fool, I know he has reservations about what we are doing, but it's not like we didn't try to fight it. The harder we tried to stay away the more we gravitated to one another. So, I do the only thing I could think of to take his mind off it. I kiss him, it takes him a second, but he kisses me back fervidly.

"Shall we go? We've still got quite a bit to drive. There's a service station five miles from here, we'll stop to use the bathroom and grab something to eat if you're hungry."

I nod and follow him, slipping into the passenger seat when he opens the door for me.

———

The rest of the drive was nice, the roads were clear, so we cruise down the freeway, Ed Sheeran's songs steaming on his music system — turns out we both share a love for Ed Sheeran's music. Talon laces his fingers with mine, his thumb brushing idly over my knuckles while we sing along to Bad Habits. "Swearing this will be the last, but it probably won't." I sing to him with a teasing smile.

Talon smiles and takes hold of my chin. "My bad habits lead to you," he sings back, smiling handsomely.

Ahh damn, those darn butterflies take flight in my stomach again.

We finally pull up at his parent's place. I turn to face Talon, "Okay, I got this. Your mother's name is Elizabeth and your dad's is Tom. Your mum is a Holistic Therapist, and your dad works in microbiology?"

Talon smiles and shakes his head, "He's a biomedical engineer."

I sigh and pinch the bridge of my nose. "God, Talon what am I doing here? They're going to hate me."

"Hey, no, c'mere, Snowflake." I unbuckle my seatbelt and Talon takes my face into his hands and gazes into my eyes. "Just be yourself and I promise you they're going to love you." He assures me sweetly, his thumbs caressing my jaw affectionately. His touch soothes me instantly and I relax. "Ready?"

I nod and smile when he kisses the tip of my nose. When he draws back a little our gaze interlocks and we stare into each other's eyes. We lean in and our lips only just touch when we hear voices and pull apart. Thank God it was dark out and there wasn't much lighting around the house.

"Tal?"

"My mother and her impeccable timing, as always." Talon utters under his breath with an eye roll.

I giggle.

We climb out of the car and Talon's parents walk toward us from the porch to greet us. "Hey Mum." Elizabeth Saxton comes flying into her son's arms. Talon wraps his arms around her and lifts her off the ground.

"Oh, my handsome boy. Welcome home. I've missed you so much." She gushes pulling back to look him over. "You look thinner, have you been eating?"

"Mum, please don't start. I've been the same weight for years. Though, I highly doubt I will be when I leave after four days of your cooking." He teases giving her cheek an affectionate squeeze.

"Hi darl, I'm Tom. Tal's old man. You must be Rein." I take Tom's offered hand and shake it.

"Yes, I am, it's so nice to meet you." Sheesh, I can see where Talon gets his height and good looks from. Tom Saxton is an absolute dream boat. They're not at all what I expected. They're both gorgeous. Well, they ought to be to produce a fine specimen like Talon who is a carbon copy of his dad. Elizabeth is petite, athletic build, big blue eyes and light brown hair similar to mine but hers is curly.

Elizabeth gives her son a light smack on the arm, and he scowls at her. "Where are your manners love? Introduce us to your friend."

"I will if you give me a minute," Talon complains and takes a step toward me, placing a hand at the small of my back. "Mum, Dad this is my friend, Rein Valdez. Rein, my parents Tom and Elizabeth."

"It's lovely to meet you Mr and Mrs Saxton. Thank you so much for kindly inviting me to join you for Thanksgiving."

"Oh no honey, no formalities needed here. We're a very informal family. Just call us Tom and Lizzie and you're very welcome." I stiffen when she wraps her arms around me in a very tight motherly hug. "We don't often get to meet Tal's friends, so this is a nice treat for us." She pulls away and smiles broadly at me. "Besides, it would be nice to have some female company while these two knuckleheads watch football and drink beer."

I chuckle when Talon and his dad gape at her, affronted. "Mum, you drink beer and watch footy too, I'll remind you."

"Put a sock in it, you. The ladies are talking so be useful and grab the bags," I grin toothily at Talon while his mother loops our arms together and we walk off toward the house.

"Rein, darling, I'm liking your energy."

My *energy?*

CHAPTER Nineteen

Talon

"Ah."

"What?"

"I wouldn't do that if I were you."

"Why not?"

"It might bite."

"I want to play with it."

"It will bite you."

"Talon, it barely has teeth, and it looks pretty docile to me." I hold my hands up in surrender and cross them over my chest while rocking back and forth on the rocking chair.

Rein reaches out to pet the chameleon on the top step of the patio. "Hey buddy, do you need a friend." She just about makes contact with it and it hisses at her and bites her finger. "Ow," She gapes at the reptile hanging off her finger. With a panic she flicks her hand, and it goes flying to a bush nearby.

I look at the bush and then at Rein before I get up and perch beside her. "See, I told you it would bite. Let me see." I take her hand into mine and inspect her finger. There's no blood however it was reddening.

"Oh gosh, do you think I killed it?" Rein says concerned and leans over to look at the bush the chameleon went flying into. I couldn't help but chuckle.

I shake my head.

"I doubt it, they're fairly resilient animals. Does it hurt?" Rein shrugs with a sigh.

"It stings."

I stand and pull her up with me. "We should wash and disinfect your finger, their bites aren't venomous, but you could still get an infection."

"Okay."

It's past midnight and my parents went to bed half hour ago, so we had to be quiet while we move around the house. Rein washes her finger while I hunt around for the first aid kit. My mum usually keeps it in the kitchen drawers. Ah, there you are.

"Found it." Rein turns to face me, drying her index finger with a paper towel. "Let's get some of this disinfectant on there. My mum puts this thing on everything."

Rein smiles watching me closely while I smear some cream over the bite mark and rub it in for her. "That should do the trick." When I look up, I find her staring at me. And I must admit, I'm becoming dangerously fond of these looks she's giving me.

After I screw the cap on to the cream and drop it in the box, I place my hands on either side of her on the counter, caging her in. "Next time, you should listen to me and maybe you'll avoid getting hurt." I tell her quietly, my eyes scanning her pretty face.

Rein smiles warmly and wets her lips, "If I start listening to you and stop get myself into these crises how will you save me, Professor?" She questions tranquilly, her head tilting to the side.

"I thought you didn't like to be saved?"

Rein's hands slip under my t-shirt. She lowers her gaze from mine for a very brief moment before they flitter up to meet mine again, "I don't," she affirms, her fingers lightly grazing my abs. "But I'm really starting to like being saved by you."

"And I've grown quite fond of saving you, Snowflake." We inch closer, our lips, like two powerful magnets luring one another in. I dip my head and brush her lips apart to kiss her when we hear footsteps right above us. I press my molars together. My parents aren't asleep yet. We draw back and I curse inwardly.

"I want that kiss, Miss Valdez."

Rein smiles and presses her lips to my jaw. I close my eyes, my jaw twitching under her lips. "And I want yours, Professor."

"Later." I whisper.

Rein nods, "Later."

TWENTY-EIGHT YEARS old and I'm lying in the bed I spent a good portion of my teen years fantasising about girls. Ten years later, I'm lying here fantasising about a girl in the room above mine. I'm staring up at the ceiling, horny as can be just itching to sneak into her room and finish what we started earlier. The thought shouldn't even cross my mind, I'm in my parent's house for goodness sakes, but this is the affect Rein has on me. I'm truly hoping that once we have sex this crazy need I have for her will disappear. I'm chalking it down to not having any action for almost three years and the fact that it's forbidden—it just makes it that much sweeter.

I didn't make the rules, it's just the way it is. By default, us mortals just want what we can't have. It's just the way we're wired.

Oh, stop waffling, Talon. We both know you're going to go up there so stop faffing around and go already.

Should I?

Before I could answer my own question I'm already out of bed. I'm a master of sneaking out of this house after doing it countless times throughout the years without ever getting caught. Let's see if I can still remember which floorboards to avoid.

I successfully manage to skip up the steps without a sound. I hear the familiar jingle of Rocky's collar as he skips up the steps following me, tongue hanging out.

"Rocky, what are you doing up, mate. Go back to bed." He blinks up at me, tilting his head to the side with that absurdly adorable pug face of his and whines. "Shh, quiet boy." I press my finger to my lips. "What? Are you hungry?" I whisper and he tilts his head to the other side. "I can't feed you right now or you get the shits and start yowling. Go to bed." I point down the stairs and he just yips at me in response.

"Shhhhh!" I roll my eyes and scoop him up into my arms and carry him downstairs quietly. "Just like our mother you sure have impeccable timing, you know that." I set him down on the kitchen floor and fill up his bowl with a couple of treats to keep him busy. "Bon appetite." Rocky dives right in stuffing his face into the bowl lapping away at the treats. I smile and sneak away before he notices me leaving and follows me again.

Second times the charm.

I make it to the guest bedroom on the third floor and knock on the door lightly. Shit, what if she's asleep? I press my ear to the door and smile when I hear the patter of her feet on the wooden floor as she walks over to the door.

It opens and Rein stands before me in a white crop top, no bra, and racy black Brazilian knickers. Fucking hell. She looks so damn good.

My eyes openly roam over her body and my cock goes rock solid. "Did you need something, Professor?"

I swallow thickly and nod taking a step forward, my hands grip her waist. "Yes, Miss Valdez. I need *you.*" Rein peers up at me through her lashes and hooks her finger in the elastic of my jogging bottoms and pulls me the rest of the way into the room with her. I close the door quietly, curl my fingers around her wrist and pull her till her body is pressed up against mine.

"I thought we were waiting?"

"I can't have you this close, looking this good and not do a damn thing about it. I've been staring up at that ceiling for an hour conjuring up all kinds of scenarios in my head." I reply, pressing my forehead to hers, my hands wander off exploring her beautiful body. Her nipples bud under my touch, she moans quietly. "I'm dying to explore your body, snowflake." I murmur teasing her hardened nipples over the thin fabric of her top.

Rein's back arches and she pushes those phenomenally full tits further into my hand, wordlessly expressing what she wants, and I don't miss a beat in obeying. I lift her arms and tug her top off, freeing her breasts. My mouth waters at the mere sight of them, so fucking perfect. Rein lowers her gaze from mine, her hand comes up to cover the glossy, whitened scar between the valley of her breasts. I tuck my finger under her chin and tilt her head up. "Look at me."

Rein's eyes lift to mine and I see a corpus of insecurities behind her striking gaze. She's ashamed of her scar, uncomfortable in her own skin which I find absurd because she's simply divine. "Don't you hide your body from me, Snowflake. I want to see, touch and taste every inch of you."

Rein winces when I lightly drag my index finger over her scar. How could she not see how incredibly beautiful she is? She shakes her head sullenly. "It's hideous."

With a shake of my head, I cup her face and force her to look at me. "It's absolutely not. Don't look at it as a defacement. This scar is simply a reminder that you were stronger than whatever tried to hurt you. It's a commemoration that you got hurt but fought on and survived." I assert solemnly, combing my fingers through her hair. Rein leans into my palm and sighs.

"I suppose it's easier for someone with no scars to see the beauty in ugly things."

"Oh, I have plenty of scars, believe me. Only difference is that mine aren't so visible, and they never really completely heal." I admit caressing her jaw affectionately. "If I wore my scars on the outside, I'd be even more hideous than you've seemed to convince yourself that you are, trust me."

Rein looks over my chest as if picturing my body covered in scars. "It's no wonder you're so attracted to me then."

I frown. "Why's that?"

"Because it's always those with broken souls that try to help and put others back together." I smile when Rein traces the outline of the infinity tattoo over my left peck. "Perhaps we're more alike than we're aware." She says stepping back a little and gestures to her right ankle.

My jaw drops slightly when I see the small tattoo on her ankle—a tattoo of an infinity sign similar to mine. Only hers had a pretty heart in the middle. How the fuck have I never noticed that before? I got mine in honour of Taylor and our baby after I lost them. Was this yet another coincidence? Noticing the thunderstruck look on my face Rein lowers her foot back to the floor. "I'm not really big on tattoos, but, my mum and I always said we would get matching tattoos once I turned eighteen. Unfortunately, we never got around to doing it, so I decided to get this after she died, a somewhat tribute to her."

I couldn't think of a single word to say in that moment. The only thing I could focus on was the overwhelming need to kiss her. So, I did just that. Those irresistibly soft and full lips brush over mine with such need and devotion it made me ache. It's been way too long since I've felt like this. There's never really been a shortage of women 'wanting' me. I've always felt wanted by all sorts of women over the years, but never needed—not until Rein. I like not only being wanted by her but being needed.

And I'm going to show her just how desperately I need *her*.

Lips still locked, we continue to kiss passionately, hands flying all over each other. I slowly walk her back toward the en-suite bathroom. I break the kiss and Rein whimpers in discontent. I turn her around so she's facing the mirror in the bathroom. "I wanted to wait till we got back to the city, but I can't hold back anymore. I'm going to fuck you and you're going to watch me do it. I want you to see how incredibly irresistible you are." I growl ardently into her ear while I pinch and roll her nipples between my thumb and forefinger. Rein moans and bites her bottom lip; her head falls back against my chest. "I'm going to fuck this pussy so good you're going to feel every ripple of pleasure in your bones." I lick up her neck and suck the sensitive spot behind her ear. "I fully intend to carve the feel of my cock buried deep inside you into your very soul, baby."

"Oh my God," Rein whimpers, curling her fingers at the nape of my neck when my fingers wander down and disappear in her underwear and brush teasingly over her clit.

"Open your eyes, sweetheart." I breathe in her ear. Rein's eyes open and she looks back at me through the mirror. "I want you to see how gorgeous you look while you ride and come all over my fingers." I sink two fingers into her tight, soaking wet pussy, and her mouth hangs open, her breath hitching. "Shh, quiet now. Don't want my parents to hear, do we?"

My thumb strokes her clit in slow teasing circles while I work my fingers in and out of her pussy. "Oh, Talon, fuck, feels so good." I groan and nip at her ear, my eyes never leaving hers.

"Show me," My free hand grips her throat. "Show me how you like to be fucked." On my command Rein begins rocking her hips against my hand, back and forth, up and down she quickly finds her rhythm and fucks herself on my fingers and I watch in enchantment, burning this memory into my brain, because it's just too damn good to ever forget. Fuck. The gasping and quiet moans secreting from her alone is making my dick throb with need. I'm so fucking ready to be buried deep inside her, though at this rate, I'm worried I'll blow my load before I even get a chance to get in there.

I feel that first squeeze of her muscles contracting around my fingers, and I know she's close. I stroke my fingers against her g-spot and she rubs her clit against my thumb more urgently as she chases down her orgasm. "Ahh fuck, fuck." I watch her fixedly. "Kiss me, please Talon, kiss me." She whimpers tilting her head back. I dip my head and kiss her, swallowing her cries of pleasure as she nears her release. Her vaginal walls clamp down around my fingers like a vice and I push deeper. "Oh God, oh yes, yes, I'm coming." She pants gripping my biceps with a death grip, her nails digging into my skin.

Her moans were getting louder the closer she got, so I clamp my hand over her mouth as she goes over and thank God I did, because she explodes with a muffled cry. Rein falls against me, her body tenses and then convulses while I stroke her through the last few seconds of her orgasm before it fades, and she collapses into my arms, panting.

I dip my head and brush a kiss on her lips. "Mm," She moans between breaths, parting her lips for me to deepen the kiss. "What are you doing to me." I couldn't resist and smile against her lips.

"I'm not done with you yet." I murmur drawing her in for a longer, deeper kiss. Rein reaches back and peels my boxers down while I continue to devour her mouth. When I feel her fingers wrap around my cock and she strokes it, it invokes a deep, feral groan from me. I can't fucking take it. Her touch sends an uncontrollable heat racing through my body. It's simply galvanic and I'm finding myself becoming addicted to it.

"Ahh fuck," I curse, pressing my forehead to her temple. "I forgot to grab a damn condom."

Rein looks up at me, "I have one."

I pull my head back and my eyes find hers, "You do?"

Rein nods and I watch as she leans over and fishes through the little pink cosmetic bag she has on the side of the sink. "I came prepared." She grins sultrily and holds up the little silver foil between her fingers.

I pluck it out of her hold and narrow my eyes at her playfully. "Even though we agreed to wait?"

"Come on, who are we kidding. We were never going to wait," She states brushing her finger along my jaw, "Which is why you came prepared too, didn't you, Professor?" she purrs, leaning closer till her lips brush over mine. "You had every intention of sneaking up into my room and having your way with me."

I stare hungrily at her mouth. "What can I say, my dick wants what it wants and right now it's just aching to be buried inside this beautiful pussy." I moan, biting and tugging her bottom lip as I cup her bare pussy and she grinds herself wantonly against my hand.

"We best let them get acquainted then, because my girl is slavering in anticipation." Rein moans sucking on my bottom lip. My dick responds perilously to her words and judders with readiness. I bite the foil and tear it open with my teeth. Rein bites her lip, her hungry eyes on mine as I roll the condom over my cock.

Lord forgive me.

"Bend over and hold onto the sink." I order and she obeys without hesitation. My one hand grips her small waist and the other rubs the head of my dick over her pussy lips again and again making her purr like the sexy vixen she is. My eyes roll to the back of my head and my head spins when I push just the head of my dick into her hot cavern.

Rein gasps, her hips that were rocking against the length of me stills at the intrusion. Slowly, inch by inch I feed my cock into her pussy, my head whirls when she clamps around me like a vice.

Fuck, she's incredibly tight. I can practically feel her stretching to accommodate me. Rein bites down on her bottom lip to keep from moaning out loud when I push myself deep into her. "Are you okay?" I whisper in her ear when she squeezes her eyes shut.

"Mhm, fuck, Talon you feel so good."

I nuzzle her neck, dragging my lips toward her ear. "Believe me honey, you feel even better."

Rein's eyes flicker open, and she holds my gaze through the mirror. "Fuck me."

That's all the affirmation I needed. With a throaty groan I grip her hips tight and slide my cock out of her and back in again. Rein moans, her fingers tightening around the sink while my hands wander off, exploring every mouth-watering inch of her body while we rock together, our heavy breathing and moans bouncing off the walls in the bathroom.

We tried our damned hardest to be quiet, but this ravenous girl somehow manages to drive me absolutely wild with desire to a point where I can't, nor do I want to think about anything but the way she feels wrapped around me. Rein Valdez has managed to unravel me in a way I'm not even sure I'll ever be able to put myself together again—and the worst part of it all is that I don't want to.

I let go of everything, every concern, every doubt and yield to the carnal beast inside that is raring to claim her, ruin her for all other men. My hips slam into her from behind and she cries out, her head falling back against my shoulder while I drive my cock into her again and again sending us both hurtling toward our desperately sought release.

"I can't get enough of you." I lick and suck at her neck till I leave a deep red mark behind, my fingers wander down and I stroke her clit, making her writhe wildly against me. Rein sucks my thumb when I brush it against her bottom lip. "Fucking. Christ. Rein." I moan throatily against her ear with every raring thrust.

Rein rocks her hips back against me, her head falls against my shoulder, our chests rising and falling with every ragged breath we take. "Ohh God, Talon I'm so close." She whimpers curling her fingers in my hair. I grip her throat, tilting her head back so I could kiss her. "Ready when you are, baby."

Rein's mouth hangs open as I thrust harder, my hips slamming against her sexy arse, fucking her savagely till I feel her walls clamping around me, squeezing so tight it was impossible to hold back any longer. "Oh my God, Talon, I'm coming, I'm coming."

I swallow her cries of pleasure, bruising her lips with a hot and dirty kiss while we both shatter together. "Watch Snowflake, look how beautiful you look when you come for me." I growl watching her through the mirror. What a stunning sight she is. "I want you to see what you do to me. Watch as I spill my hot cum deep into your greedy little pussy." My knees start to tremble, my balls tighten and that all-consuming rapture fires through me rapidly, momentarily paralysing me just as I hit the apex of my climax and fire my load into the condom with a guttural moan.

"Fucking *Christ*, Rein."

"Talon." Rein whimpers, unable to hold herself up any longer she falls back against me, sucking in mouthfuls of air to catch her breath, her beautiful face flushed. I press my forehead to her temple, while I calm my own hasty breathing. "Wow."

My lips brush along her jaw, my fingers caressing her hips while our bodies calm. "You all right?"

Rein smiles lazily and nods biting her bottom lip. "So, that's what sex is supposed to feel like..." She stops to catch her breath and shakes her head. "That was unlike anything I have ever experienced with anyone, including myself."

I chuckle and kiss her temple. "It only gets better, Snowflake."

Rein pulls her head back, her eyes gleaming. "Better than that?"

I nod and tilt her head back so I could brush a soft kiss to her lips. "So much better," Rein twists in my arms and pushes herself up on her toes and responds readily to my kiss, her arms snaking around my neck.

"Show me what I've been missing, Professor."

I scoop her into my arms bridal style and carry her out of the bathroom toward the bed, "With pleasure, Snowflake."

CHAPTER *Twenty*

Rein

"Mum, please, I'm begging you stop." Elizabeth Saxton pins her son with a pointed look, her right brow raised she smacks his hand away when he reaches for the photo album. "Ow, I'm going to burn that thing one of these days." He threatens her with a playful scowl.

I giggle and take the photo his mother hands me. It's a photo of Talon as a toddler, running around with no clothes on. "Look at this one, he was two years old. I think he spent a good portion of that summer in the nuddy."

"Oh my Gosh, look how cute you are!" I coo and pull the photo away when Talon tries to grab it from me.

"Give me that." I slap his hand away when he pokes me.

"Of course he was, he gets his good looks from his old man." His dad drawls teasingly, wagging his dark brows at his wife who rolls her eyes and takes a long sip of her glass of Rioja.

"Fucking hell, someone kill me now." Talon groans pinching the bridge of his nose and shaking his head clearly embarrassed.

"I don't know why you're so embarrassed, you were such a cutie." I state with a grin, and he responds with a not so amused glare.

"Cutie my arse, it's a violation if anything." He grumbles taking a sip of his glass of wine.

"Oh, stop spitting out your dummy, you big baby. I'm a proud mum, let me enjoy it will ya." His mum complains and closes the photo album. "I can always show her the ones of when you were in high school if you prefer?"

Talon's eyes go wide in alarm, he shakes his head. "You dare, that album comes out and I swear to Jesus I'm out of here." Talon grumbles and his mother cackles putting the album to the side of the dinner table.

I look over at Talon. "I'm intrigued now, what's in this high school album, hm?" I question curiously and he smiles.

"Nonya."

I blink, "Nonya?"

"Yeah, none of your business." I give him my best pleading look and he smirks back at me. "You can give me the puppy eyes all you want, it ain't happening... ever."

"Meanie." I sulk and sink back into my seat.

"Ignore him darling, don't be fooled by the composed demeanour, Talon was a little terror growing up. Oh, the stories I could tell you."

"But she won't, will you mother." He utters through clenched teeth, his blue eyes wide as he stares at her meaningfully.

Tom chuckles, "Honey, stop embarrassing him in front of his friend. You're making the poor kid sweat." Tom scolds her playfully and she waves him off not even acknowledging it. Talon exhales audibly through his nose and picks up his glass of wine. I am enjoying watching him squirm.

"Serves him right for not coming to visit more often. Oh, you need to see the first picture he ever painted." Elizabeth gushes proudly.

"Bloody hell," Talon complains sinking further into his chair. "Pop, game of chess?"

"Oh yes, you know it. Someone's itchin' for an arse whoopin'." Tom gets up and wanders off out of the dining room.

The Saxton home is stunning. As you would envisage living in the suburbs, the house has three massive bedrooms, a modern kitchen with a marble island in the middle, a spacious back garden where they grow their own organic vegetables and beautiful flowers. They're literally living the American dream. But you know the best part? You could feel the love and warmth of a happy home the moment you step in. It's just so comforting. There are photos all over the house of Talon throughout his years growing up and his parents all loved up.

Perhaps true love does exist after all or maybe one must be lucky enough to find it. Unfortunately, the women in my family aren't so auspicious when it comes to love—if anything it's quite the opposite.

I listen to Talon's mother talk animatedly about her work and you could really feel how much she loves what she does. We all laugh hysterically when she tells us a hilarious story of her client falling asleep on her massage table and talking in his sleep about what he wanted to do to his wife.

An enchanting warmth engulfs me from head to toe when I feel Talon's fingers discreetly lace with mine under the table. There go those darn butterflies again, flapping around in my stomach making me feel all kinds of frivolous. I turn my gaze to look at him, he's talking with his dad about the football match the next day while they setup a game of chess. He takes a sip of his wine and smiles into his glass, his fingers tightening around mine giving my hand a gentle squeeze.

"Rein, why don't you come with me, sweetheart, and we can plate up dessert. Let the boys talk sports."

Talon lets go of my hand and I follow his mother into the kitchen. I couldn't even think about eating a crumb of anything else. I was absolutely stuffed after the delicious Thanksgiving dinner. Probably the best meal I have had in a very long time. Lizzie made a strawberry trifle and bunch of other desserts that are supposedly Talon's favourites.

"I'm so full, but all these desserts look so good. I can't remember the last time I had a home cooked meal. In fact, I can't remember a time I've ever eaten so much in my life. I think your dinner will keep me full till Christmas." I say taking the bowls she hands me after she carefully takes them out of the drawer.

Lizzie laughs while she serves the trifle into crystal bowls, "Nonsense, there is always room for dessert. I've never made trifle before, so I really hope you like it." She smiles at me warmly.

"After just devouring your food, I have absolutely no doubt that it tastes amazing. Though, you really didn't have to go to so much trouble on my account."

Lizzie shakes her head and waves me off flippantly. "It's no trouble when you do it with pleasure, darlin'. I love to cook, after my therapy room the kitchen is my second favourite place." She stops for a beat and her brows fuse together slightly as if she's remembering something upsetting. "I should be the one thanking you."

Thanking me? What on earth for?

Noticing the bemused look on my face, she proceeds. "It's been a long time since I've seen my boy in such high spirits. He's not been himself since he lost Taylor three years ago..." the spoon in my hand almost slips out of my grasp. I tighten my fingers around it and lift my gaze to look at her, my mouth suddenly feeling very dry.

Who's Taylor?

"I honestly thought we'd never get him out of that dark place he was adamant on keeping himself in. He shut himself off from everyone, blamed himself for so long over what happened, but now, I can see he's got that sparkle in his eyes again," she explains with an adoring smile. "And I've got a feeling you have something to do with it."

I shake my head, lowering my eyes to stare at the spoon in my hand. "Oh no, Talon and I, we're just friends."

Elizabeth smiles, the knowing look in her eyes telling me she's not buying a word of what I'm selling.

"Rein, I'm a holistic therapist. I can feel the tangible energy pulsing between the two of you. The chemistry, when you're both in the same room, is honestly making me sweat."

I blink and force myself to look at her, I can feel my face getting redder by the second. My stomach constricts with guilt. I hate lying, I'm not very good at it. Talk about awkward. "It's okay sweetheart. You kids these days aren't so big on labels. I'm just happy to see my son is smiling again. Come on, let's go join the boys."

I watch her walking out of the kitchen and exhale deeply before I pick up the two remaining plates and follow her.

"So, I want to hear all about how you two met." Talon's mother says taking her seat and looking between Talon and me. I shove a mouthful of trifle in my mouth and look over at Talon who rubs the back of his neck.

"Uh, we met at the bar Rein works at." Talon explains with a shrug, pushing around his dessert with his fork. "I went there a couple of times after work with some friends and one night she stole my cab and we've been friends since."

I gape at him in scepticism. "I stole *your* cab?"

Talon looks at me and smirks cheekily. "Yes, you did."

I shake my head and point my fork at him. "No, as I recall that was my cab that you so rudely jumped into." I point out and narrow my eyes at him. "While it was pouring out, might I add."

Talon laughs and scoops up a bite of his dessert and eats it, licking his lips "I insisted we share, if you *recall.*"

Lizzie and Tom watch on amusedly as we continue to bicker back and forth. After dinner was over and Talon wrapped up his game of chess with his dad... which he sorely lost. I can't lie that did gratify me. Want to know what else gratified me? The concentration on his absurdly gorgeous face, while he thought about his moves. The sexy manner his eyes narrow and the way his index finger glides over his bottom lip.

"All right, I'm officially stuffed, if someone pokes a needle in me I may actually explode." Talon complains rubbing his muscular stomach. "I need to walk off some of this food."

"That's a great idea, Darling. Why don't you and Rein go out, you can show her around. Ohio is magical during the holidays." She suggests snuggling into her husband when he wraps an arm around her shoulder.

Talon looks over at me and smiles, silently asking if I was up for it. "I did have plans to show you around tomorrow, but we can go for a walk and grab some hot chocolate if you're up for it?"

Some one-on-one time with my hot professor? Hell to the yes, I'm up for it. I nod without hesitation and stand up. "Sounds good, my legs could use a stretch."

"Make sure you wrap up warm, it's freezing out. I don't want you catching a cold," Lizzie insists.

"Yes mother." Talon drawls with a playful roll of his eyes. He places his hand at the small of my back and guides me out of the dining room.

I thought Chicago was freezing, boy was I wrong. Ohio is brutally cold. The second you step outside you feel the chill in your bones, even through the three layers I was wearing. The glacial wind hits you in the face, momentarily catching your breath. Talon and I walk side by side down the sidewalk. He pulls up the collar of his overcoat to further shield him from the bitter weather.

It wasn't till we were a good distance from the house that Talon wraps his arm around my shoulders and draws me against him. I smile and nestle into him, soaking up the warmth while we stroll along the quiet street.

"The town isn't too far from here; it's buzzing this time of year and there's this cosy coffee shop that serve the best hot chocolate."

"You had me at hot chocolate." I reply tilting my head up to look up at him. Talon looks down into my upturned face and grins, he reaches over and tugs my beanie hat over my eyes and drops a lingering kiss on my lips.

"Hey!" I laugh and shove him away playfully, pushing the hat up over my eyes and glower at him. Talon laces his fingers with mine and throws his arm around my shoulder and we continue our walk toward the town.

"You know, I must say American's sure know how to do Christmas right." I acclaim looking around the stunning Christmas decorations.

"Compared to back home in London, it's just something else. I remember my first ever Christmas here in the states, I was so stunned at how beautifully everywhere was decorated."

Talon nods in agreement, his blue eyes darting around the various Christmas decorations and huge colourful lights lighting up the entire town wonderfully. I stop and stare in awe. This is what they call a town? It looks more like a mini winter wonderland. Christmas music plays from the speakers fixed to the trees, robed in twinkling fairy lights. "Wow," I breathe taking in the magical sight before me. "It's so beautiful."

Talon watches me, wetting his lip. "Sure is."

Despite the freezing weather my cheeks burn hot under his intent stare. Talon reaches over and takes hold of the ends of my scarf and tugs me closer. "Miss Valdez are you blushing?" he murmurs, his lips inching closer to mine.

"No, it's wind burn." Talon smiles and brushes a kiss over my lips.

"You lie." He whispers, coaxing my lips apart with his. "I've been dying to kiss you all day." I respond with a moan when his velvet tongue sneaks into my mouth and languidly caresses my own. My fingers curl at the collar of his jacket, my knees wobbling when he deepens the kiss, his thumb stroking my jaw as he slowly pulls away.

"Come on," his long fingers slide into mine and he tugs me toward a homely coffee shop on the corner of the street. This must be the coffee shop he was referring too. It really was small but with a couple of seats inside and another two outside which were all occupied. "Do you want to wait here and I'll grab us the drinks?" Talon ask and walks off toward the coffee shop when I nod. I watch him blowing into his hands to warm them up.

"He's not been himself since he lost Taylor..."

Lizzie's words from earlier keep drumming around in my head. The more I'm trying to ignore it and convince myself it's not my business the more I'm bursting to ask him who Taylor was and what happened to her.

It's obvious who she was, clearly his girlfriend or someone he cared a great deal for. I can't seem to pinpoint why, but I feel a twinge of jealousy.

Oh, for the love of God Rein, what are you doing? Don't go poking your nose where it doesn't belong. If he wanted you to know, he would tell you. Don't you dare go and let yourself catch feelings for him. This thing between you is nothing but a meaningless fling. You're inconsequential. Just a momentary thrill.

My stomach sinks deep into my gut. I swiftly shake my head ridding myself of such thoughts. I don't care. It's just sex. I'm just getting caught up in the passion. That's what we agreed, no emotional attachment.

My eyes wander around and stop when I see a massive mural on the wall opposite the coffee shop. I stroll over to it and study the picture. It's a painting of a mother holding a baby close to her chest, her lips pressed to her baby's forehead, both their eyes closed.

The colours, every small detail of the subjects was astounding. The hair, the eyelashes, down to the last freckle on the mother's nose. Whoever painted this has some serious talent. I stand there staring at it utterly speechless. There are names painted at the bottom of the picture.

Katie and Isabella Franklin 2015

"Hey you." I jump, startled when I feel Talon's warm breath and deep voice against the shell of my ear.

"Jesus Christ." I gasp pressing my hand to my chest to calm my wildly beating heart.

Talon smiles gorgeously, "Actually, Snowflake I only go by 'Jesus' after hours."

I chuckle and take the plastic cup of hot chocolate from him when he holds it out to me. "You're insufferable, I hope you know that."

Talon winks at me and turns to look at the painting on the wall, his face falls almost instantly. "It's incredible, isn't it?" I sigh, wrapping my cold fingers around the hot cup while I stare up at the painting. Talon remains quiet. "I feel like there's a significance to this painting."

"There is." He replies sombrely, his blue eyes scanning the faces on the painting. "Katie and her six-month-old Isabella were both shot to death in their home, right here in this town.

"Oh my God, that's awful. Who would do such a thing?"

"Her husband, believe it or not. First, he shot the baby, then Katie and then killed himself." Talon explains with a drawn-out sigh, his breath steaming in front of him when he exhales.

I stare up at the image of Katie and her baby girl and my eyes water. It hits a little too close to home for me. "Was he abusive toward her?"

"No. As far as everyone knew they were happy and in love and then one day it's like a switch went off in his head and he decided to murder his family and end his own life." Talon explains turning to look at me.

"How can you claim to love someone one moment and then pull out a gun and kill them the next?"

"The mind is a fragile thing. Who knows what was going through his head." I bite my lip and look at the painting again. It's so tragic.

I read the names again and notice a signature at the bottom right. Hold on. I recognise that scrawl. I lean over to take a closer look. "Talon, Isn't that *your* signature?"

Talon takes a sip of his hot chocolate but says nothing. "Did you paint this?"

He nods.

"Wow." I move to stand beside him and we both stare up at the painting... his painting. I feel my heart swell in my chest. "Talon, it's incredible. How long did it take to paint this?"

Talon shrugs, licking his lips. "A week or so."

I look over at him and he smiles. "You're not so bad, Professor."

"Oh gee, thanks Valdez." Talon drawls dryly, but his gaze is playful.

We walked around for a while and talked. Talon told me about his years growing up in Ohio.

It was gone eleven by the time we got back to the Saxton manor. His parents were already in bed, so we snuck in quietly to not wake them. I giggle hysterically while I climb up the steps to the guest bedroom, Talon close behind me. "Shh," he chuckles following me to the guest room.

"I wasn't expecting to have as much fun as I did on those bumper cars at my big age." I admit, taking off my beanie hat and tossing it on the bed, followed by my scarf and jacket.

"It's good to let out the inner child in you occasionally. We often get so busy trying to make a living that we forget we need to actually live." Talon declares with a rapacious smile as he sits on the bed and beckons me to him.

I walk over to him and stand between his legs. "Well, my inner child had a great time, so thank you."

My eyes meet his blue ones and his smile grows into a full-on grin, "It's not over yet, Snowflake. We've a long day tomorrow. My mum will have us up at the arse crack of dawn to go and pick a tree, then we'll come home to put it up and decorate it. After that, we'll have lunch with my parents and then you and I are going out for the day for some more juvenile exuberance."

My brows rise with interest. "Oh? Juvenile huh?" I question, raking my fingers down the side of his face.

Talon's eyes close at my touch and he sighs, "Mhm." His strong arms snake around my waist and he presses his face against my stomach, his eyes lift to look up at me. I couldn't ignore the apprehension lingering behind his gaze. Why do I have the gnawing feeling that whatever this is between us is going to come to an end real soon. I mean, we both knew it wasn't going to last. I don't think either of us expected our fling to go on as long as it has.

"I think I better go back to my room." Talon sighs but makes no move to actually get up and go. I brush my fingers through his hair and smile knowingly.

"How about you *don't*?" I whisper tilting his head back and dropping a lingering kiss on his chiselled jaw. Talon licks his lips, his hands gripping my hips.

"I really, really, think I should." He whispers back, biting down on his lower lip when my lips glide along his jaw toward is lips. "We're out of rubbers, Snowflake and if I stay in here with you, I won't be able to keep my hands off you." He declares gazing up at me, his eager fingers sliding my top up, exposing my stomach.

"There are other ways of satisfying one another that doesn't require condoms, Professor." I point out sultrily.

Talon's lips quirk, "Mm, Miss Valdez, you do make a valid and very tempting argument." I gasp when he pulls me down on the bed and rolls me onto my back, his strong and strapping body covering my own. Those sinfully soft, full lips descend upon mine, our tongues glide over one another sensually making it impossible to hold back the moan that escapes me. His kiss steals every last drop of oxygen from my lungs till I'm gasping for breath.

One by one, each item of clothing we discard joins the growing pile on the floor beside the bed. We may not have been able to have sex, but we certainly enjoyed every steamy second of leisurely exploring one another.

After we slaked our urges, we lay in bed whispering to one another. Me on my back and Talon on his front, his chin resting on my stomach. I play with his hair while his index finger strokes my scar. I can see the curiosity burning in the depths of his blue eyes. Maybe if I open up to him, he will do the same. "It was a car accident."

His eyes lift to meet mine, for a very fleeting moment he looks almost startled. "My mum started seeing this guy, Donny Santos, he was a real piece of work. I didn't like him the moment I met him, despite all his efforts to woo my mum I just saw something she couldn't. I didn't say anything, though, because she finally seemed happy and to me that's all that mattered. I only wanted her to be happy after the dozen heartbreaks she suffered over the years, I truly wanted her to find her 'one true love'." I explain while I absent-mindedly trace circles over his bicep. I smile sadly, "She was forever looking for the love of her life and she really believed she found it with Donny, until a year later when his true colours started to show."

Talon listens intently, his eyes narrowed slightly. "What happened?"

I heave a sigh, the back of my eye lids already burning with the tears that threaten to fall when my mind travels back to the day that I lost my mum. "After we moved in with him, it's like he had a complete personality change. Though he was adamant that he loved her, he treated her like she was a piece of property he owned instead of cherishing her as the woman he was supposedly in love with. Donny was always good at manipulating her to get what he wanted, and my mother being the ever-trusting person she was always fell for his shit, believing he would change, but he never did. If anything, he got worse." Talon likely sensing my distress wraps his fingers around my hand and presses it against his lips to comfort me.

"It's okay Snowflake, you don't have to talk about it if you don't want to."

I wet my lips and a quivering breath escapes me, "I begged her to leave him and finally she had enough of being his doormat. They got into another heated argument and my mum told him she was done with him. We packed up our bags and left to go back to my Grammy's, but he insisted on driving us there. I sat in the back of that car just listening to him try and convince her yet again that he loves her more than anything and he was sorry. My mum didn't say anything, she just gave him this look... one full of defeat and then said, 'I don't love you anymore Donny. It's over, just set me free'." I blink and tears roll down my eyes.

"He went all quiet and slowly the car started shifting faster and faster, my mum begged him to slow down, but it's like it didn't even register and then he whispered, 'Even in death, it's you and I, cariño' and drove straight into oncoming traffic. My mum screaming my name was the last thing I remember before we drove straight into a truck." I sob woefully into my hand.

Talon crawls up and without a word gathers me into his arms. "They both died upon impact. The doctor said it was a miracle that I survived considering I wasn't wearing a seatbelt. The impact of the crash left my heart significantly damaged, and I was on a ventilator for over three weeks until they found a heart that was a match." Talon presses his lips to my forehead, his fingers brushing through my hair. "I don't belong here, they should have let me die with her, I should have been with my mum."

"Rein don't talk like that. Of course you belong here. I can bet my life your mother is relieved that you survived. You were given a gift, a second chance at life and you should be living it to the fullest. If not for yourself then do it for your mum and the person whose heart is beating inside of you." Talon asserts, tilting my head so he could softly brush away the tears that just kept rolling down my cheeks.

"I know I should be thankful and a big part of me is, however, when you have somebody else's heart beating inside your chest you can't help feel a little... out of sorts. It might sound silly or trivial because it's just an organ but..." I feel like a part of *me* is missing.

"But what?" Talon presses and I shake my head dismissively.

"Doesn't matter, it's stupid."

"Hey, your feelings are absolutely not stupid. If it helps you to talk about it, I'm here to listen." He assures kindly.

"Thank you, I've not told anyone the truth behind the scar, you're the first person outside of my family that I feel comfortable speaking to. It's nice to talk about it." Talon smiles a little and nods.

"Well, you make being a good listener pretty easy." He states, my eyes search his and I'm comforted by his sincerity.

My fingers caress his jaw. "So do you."

Talon kisses my fingers when I brush them over his lips. "Can I ask you something?" Talon nods.

Fuck it, I'm going to ask. I can't live with this burning curiosity any longer.

"Who's Taylor?"

Her name hadn't even properly left my lips before his face fell and a melancholy look overshadowed his beautiful eyes. Talon draws away from me and I watch him shift to the edge of the bed, his shoulders tensely gathered up, the muscles in his back stiff. "No one that concerns you."

Ouch.

My heart squeezes and slowly sinks to the pit of my stomach at the terse tone of his voice. Talk about having the rhetorical door slammed right in your face. I suppose I was hasty in assuming we were in a position where we could share more than just bodily fluids. Boy was I wrong.

The air in the room suddenly feels suffocatingly thick or maybe that's the lump forming in my throat where my emotions were starting to choke me. I need to get it together. While Talon's head hangs low between his shoulders I fumble with my fingers resting in my lap. "I'm sorry, I didn't mean to overstep. I was just curious."

Talon sighs heavily and turns his head to peer at me over his shoulder. "Don't be."

Bloody hell. It's clear whoever this Taylor was, she's a hard limit for him. The passionate and considerate guy I've grown accustomed to vanishes and is replaced by the frosty jerk-off he was when we first met.

"Noted." I utter ineptly, veering my eyes to look anywhere but at him. I'm honestly trying my best to not show him that his sudden indifference is affecting me. Damn my curiosity, why did I go and open my big mouth? Last thing I want is to make things awkward between us which it is now.

Talon stands up and proceeds to get dressed, I watch him with a frown. "Where are you going?"

"I think it will be best if I sleep in my room tonight. My parents will be up early, and I don't want to get caught sneaking out of your room." He answers stiffly pulling his jeans on and looking around for his black t-shirt.

Seriously? I ask one question about his ex, and he goes cold turkey on me? "Talon your mother already suspects there's something going on

267

between us." I state matter-of-factly and he licks his lips, not even regarding me with a look.

"Even more reason for me to stay in my room." I sit up on my knees and blink up at him a little shell shocked at his response. Wow, he's really gone and done a complete one-eighty on me. What the ever-living fuck.

"Fine, Talon," I shrug, "If that's what you want."

He finally looks at me, jaw set tight. I pull the sheet up, covering my bare chest and hold his gaze. Why is he looking at me like that? I couldn't decipher the look in his eyes. The dejection I felt moments ago vanishes and is quickly replaced by exasperation. What was he expecting exactly, that I would beg him to come back to bed? I don't think so.

"Rein—"

"Don't." I hold up my hand and shake my head, "I get it, I may have inadvertently overstepped, but if you don't want to open up or talk to me, that's fine, you don't have to be an arsehole about it." Talon closes his eyes, and he rubs the back of his neck, muttering something under his breath. "Don't mutter to yourself, I'm right here, if you have something to say I'd love to hear it." I grouse irritably, crossing my arms over my chest and glaring at him.

"Why is it every time you don't get your way, I somehow become the arsehole?"

"Oh, I don't know, could it be because you're incapable of communicating with me like a normal person instead of reverting back to your callous manner every time shit gets a little too real." I argue valiantly not even flinching when he throws a sharp look in my direction.

"I believe I've been perfectly clear with my communication with you, Rein. There's no need to complicate things between us by getting too personal. This, between us, can never be anything romantic, nothing more than just sex. That's what we agreed, right? In fact, I think we should put a stop to it after this weekend because evidently, lines are starting to get blurred." Talon explains evenly and takes a step toward me.

There goes that imbecilic feeling of heavy-heartedness making my stomach ache again. I hadn't noticed until he uttered those words how much I'm actually starting to like him. I must suck at hiding my feelings because he's clearly picking up on my disappointment and moves closer until he's standing at the side of the bed. "The last thing I want is for you to be left disillusioned and I fear if we carry on one or both of us will eventually start developing feelings."

I sigh and nod, "If you're concerned that I'll go and fall in love with you, you don't have to worry Professor. I have no intention of falling 'in love' with anyone ever. I don't trust enough to ever allow myself to get that close to someone. However, if you want to end whatever this is between us then that's fine with me."

Talon's eyes narrow a little and he scans my face as if in search of something. Is he looking for some trace of ambiguity? Did he expect I would sulk and kick up some dust because he wants to end things? God, a part of me wishes I had the power to read minds just so I could figure out this look he's got lingering deep in those magnetic blue orbs of his.

Talon regards me closely, "I understand your reluctant to allow yourself to feel something for someone after you witnessed your mother suffer the way she did with her relationships "

"—it's not reluctance." I interrupt. "I just don't believe in the whole fairy tale, happily ever after waffle like everyone else does. Love is nothing but a chemical reaction designed to make two people like each other long enough to procreate. That's it. There are no soul mates, or one true love. People associate love with the heart when it has nothing to do with the heart at all, it's all a reaction of the brain."

Talon's brows rise to his hairline, and he looks at me as if I've sprouted a second head. "While you may be right, love is only a chemical reaction inside your brain that eventually subsides after a while, but if you want that flame to keep burning you need to feed it." He says inching closer to me. "Nothing beats being in love and being loved unconditionally in return."

My gaze lowers to his lips. "For someone who stood there a moment ago concerned that I would foolishly fall for him you're pushing awfully hard to convince me, Professor."

The corner of Talon's lip lifts and he licks his lips. He reaches up and brushes a strand of my hair away and tucks it behind my ear. "Had the circumstances been different and we didn't have the hindrances that we do. I assure you; I would have had a real tough time preventing myself from falling for you, Snowflake, because you make it so easy." He affirms. "If we don't stop this and nip it in the bud now, there is only one of two ways it will end for us, neither of which is favourable." He adds, his voice low and hoarse which sends tremors of desire sparking through me.

Our eyes lock, lips inching closer. "Then you should go, Professor."

"I will."

"When?"

"After one last taste of you."

CHAPTER Twenty One

Rain

THANKSGIVING WEEKEND WENT BY FASTER THAN A BLINK OF AN eye. The four days I spent with Talon was bittersweet, especially now we're back in Chicago and agreed to end things between us before things got more complicated. I honestly don't know how I'm going to see him around school and withstand the urge to not rip his clothes off and kiss him. I feel so utterly thwarted, but I understand it's for the best for us both. He's sitting right beside me, but I miss him. I miss his touch, the taste of his kiss, the heat of his breath on my skin.

The car ride back home was quiet compared to the Wednesday when things were hot and heavy, and we couldn't keep our hands off each other. We pull up outside my apartment building and my state of discontent grows tenfold, so much so that I can feel it in my bones. Talon pulls the handbrake up and stares ahead pensively. I wonder what he's thinking. Is he feeling as disappointed as I am or is he relieved?

This awkward silence and unspoken words between us is killing me. It seems we both had the same thought because we turn to face each other and start to speak.

"I had a—"

"I had a—"

We say in unanimity and laugh, albeit a little gawkily, "I had a great time this weekend Talon, thank you for inviting me." I say fumbling with the keys in my hand.

"I did too, and I'm glad you decided to join me. You managed to keep my mum happy and off my back the whole weekend which I'm eternally thankful for." He voices with a genuine smile.

I match his smile and nod, "Count yourself lucky you still have a mother around who loves you."

Talon's smile falters and a look of sorrow quickly takes its place. He turns to look at me apologetically. "Fuck, Rein, I'm sorry I didn't mean to be tactless," he apologises, and I wave it off.

"No, it's fine, don't worry about it." I assure him with a smile, and he winces, seemingly annoyed with himself for neglecting to recall that I lost my mum. He reaches over and takes hold of my hand and presses a kiss to my knuckles, his eyes on mine.

"Would you like to come up for a night cap?"

Talon sighs and looks down at my hand clasped with his and shakes his head. "As tempting as that offer is, I shouldn't." He replies. I see his Adam's apple rise and fall when he swallows when he looks up and our eyes meet. "I'll see you in class tomorrow."

I nod.

"You will."

"Good night, Snowflake."

"Good night, Professor."

We gaze longingly at one another and smile. It's obvious we're both itching to lean in and close the small gap between our lips and once again savour in the taste of the other, but regrettably that's no longer a possibility for us. "I should go."

Talon's eyes lower to my mouth and he nods meekly. "You better."

Jesus, when he looks at me like that, he makes it so damn hard to leave. With a heavy heart I reach for the door handle and push the door open. I look back at Talon once more and he bites his bottom lip and smiles handsomely back at me. "Stop looking at me like that."

Talon half laughs and groans and rests his head back against the headrest. "Rein I'm fighting every urge in my being to not pull you back and kiss you right now, please go, before I lose all control and tongue fuck that addictive mouth of yours."

Liquid heat coils between my legs and my clit pulses with need. "Talking to me in that manner isn't going to make me go any faster, Tal." I say with a shrug, and he groans rubbing his large hands over his face in frustration.

"Good Lord, give me strength." He beseeches with a growl, gripping the steering wheel so tight his knuckles turn white. As hard as it is I need to respect our decision. I sigh and lean over to brush a kiss on his cheek.

"I'll see you Professor," Talon watches me open the door and get out of the car. I can feel his penetrating gaze burning a hole in my back while I walk to the entrance. He lingers till I push the code in and open the door. We share one last look and I force myself to walk in. My eyes closed I lean against the wall beside the door, my heart suddenly so heavy in my chest I thought it would snap and fall at my feet.

My phone vibrates in my hand, and I lift it to see a message from him.

Adonis:

"I'm sorry, Snowflake."

I stare down at the message and my vision blurs when tears fill my eyes. I touch the tears that roll down my cheeks. I've grown quite attached to him over the last four days. It's been less than a minute and I'm missing him terribly.

Me:

"I'm not."

Goddamn it. Walking away from this is going to be harder than I ever anticipated.

ONE WEEK DRAGS on painfully slowly. Each day feeling longer than the last. I've been fighting temptation all week to not text or call Talon. I'm looking for excuses throughout the day to go to his office, so I can talk to him, but he's keeping himself busy. Whenever we cross paths in the corridor, our eyes meet until we pass by. My heart races just a little faster when I get glimpses of him in between classes. Like a hawk my gaze is on the constant look out for him. It's Wednesday today, so I've got him for my next class. Two and a half hours where I can somewhat satisfy my longing and let my eyes feast on him while he pretends to work.

"Ugh, I am so done with finals week." Paris complains and plops herself in the empty seat beside me.

"Huh?" I was so lost in thought I didn't hear a word she just said. Paris looks at me and then my plate full of food and frowns.

"What is up with you? You've been in a miserable mood since Thanksgiving." She queries, eyeing me curiously.

"Nothing, I've just got a lot on my mind."

"Well, say no more. Your best bitch is here to help you unload, sugar tits." I look over at her with a frown and she grins widely, wagging her brows at me.

"I'm afraid to ask."

"You are coming out on a double date with me."

My jaw drops a little and I scowl at her. "Am I fuck."

Paris pouts and pins me with a pleading look, "Please Rei Rei, Dean has been asking non-stop about you."

I roll my eyes and go back to pushing the macaroni and cheese around my plate. "So?"

"What do you mean so? It's time to hop back on, grab that bull by the horns and ride it till you're out of this funk you've been in since you dumped Hunter."

Hunter? Good God, I've not spared that idiot a second of my time since I dumped his sorry arse. "P, I'm not in a funk okay, and it certainly hasn't got shit to do with Hunter, I promise you."

Paris rests her elbow on the table and plops her chin in her hand while she observes me with those wide and probing hazel eyes of hers. "So, what's the prob dog?"

"It's nothing." I drop my fork with a clatter.

"Then you're coming out on a double date with me and Miles," I open my mouth to refuse but she holds her finger up in my face. "Ah! I would hate to do this but I'm going to have to pull out the BFF code card."

I groan, "P, come on, a double date doesn't warrant the use of the BFF code card. It's for *emergencies*."

"Bitch, this is an emergency!" Paris utters sitting upright. "I already spoke to Clay, he said you could have the night off tomorrow. So we are going out with Miles and Dean and you're going to get railed until you're more pleasant to be around."

"You did what?!"

"You'll thank me after Dean has screwed you in every position till you see God himself." She points out with a sugary smile. I don't want Dean to screw me. There is only one man I want and he's the one I can't fucking have.

"Oh, speaking of screwing. I have juicy gossip."

I sink back into my seat and rub my temples tiredly, wondering how the hell I'm going to get out of this double date now without breaking the BFF code. "I heard from the grapevine that Professor Hottie is dating someone."

I choke on the bottle of water I'm sipping when it goes down the wrong hole and I cough hysterically. Paris slaps my back with a panic. "Geez, you good?"

"I'm good." I wheeze rubbing my throat. "Who is he dating?" I croak after clearing my throat to clear the liquid out of my windpipe.

"I don't know, someone on the faculty. That blonde chick that's always batting her eyes at him from Media, what's her name? The one that looks like a royal betch."

"Professor Montgomery?" I probe, and she nods sipping her iced latte.

"That's the one." She confirms after swallowing her coffee. "One of the girls from my dance class overheard them talking in front of his office yesterday. They're going to Le Bouche, tomorrow night."

Well, that's just fragging fantastic. It didn't take him very long to move on and find another play mate.

That rotten bastard!

"Rein." Paris calls my name, waving her hand in my face. I look at her and she blinks looking rather confused. "Why are you grinding your teeth like that?"

"I wasn't."

"Oh, you were, you had this faraway look like you wanted to murder someone. You might want to check you've not lost a couple of teeth there girl. You just as pissed as I am that our eye candy is off the market now?"

I huff and stand up. "I got to go, I can't be late for Professor Dipstick's class, or he'll reprimand me in front of all my peers again." I complain, picking up my tray of untouched food. "Oh, and you can tell Dean I am really looking forward to seeing him again too." Paris claps and squeals excitedly.

"I'm all over it like a fly on hot shit, boo." Paris calls after me as I walk off to empty my tray. I shoot her a look of disgust and shake my head.

So, Professor Saxton, so eager to move on, are we?

THE NEWS of Professor Saxton's date spread like wildfire around the school. Hushed whispers filled the corridors, envious looks followed Professor Polly Montgomery whenever she walked through the corridors. I've never paid mind to the woman once in my two years at this school, but now, I'm watching her in scrutiny. Wondering what Talon sees in her. Sure, she's beautiful in an obvious kind of way and they're both Professors which means they'll have a lot in common, they can openly date without the burden of getting caught.

I should be happy for him, right? So, then why won't this pain in my chest go away? Why does a part of me want to run away as far as possible than face him and the other throw everything I can get my hands on at his beautiful head? Why do I have this rage in the pit of my stomach scalding me slowly from the inside out every time I picture him kissing or touching her?

Sounds to me like you're jealous. The neurotic voice inside my head points out. I shake my head. I am no such thing. To be jealous means you're emotionally invested in that person and I... I'm *not* invested.

You've fallen for him.

No, I haven't. I refuse to believe all these jumbled up feelings inside of me is associated with... *love.*

I sit staring at my canvas, brush in my hand but my mind a million miles away. "Afternoon class." I snap out of my thoughts and almost drop my brush when I hear his deep voice as he enters the room. I sit a little straighter, ignoring the sudden increase of pace in my heart.

He's moved on, he has the right to move on. You can't be angry with him; he's doing nothing wrong.

"The fuck I can't." I grouse bitterly under my breath and focus on mixing the paint on my palette board.

"I've got some exciting news I would like to share with you all. There is an open art competition and I've been asked to put forward three candidates to enter. The winner will get five thousand dollars and the painting will be exhibited in the Eclipse Art gallery on their grand opening night." Talon states elatedly, walking back and forth, his eyes wandering around the room. "You have two weeks to finish the paintings you've been working on; I will pick the top three for submissions which will close on the seventeenth of December. It's going to be a tough choice for me because you're all very talented young artists with an exceptional eye." He adds and his eyes fall on me and linger, then just as quickly he turns and walks back to the desk.

Hard to believe this was the same man that had his head buried between my legs one week ago while telling me he couldn't get enough of me.

Agitation imbues my body the more I allow myself to think about him, so I plug in my earphones, blast the music at a deafening volume and pour all my focus and energy into my work.

As usual two hours fly by quicker than I would have liked. The painting was helping me fuel the annoyance I was currently feeling. I've always found it therapeutic to paint. It distracts me from all the chaos in my head and I desperately needed that now. I can't think about these stupid feelings I'm harbouring for Talon.

I feel a tap on my shoulder and tear my eyes away from the canvas and see the man himself standing before me. Shit, the studio is empty. I stop the music and pull the earphones out of my ears. "You've lost yourself in your painting again. I do wonder if I didn't break your concentration at what point you'd realise that class was over."

I exhale and nod, veering my gaze to the canvas before me. My stomach ties itself into knots when he moves closer to study my painting and the familiar smell of his aftershave surrounds me. "Painting has always been my escape when life gets a little too much, which is why I find it easy to shut off from everything while I paint."

"I get that." He says, pushing his hands into his pockets. "It's really something, Rein."

I chew on my bottom lip and gaze at my painting pensively. "The outlawed love of the Moon and Sun. The greatest and bittersweet love story of all time."

"Rather ironic for someone who doesn't believe in love to be inspired by the very thing they're contesting, no?"

"Shocked me too, but something about their story spoke to me. Legend has it that the sun and moon loved one another so much they were inseparable, always side by side which confused people so much no one could tell whether it was night or day. In order to fix the problem, they were separated by the Gods, cursing them to chase one another in the sky forever, never to be together."

Talon turns his attention to me. Listening intently while I speak. "But their love was so strong the Gods couldn't keep them apart forever. The force of their love would bring them together once every two years, the world would align so they could meet fleetingly for a total of seven minutes."

"The solar eclipse." Talon whispers looking at the painting of the couple entwined in one another. The female painted with a deep navy blue and white, with long dark hair has her head thrown back while the male, burning bright like the sun has his face pressed against his lover's—the moon's—chest.

When I feel Talon shift beside me, I turn to look up at him from my seat. "When I read it, I just couldn't get it out of my head and this painting seems... fitting with the way I'm feeling at the moment."

Talon exhales heavily and closes his eyes, "You've heard the rumours floating around about me and Polly."

I slide off the stool and start to clean my brushes in the warm water on the table to my right. "Hard to miss when the entire school is talking about it."

"Rein, listen—"

I shake my head dismissively and turn so I could face him. "Talon, you don't owe me an explanation or anything at all for that matter. You're free to date whoever you want and so am I."

Talon's eyes that were glued to his feet snap up to mine and he frowns. "You're dating someone?"

"Mhm"

He straightens and clears his throat. "That's great, someone from school?"

"Nope," I sigh cleaning the paint off my hands. "He's an older guy I met a couple of weeks ago when I was out with Paris. I think he said he's in finance."

Talon moves to stand beside me, "An older guy?"

I force a smile on my face and peer up at him over my shoulder, "Mm, I've recently discovered I have a thing for older guys." Talon's eyes darken and he looks less than enthused at my remark.

"Well, I'm pleased for you. Just do me one favour and be careful okay, some men can be real bastards when they want to be."

My head tilts and I smile, eyeing him, "Are you worried about me, Professor?" I question him coquettishly and watch avidly when his tongue glides along his bottom lip while fixing me with a stare.

Fucking Christ, why does he have to be so hot. "Perhaps, I am. Would you blame me after all your misadventures the last few weeks?"

"I didn't realise you were still so willing to be my saviour, Professor." My voice wavers when he takes a step closer. I crane my neck to look up at him, our lips a breath apart.

"Do you have a better option, Miss Valdez?" I swallow hard and my eyes close when he leans in close and whispers in my ear.

"Maybe."

Talon pulls back a little and stares deep into my eyes, a knowing smile gracing his face before he turns and walks toward the door once again leaving me burning with desire.

THE FOLLOWING day Paris and I were at my apartment ready for our double date with Miles and Dean.

I have absolutely zero interest in Dean, while he's handsome in his own right and evidently successful given the two Porsches that are currently pulled up outside my apartment building.

"You look... beautiful." Dean drawls, brushing a kiss over my knuckles, his eyes full of want. I smile waiting for the burst of butterflies but they're either already as bored as I am or dead. Paris forced me into wearing a tight, black mini dress and bright red stilettos for this stupid date.

Okay Rein, no thinking about Talon tonight. He's on his date probably charming the panties off Professor Montgomery right about now. God, I bet she's loving every second of it too, lucky cow.

Dean and I make small talk on the way to the restaurant which was a good thirty-minute drive. I pretend to listen, nodding occasionally whilst he drones on and on about his firm and how he's been thinking about branching out in London.

I say a silent prayer when we finally pull up at the restaurant. My door opens by the valet, "Welcome to Le Bouche." He greets with a welcoming smile and holds his hand out to me to help me out of the car. I peer up at him like a deaf mute. Did he just say welcome to *Le Bouche?*

I must be hearing things. The bright neon sign behind the valet confirms my panic. Thousands of restaurants in this city and this idiot brings me to the one Talon is dining at with his date.

This has Paris' stench all over it. I can bet my left tit she suggested this to them just to be nosey just so she could get the scoop on Talon's date with Polly.

I'm going to kill her.

Oh hell, he's going to think I'm a psycho for following him and showing up on his date. Maybe I should fake being sick and cancel the whole bloody date.

"Le Bouche." I grit out when Paris comes to stand beside me. "Isn't this where *Professor Saxton* is having his date with Professor Montgomery?"

Paris turns her hazel eyes to look at me and shrugs, "Coincidence? I mean, it is the best restaurant in Chicago babes."

My hands and knees start to tremble with nerves. It's bad enough knowing he's on a date with her without having to witness it. The restaurant is stunning, I have to admit. Fine dining galore—which is something I detest if I'm honest. Crystal chandeliers, expensive décor. The restaurant was intimate and elegant; a dimly lit space filled with two-seater and four-seater tables, a piano bar, and an entire wall that was a fish tank, with exotic fishes curiously swimming back and forth.

After being greeted by the host we are directed to a small booth toward the back of the restaurant. My eyes scan the area in search of him and my heart thumps against my ribcage when I spot him at a table for two almost adjacent to ours.

Talon looks up and does a double take when he hears the clicking of heels approaching. He stares at me, and I stare back as we pass by his table.

"After you sweetheart." Dean pulls out the chair for me and I smile and take my seat. Of course, I'm directly facing Talon who is scowling in Dean's direction. The way he eagerly drank the wine as soon as it arrived at his table, I could tell he was agitated.

"What are we drinking?" Miles questions picking up the wine menu. "Champagne for the ladies?"

Paris nods smiling in my direction. "Yes please, we do love champagne."

"Excellent. A bottle of Cristal, and your finest bottle of red." Dean orders, his arm sneaking around the back of my chair, his thumb stroking my bare shoulder.

Well, he's forward.

I shift in my seat and subtly pull my shoulder away from his touch when it raises every hair on my body... and not in a good way.

My phone vibrates in my clutch which is resting in my lap. I look over at Talon and see he's setting his phone down on the table, his expression grim, his chest rising and falling quicker than usual.

Oh boy.

I take out my phone while Dean and Miles have a conversation about the drinks menu and see Talon's name flash on my screen.

Adonis:
"What the fuck, Rein?"

I don't respond to his message. I put my phone on the table and force myself to not look in his direction, all the while every nerve in my body seemed to be heightened, turning my limbs to jelly.

My gaze keeps inadvertently flittering over to Talon's table and as if sensing me he catches me looking at him every time.

"You okay, sweetheart? You're awfully quiet?" Dean questions, brushing my hair away from my shoulder. I smile and nod, taking a large gulp of the champagne. The bubbles burns as it slides down my throat making my eyes water. The waiter fills my glass again.

Third glass before the main course and my head is starting to feel fuzzy. "I saw Rein the first day of school, she was unlike any of my other friends, I was just drawn to her." Paris explains, reaching over to take my hand. "She's like the sister I never had,"

I smile and give her hand a squeeze. "Likewise."

My phone buzzes again.

Adonis:

"Bathroom. Now."

Talon excuses himself from his table, his stern gaze holds mine as he walks by. I give it a minute before I follow suit

"I just need to make a quick phone call. I won't be long." I stand and set my bag on the table.

Paris eye's me curiously. "Are you okay? I'll come with you."

I shake my head, "No, it's fine. I just need to call my aunt in London. I've not got service here. I'll be back in a bit. You guys enjoy your dinner." I lie and hurry away in the direction of the bathroom.

Where the hell is he?

I gasp when I feel a firm grip on my upper arm before I'm hauled into a disabled bathroom. My body relaxes when I see Talon glaring down at me looking mighty angry and sexy as all hell. "First of all, don't you *ever* ignore me when I message you." He rasps backing me up against the tiled wall of the bathroom. "Secondly, would you like to explain what the fuck you think you're doing rocking up here? What are you trying to pull, Rein?" He demands hotly.

"I'm not trying to pull anything. I didn't exactly know they would bring us here. I was just as surprised when we pulled up and saw you sitting there. No offence Professor, but stalking really isn't my thing nor am I so desperate for your attention that I need to play childish games to provoke you." I answer calmly. "Now if you'll excuse me, I have to get back to my date and you shouldn't keep yours waiting either."

I go to slip away, but Talon presses his palm against the wall caging me in. "Not so fast." His eyes narrow and lower to my mouth before they slowly rise to meet my quizzical gaze. "I don't like the look of this guy."

"Don't date him then." I retort tongue-in-cheek.

"I'm being serious, Rein. I know his type; they throw around cash to impress and lure young women like you and by the end of the night you'll find yourself too boozed up and unable to see straight and you'll wake up in his bed with no recollection of how you got there or what went down."

My heart swells and I almost swoon at the deep and protective under-tone to his voice. If I'm not careful I'll go and get used to being fended for. "Thank you for your concern, but I think I'm old and sage enough to take care of myself." I assure him brazenly and raise a brow. "Or is it the fact that he's here with me that's got you all uptight?" I purr sultrily, looking up at him through my lashes and lazily drag my index finger down the length of his chest.

Talon tilts my head up so my lips are aligned with his, "You want the truth? I'll be honest, it bothers the ever living shit out of me. Every time he touches you the urge to slam his head into the table gets stronger. Unfortunately, there isn't a whole lot I can do about it and I'm no neanderthal. As much as I would like to claim you as mine, I don't make a habit of imposing upon women. You're not an object, you're an intelligent woman more than capable of making your own choices and I have to respect that."

This man just gets sexier and sexier to me. "If I had the choice, I would choose you every time."

"Me too, Snowflake." Talon whispers pressing his forehead to mine, his large hands cup my face. "You should head back before they come looking for you, and don't drink anymore, it's clear the arsehole's trying to get you legless."

I couldn't contain my smile. "Why are you always saving me, Professor?"

Talon's smile matches my own, he drops a kiss on the tip of my nose and pulls back, his eyes searching mine. "Because you seem keen on getting yourself into one treacherous situation after another, Snowflake." Talon says and takes a step away from me.

"Wait."

It may have been the three glasses of champagne, but I smile and slide my black thong down my legs and hold it up for him. Talon eyes me hungrily, his eyes go dark with lust as I near him and push the underwear into his pocket. "Just a little reminder in case you've forgotten how wet I get for you." I whisper and kiss the corner of his mouth.

"Fucking Christ." Talon sighs heavily, "What are you trying to do to me? How am I supposed to focus on my dinner when I know you're sitting there with no underwear on while on a date with another man. Are you trying to drive me in-*fucking*-sane woman?"

"I don't want you focussing on anything but the thought of me, Professor."

"You're playing dirty, Snowflake." He growls through gritted teeth, his hand gripping my waist. "All I can think about right now is taking you home and fucking you till you scream with nothing but those red heels on."

I moan, my pussy moistening even more. "Then ditch your date and take me home, Professor."

"I really wish I could, but I can't Snowflake."

I shrug, "Have fun on your date then."

I open the door and walk out of the bathroom leaving him muttering profanities under his breath. "That ought to keep your mind occupied for the rest of the night, Talon Saxton." I whisper to myself with a wicked grin and saunter off toward our table.

"There you are, I was about to send out a search party." Paris complains as I take my seat.

"Sorry, my aunt just loves to chat. Mm, food smells good. I'm starving."

Two HOURS, four courses and many discreet glances with Professor Saxton later, Paris, Miles, Dean and I leave the restaurant. "Thank you for agreeing to come out with me," Dean says.

"Thank you for asking, I had a good time."

He smiles and nods, looking from me to the road. How much did he have to drink? It didn't even occur to me to keep an eye on his consumption. "I'd like to see you again."

I wince inwardly. God, I hate having these types of conversations. "Might not be for a while, I have finals coming up, so I'll be pretty busy between studying and working."

Dean nods, reaches over and runs his finger along my bare thigh. "I have a feeling you're worth the wait." He drawls, licking his lips ravenously.

I rack my brain to find a plausible excuse to avoid seeing him again. Just as I go to speak a honking of a car horn interrupts me. Miles and Paris pull up beside us at the traffic lights. Paris waves at me and I wave back. Miles revs his engine challengingly. Dean laughs and turns to look at me.

"Might want to sit tight baby, I'm about to take you on the ride of your life."

Panic fills me.

"What?" I shake my head, staring at the red light in horror. "Dean..." I say in warning, but he ignores me and revs his engine back at Miles. I look at the dial on his speedometer jumping back and forth and my panic grows, sending my heart rate spiking through the roof. "Dean, please don't."

"Sit back and relax baby, it's okay." The light goes green, and I gasp out loud when the car lurches forward. I grab onto the doors handle for dear life; flashes of the night we had the accident comes flooding into my mind's eye. "Dean, please, please, slow down, you've been drinking. What are you doing, this isn't funny?!" They weave in and out of traffic racing each other like a pair of lunatics.

My entire body shakes uncontrollably, I look at dial and see we're pushing hundred and ten mph. "Dean! Dean, stop the car. Stop the car, I want to get out!"

Through the wild thrashing of my heart, I hear my mum screaming Donny's name in my head. The car in front of us pulls into our lane. "Dean, look out!"

The last thing I recall hearing was that sickening screeching of the tyres on the asphalt and the smell of burning rubber before I suck in one last breath and squeeze my eyes shut tight once again bracing myself for the impact.

To be continued...

Dear Reader,

Thank you for taking the time to read Hook, Line, Professor. I truly hope you enjoyed reading Talon and Rein's story. It's not over just yet. Their story is only just beginning. You'll have to wait a short while to find out what happens next, but I promise, it will be so worth it.

Part II will be packed with even more steamy and romantic scenes as we delve deeper into their relationship together and individually, and you'll see more of the secondary characters too.

Before you go.

Please kindly share a review of your thoughts on the book. I would love to hear your feedback.

Printed in Poland
by Amazon Fulfillment
Poland Sp. z o.o., Wrocław
24 October 2023

9e7c4bf4-9349-4cae-af5f-0c3f338bdd12R01